André Caroff's
MADAME ATOMOS

The Wrath of
Madame Atomos

also by André Caroff:
1. The Terror of Madame Atomos
(translated by Brian Stableford)
2. Miss Atomos
(translated by Michael Shreve)
3. The Return of Madame Atomos
(translated by Michael Shreve)
4. The Mistake of Madame Atomos
(translated by Michael Shreve)
5. The Monsters of Madame Atomos
(translated by Michael Shreve)
6. The Revenge of Madame Atomos
(translated by Michael Shreve)
7. The Resurrection of Madame Atomos
(translated by Michael Shreve)
8. The Mark of Madame Atomos
(translated by Michael Shreve)
9. The Spheres of Madame Atomos
(translated by Michael Shreve)

André Caroff's
MADAME ATOMOS

The Wrath of
Madame Atomos

By
Michel & Sylvie Stéphan

Translated by
Michael Shreve

A Black Coat Press Book

Acknowledgements: Thanks to Françoise Carpouzis & Catherine Losserand.

Madame Atomos sème la tempête and *Madame Atomos parie sur la mort* Copyright © 2013 and 2014 by Michel & Sylvie Stéphan & The Estate of André Caroff; English adaptation Copyright © 2014 by Michael Shreve.
Introduction, Copyright © 2014 by Jean-Marc Lofficier.
Cover illustration Copyright © 2014 by Jean-Michel Ponzio.

Visit our website at www.blackcoatpress.com

Table of Contents

Introduction

The saga of Madame Atomos was a series of 18 novels published between 1964 and 1970 in the *Angoisse* horror imprint of French publisher Fleuve Noir (except for the 18th novel published in 1979 in the *Anticipation* sf imprint).

Our introduction to Volume 1 contains a biography of its author, André Carpouzis, a.k.a. André Caroff (1924-2009), one of Fleuve Noir's most popular authors. More information about Fleuve Noir itself and its popular brands of science fiction and horror can be found in the introductions to Richard Bessière's *The Gardens of the Apocalypse*, Gérard Klein's *The More in Time's Eye* and Kurt Steiner's *Ortog*, also published by Black Coat Press:

Briefly, the saga of Madame Atomos (her real name is Kanoto Yoshimuta) is about a brilliant, but twisted, middle-aged female Japanese scientist who is out for revenge against the United States for the bombings of Hiroshima and Nagasaki—where she was born, and where her family died in the nuclear holocaust.

Madame Atomos seeks to repay the United States by unleashing deadly threats, such as radioactive zombies, giant spiders, a madness-inducing ray, flaming tornadoes, etc., etc. The heroes opposing her are Smith Beffort of the FBI and Yosho Akamatsu of the Japanese Secret Police. In the third volume of the series, Smith was joined by Mie Azusa, the former "Miss Atomos," a younger version of Madame Atomos, initially groomed to continue the fight in the event of her death, but who betrayed her mistress by falling in love with Beffort and, ultimately, marrying him.

There is no love lost between the Befforts and Madame Atomos. She increasingly devotes all her energies to achieve revenge on Smith and Mie for continuously thwarting her schemes. Conversely, the Befforts will do anything to destroy the deadly Japanese *femme fatale* in order to repay her for killing both Dr. Soblen, one of Smith's best friends, and Bob, their baby son.

In Volume 7 of the series, Madame Atomos discovered that her frequent use of teleportation rejuvenated her body, and she now looks like a very attractive young woman. Not only does this help her to evade the FBI, but she uses her charms to seduce Yosho, who is, of course, unaware that the beautiful "Miss Icho Fuj" is, in reality, his deadliest enemy.

There is a real life as well as a fictional gap of almost ten years between the last Atomos novel written by Caroff for the *Angoisse* imprint, *The Slaves of Madame Atomos* (1970), that takes place in April 1969, and *The Spheres of Madame Atomos* (1979), which takes place in 1978.

A few short stories tried to fill that gap: *On an Ill Wind...* (published in Vol. 7) deals with the July 1969 Moon Landing. *A Day in the Life of Madame Atomos* takes place in the swinging London of 1972 (Vol. 9) and *Madame Atomos' Holidays.* (Vol. 9) takes place in January 1976 and shows how the deadly Madame Atomos rebuilt her criminal empire.

But that was it until Michel Stéphan, ably assisted by his wife and writing partner Sylvie, proposed to do a series of novels that would more completely tell the story of Madame Atomos' fearsome exploits during the rest of the 1970s.

Michel was born and lives in Brittany with Sylvie and their two children. He has been a fan of science fiction, fantasy and horror since age 10. In particular, he loves the Universal monster movies (especially the *Frankenstein* series), sci-fi serials and collects Aurora model kits. He is also a regular contributor to our *Tales of the Shadowmen* series, for which he has penned the following stories:

- "The Red Silk Scarf" (Vol. 6)

- "The Three Lives of Maddalena" (Vol. 7)

- "With the Compliments of Nestor Burma!" (Vol. 8)

- "Vampire in the Fist" (Vol. 9)

- "Nestor Buma in New York" (Vol. 10), and

- "The Submarine Gustave Le Rouge," to be published soon in Vol. 11.

Michel also wrote "The Woman in the High Castle" published in our Vol. 8 and "Moreau Lives!" in our collection *Harry Dickson vs. The Spider*.

The Stéphans' first novel, *Madame Atomos Sows the Whirlwind*, opens in May 1970, almost a year after the infamous Manson murders in Los Angeles. The second, *Madame Atomos Bets on Death*, follows a few months later, in Nevada.

Now read on...

Jean-Marc Lofficier

MICHEL STEPHAN
d'après ANDRE CAROFF

LA SAGA DE 7
MME. ATOMOS

RIVIERE BLANCHE

ANTICIPATION
BCP
FICTION

Madame Atomos sème la tempête

MADAME ATOMOS SOWS THE WHIRLWIND

Chapter I

Sergeant James Bundick and his partner Danny were riding in an unmarked green car that had seen better days and would certainly not last another winter. They had just exited Highway 23 and could already see the first breathtaking lights of the Mojave Desert in front of them. In the early morning heat of the spring the mist rising off the Pacific was starting to spread over the suburbs of Los Angeles.

Danny, the younger of the two police officers, glanced quickly at his colleague. He wondered whether he, too, would change like that in 20 years and become a paunchy civil servant like Sergeant Bundick, who was reaching retirement age and did not seem to think much about anything. Danny was only 23 and still very gung-ho about the career he had chosen: to defend widows and orphans, as he liked to tell himself. It might seem kind of overrated, a tad old-fashioned, especially at the dawn of the 1970s when most young Americans felt radically opposed to the established order and went around preaching about free love and anti-war. The demonstrations in San Francisco last month had proved this point once again. Danny understood all this. He understood how you could have doubts when you saw all those policemen marching around and when he looked at Sergeant Bundick with his clammy hands and his face that looked like it was melting in the heat of the Californian desert. But Danny was young and his belief in a better world was still intact.

With his sweaty finger Bundick pointed to the glove compartment. "Go on, boy, open that up. With a little luck you'll find a road map buried in that mess."

"Don't you ever get sick of the police, Bundick? Always the same thing, watching the same places…"

"First of all, I don't always do the same thing. I don't know who you were out on patrol with before, but you'll see that our mission orders have changed a little."

"You officers have briefings. They keep you up-to-date. Us others never get told anything."

"Yeah, well, try to find that goddamn map," the sergeant grunted. "It may be a mess but it's still a glove compartment."

Danny's eyes rolled up. He was holding what must have been a road map from the 40s. The sergeant nodded to him that it was the right one and that for a rookie he was getting by just fine. Then he slammed on the Ford's brake in order to kick up as much dust as possible before pulling over to the side of the road. Danny was stunned by the brutal silence of the desert. He had never liked the place and surely never would.

Sergeant Bundick tried to unfold the map without looking too ridiculous, but it was a lost cause. The tattered sheets started flying all over the place. Danny looked apologetic before deciding to come to his aide.

"Do we really need a map to drive through the desert? Don't you know it like the back of your hand after all this time patrolling it?"

"Where do you come from, pal?" Bundick laughed. "Certainly not from this state or anywhere around."

"I was born in L.A. and I grew up there."

"You must not have left the city much!"

"I went to New York a few times and…"

"No, I mean, you must not have ventured into this neck of the woods very often."

"Just since I joined the police force. A few patrols with and without you."

"That's exactly what I thought."

The sergeant looked at the map one last time. Figuring it was useless he tossed it lazily out the window before starting the car up again and speeding off.

They drove for a good half an hour in silence. The car glided down the road, smooth and steady in spite of the speed, which impressed Danny to no small degree. The sergeant was very concentrated on his driving.

In the distance the landscape slowly took shape. The dry, sharp rocks of the desert presented a vision that was far from monctonous. The elements seemed to transform themselves constantly. The asphalt was long gone by now, but they could still make out a highway running parallel in the distance that a number of big trucks were rolling down. Danny thought he it might be Route 66, but he was not really sure. It gradually veered off as the car seemed to head into an area totally cut off from the world.

Bundick stopped again. First because he had something to say and the sound of the engine combined with that of the gravel under the tires drowned out any normal conversation. Then, also, because he needed to get some air and relieve himself.

"Hell, it's not even noon and already this hot!" the sergeant commented, scrambling out of the car.

He opened the trunk and took out two beers.

"Get out, son. Come and have a drink. I gotta explain something to you."

Danny did not have to be asked twice and he guzzled one of the cans in one go.

"Okay, one beer will do. We're on duty. And with this sun another might just prove fatal. And not to worry, we've got enough to feed an army back here in the trunk. So, the good news is that you're going to be able to eat lunch if this goddamn sand hasn't scoured your throat."

"Are we planning to sit out here a long time?" Danny asked. "You could tell me a little more about what we're doing?"

"You know Manson, boy? The family and all that mess?"

"To tell you the truth I was kind of expecting as much. Since those crazies massacred a whole family last year I imagine all the cops in California are hunting the commune that was living in the desert or around Los Angeles."

"A little like that, boy. A little like that... but not quite."

"I'm all ears, Bundick. Are you and me going to arrest a new Manson this afternoon?"

"It's just a routine inspection, maybe a little bit premature. We're going farther into the desert where nobody lives unless they have to. You know, I've got nothing against the youth of today. Your fashion, your stuff and everything, long hair, love fests like wild pigs... I know that you're a nice guy, young and all. No, what I'm talking about is living in those communes and eating cactus. But, you see, Manson wasn't young. He was older and used the young, the innocence of the young."

"Say, Bundick, you talk pretty good. Ever think of teaching philosophy?"

"Go on and joke, kid, but you can't imagine how sordid the desert is. There are places that won't ever be put on maps and in some of those places they still worship Satan. It's become a fad after Manson. More and more junkies are gathering around these pseudo-gurus. Satan and all that is hogwash, but the murders are real."

"You shouldn't paint everything black either, Sergeant. Mansons aren't running around the streets. I mean the communes. And over the last ten years we've had ten times worse than him too with that crazy Japanese woman."

"In fact, speaking of Japs, I understand you're related to Smith Beffort?"

"Smith Beffort is my uncle. He's my father's brother."

Bundick took two more beers out of the trunk. "You deserve a second drink, kid. With my respect," he said somberly.

Danny smiled. He liked Bundick. While drinking his beer he thought again that he would not mind being partners with him.

"In conclusion? What's the program for the day, Sergeant?"

"Like I said, we're going to make a little premature inspection of the communes in the desert where people don't usually go."

"What? We're going to check out all the hippies in the Mojave?"

"Not exactly, not exactly. Let's say that we're going to check out one commune. And I'll add that even if it's not really dangerous, it does present certain risks."

At that moment the sergeant was looking for some kind of change in his young partner's expression, but Danny remained unfazed.

"That's good, son. You've got guts. An old cop about to retire and a young one like you ought to have no problem at all."

"Tell me a little more, Sergeant. Where are we going?"

"To a guy named Vargas."

"Vargas? Who is he? A Manson copycat?"

James Bundick spoke in all seriousness. "There are a lot of youth moving around today," he said, scrutinizing the horizon like an old Indian waiting for a cavalry that will never come. "A few murders in remote spots and some of them even on the edge of the Mojave, not your usual thing, no, ritual murders and all that. As I said, I don't believe in all that hogwash, but on his last patrol Sergeant Braddock, who was a heartbeat away from retirement like me, left early after finding one of these things."

"What is one of these things?"

"The youth are turning crazy because of drugs. They kill more and more violently and gratuitously. There was even a massacre not far from here last month. That's all I'll say because I don't want you heaving your breakfast. But believe me, it was not a pretty sight."

"I didn't hear anything about it."

"Nobody heard anything about it. But things are moving a lot, believe you me. Manson has become a hero to all the trash."

"And Vargas?"

"Vargas would be more like a poor boy's Manson, or so I hope. For the moment we don't have anything against him, but we're keeping a close eye on him. He's pretty young, not yet 40, but with his eyes, his past and his gift of gab he could pass Christ off as a conman. He lives in a commune close to here with 20 or so morons, some more dangerous than others. That's where we're going."

"And we're just going to barge in on them?"

The sergeant turned away from the horizon and stared at Danny straight in the eyes. "For a young man you're not too with it. Haven't you heard of the Hollywood Bowl? Three days of love, booze and drugs. And maybe some music if they're able to listen."

"My girlfriend might be there, but it's not my sort of thing. I didn't know about it."

"Yeah, well, the police know about it, imagine that. And I can tell you that right now all these kids with Vargas are having themselves a time in Los Angeles. We'll have all afternoon to search their camp. Come on, let's get going. We'll check it out and then go home."

After fifteen minutes on the road the Vargas ranch came in sight. It was located in a small, sunken valley. From their vantage point the two men could see the whole set-up: a big building with a flat roof and a few small shacks to the left and right. Everything looked covered in sand, but it might have been just an optical illusion.

No sign of life could be seen on the ranch.

The policemen parked right outside the front door. Danny noticed that the door was missing a few square panels, which made the building even more ghostly.

The sand must get in through all those holes, he thought. *How can they live in there?*

Then he remembered Manson. He had read a bunch of stuff after they arrested the guru and his family. Manson was way out there. Of all his twisted ideas there was one that had caught the young policeman's attention: Manson was convinced that there were subterranean people living in the desert. The idea had fascinated Danny also and it took on its full meaning as he stared at the gaping holes that seemed to invite into the realm of the fourth dimension.

"Don't start daydreaming, boy," the sergeant said. "Don't let it affect you. It's just an old wood shack. It's not going to swallow you up."

The two police officers climbed out of the car. Danny was ready to draw his weapon at any moment.

If there's danger, he thought, *I'd be surprised if my gun did any good.*

He shook that idea out of his head. He was certainly not going to let himself get upset by the evil spirits of the desert.

"You see, my boy, we don't even have to break down the door."

Sergeant Bundick entered the house. Danny was right behind him. They were surprised by the darkness and the foul smell in the room. Groping around the sergeant flipped a light switch, hoping that the generator was not broken. The light revealed a room full of dust.

"They should have more holes in the doors. It stinks pretty bad in here," he said.

Danny felt reassured. With the nauseating stench he was expecting to see a rotting corpse or some other squalid remains, but it was only the smell of must and grime.

The two men opened the windows and the creaking shutters so that the sun could shine in and give a semblance of life to a place that truly looked dead.

"Are you sure they only just left?" Danny asked. "I'd swear the house has been abandoned for months."

"Who cares," Bundick replied. "Nobody's here and we can inspect the place."

He had already started searching a closet in the main room, which was big and must have been used as the living room. There was a tiny table in the center piled with dirty dishes and several beat-up sofas that were, in fact, nothing but backseats of different cars. One of the posters pinned to the wall showed a soldier standing up, being hit by a bullet and about to fall, his final gesture frozen before death. Below it was printed "Why?" but some jokester had written in "Why not?", which made Bundick smile as he kept searching with healthy enthusiasm.

"What exactly are we looking for?" Danny asked.

"Weapons. Mostly weapons. These communes are used as stashes. When we've found them, we can trap Vargas. I'm sure the bastard's hiding them here."

"Right now I see nothing but spilled tea."

"We should find some dope too. But don't worry about that for the moment, unless it's big bagfuls. Why don't you go check upstairs?"

Danny started up the stairs to the second floor.

"Watch yourself," Bundick shouted after him. "Step carefully and call me if you find anything. And don't hesitate to pull your gun if you need to."

A bright, almost blinding light was shining upstairs, in strange contrast to the darkness on the first floor. Danny examined the sun-drenched room. Seeing the mattresses lying on the floor, he figured it must be the dormitory. The room had an extremely relaxing air about it. The young policeman caught a few whiffs of incense and was amazed by the feeling of quiet wholeness that filled the room. No trace of satanic objects here. No sacrificed animal corpse. He tried to imagine the people living here. It was like a parallel world that he knew nothing about but that he would really like to get a little closer to.

A few ashtrays on the ground, blankets lying around and a big bay window where all the light was coming in. The room was certainly going to become an oven in less than an hour.

Danny was shaken out of his daydream by the shouts of Sergeant Bundick, who must have found something.

"Get down here, boy! It's the jackpot!"

On the first floor he found the sergeant panting at the stairs to the basement and motioning him to follow.

"There's a cellar down there. It's full of guns. For a bunch of non-violent groupies, it doesn't look good."

They scrambled down the stairs. The cellar preserved a certain humidity that was refreshing after the heat outside. Gun racks stood against the stone walls, lined up with weapons of all sizes. Danny was impressed by their number.

"There's at least a hundred here," he said. "What in God's name have we stumbled onto?"

"We've gotta go," Bundick grunted. "Mission accomplished. Let's get back to the station."

On hearing this, the young policeman felt a shiver run down his spine. The sergeant's voice was a little shaky. And his anxiety was catching.

What caught Danny's attention was a group of weapons lying on the ground: a few rifles and shotguns, some with the barrel sawed off, and a 38 special, but also a small, shiny object. Danny bent down to pick it up. He weighed it in his hand.

"This must be a weapon," he said, "but it looks like a toy. Have you seen anything like this, Bundick?"

Before he finished a muffled din rumbled outside. The two men rushed upstairs and saw an unexpected number of motorcycles roaring and backfiring furiously. 50 or so bikers were encircling their car. Not too many women by the looks of it. Big, solid guys riding big, solid bikes.

"They came back sooner than I expected. Don't you worry, kid. I'll have a talk with them."

The sergeant motioned to Danny to stay in the room like a father giving an order to his son. The young policeman watched Bundick walk through the doorway and face the pack. The engines stopped. There was total silence.

All of a sudden Danny remembered an image from a science fiction film whose name he could not recall. An image of a priest walking forward, bible in hand, in front of a crowd of warmongering extraterrestrials. He never knew whether his mind had foreseen the following scene or things happened so fast that he confused dream, reality and the nightmare that he witnessed.

Nonetheless, the white lightning that struck Sergeant Bundick must have been faster than his brain because his reason refused to believe what his eyes were seeing. The body of his partner vanished leaving behind only a wisp of blue smoke that very quickly faded into the desert dust.

Chapter II

Smith Beffort watched Sergeant Wood talking. He watched more than he listened. Since his arrival the night before in Los Angeles Beffort had not stopped observing. His hunt for Madame Atomos had sent him so far into spheres which he had not even suspected existed before that he had to come back down through stages of decompression. It was always the same thing: the incessant battles with the Japanese woman slowly but surely detached him from reality and the return was becoming more and more difficult.

Luckily he had his Mie, his wife. He also had a few friends with whom he figured it was vital to keep in touch.

Sergeant Wood was a relief because he looked exactly like what he was: a sergeant. Beffort was in dire need of people who could bring him back down to earth by their normality.

He was always surprised by the faculty of the human brain to adapt itself to extreme conditions. How could Mie, for example, after their child had been killed by the sinister Japanese woman, still keep that astonishing clear-headedness? How could he himself, after all the trials and tribulations, still be able to talk about frivolous things with his colleagues? It was precisely these frivolous things that helped him stay in control by scattering their beacon lights along his way. The ability to be interested, even for a short time, in sports or a book kept his mind from sinking for good.

Madame Atomos had shown no sign of life for a while and he needed a vacation. That was why he had come to his brother Alan's house at the request of his nephew who had recently joined the police force and had desperately wanted to talk to him about something on the job that had badly affected him. Smith Beffort had made one requirement: no more than two weeks with family; no more than two weeks without Mie. He was here to decompress and he had to do it gently.

This little visit to the Los Angeles police station was not a problem. He was going to listen to Danny and Sergeant Wood. He was going to pretend to be interested for the sake of his nephew. But his mind was elsewhere and his main concern was to recover some inner strength.

He was in the north annex of the police headquarters in a small office that he examined attentively. God, how cramped the place was! So, the L.A. cops did not have very many resources! Sitting in front of a tiny desk Beffort watched the sergeant struggling to explain as best he could what had happened. He looked like he was a having quite a problem at it too, but everyone had their problems. The death of a police officer, even though it was a terrible thing, did not make him forget that he had nothing to do with any of this.

"Your nephew will get here soon," the sergeant said. "He'll give you his version of events. I'm just trying to show you the big picture."

"The connection to Madame Atomos seems pretty flimsy, not to say completely groundless," Beffort said.

"Maybe so, but your nephew thought there was something you might be interested in."

"You're talking about the weapons they found there?"

"No, I'm talking about an idea that doesn't sound too crazy, even if it's a little far-fetched..."

"I'm listening."

The sergeant looked up from the map he was studying and stared hard at Beffort. "First of all don't take what I'm about to tell you in the wrong way. You're a very famous person, Mr. Beffort. Famous for having spent most of your life fighting against this monster, this horrible woman…"

Clearly embarrassed he paused for a minute.

"You see, Mr. Beffort, it could be that this fight you're leading, and we know the effects it has had on your family, it could be that this fight has cut you off a little from reality…"

"Is that really why I'm here?" Beffort burst out. "To get some perspective? Where's all this going?"

"You can't really understand your nephew's theory unless you understand the problems we're having right now on the West Coast, especially here."

"There's only one problem for me and that's Madame Atomos. I know very well there are other problems, but that's police business. Everyone's got his job. I've paid a pretty heavy price for mine."

"That's not what I mean," the sergeant replied, almost apologizing. "But the situation in California, this atmosphere of revolt that's looming over our young people, not to mention the war in Vietnam that looks like it will ever end… all of this could help you understand…"

"I know there's a war in Vietnam," Beffort blurted out impatiently. "I'm not a complete idiot!"

"I don't know how to broach the subject," the sergeant stammered. "To us you're the most respected man in the United States…"

"Right, then tell me the situation. I'm sorry but I'm a little edgy. So, what's going on in California?"

"I'll give you a rough sketch. Your nephew can explain it better than I. He's young and therefore better informed. There's a climate of protest that's more and more serious for the U.S. The young men don't want to be sent off as cannon fodder in a conflict they don't understand and that they see as pointless."

"I agree with them on that. But what's it got to do with Madame Atomos?"

"Your nephew Danny is of the opinion that all these young people could be led anyone with a silver tongue. It would just take a charismatic leader, as we've already seen, to turn them against their elders. Plus, the revolution that's brewing in the country right now is proof that we're close to the breaking point. The adults are all considered perverse. Most of youth don't trust anyone over 30."

"And you think Madame Atomos could be this charismatic leader who will get the youth to rise up against the adults?"

"That's what your nephew thinks."

Beffort started laughing. "Nothing you're saying holds water. Why would Madame Atomos take the trouble to pass herself off as the grand guru of our youth? All she has to do is plant a micro-transmitter in anyone's brain and turn them into a zombie at her command. Everyone knows that. We also know that she's improved her technique over the years. Believe me, she doesn't need to go around preaching gospels. Her methods are more radical."

"Your nephew Danny thinks she might have armed the young people living in all these communes around Los Angeles."

"Sergeant Wood, I need a vacation, that's true, but you should learn more about the methods of the Japanese woman. You're way off the mark."

"We found weapons…"

"You found disintegrators. There are a number of them in the U.S. In our various battles with the diabolical woman weapons got scattered around. There's a whole department of the FBI in charge of tracking them down so they don't fall into the wrong hands."

"Very well," the sergeant admitted. "It's our problem then, routine work. Even if things get ultra-violent, violent like we haven't seen in years. That's not your problem. It's true that we can blame Madame Atomos for all the evils in the world."

"Don't think I don't care about the death of your colleague. While waiting for Danny, you can tell me all about it."

"The Mojave desert is huge. There are more and more communes there, which comes from the fact that our children are completely denying our way of life and trying to invent one that fits them better, without all the violence and the alienation that comes from money."

"Utopia."

"Unfortunately that's not considering the drugs. There are more and more dropouts among the youth. I'm not going to give you a speech on it but all these ranches, all these shacks where they get together are fertile ground for the proliferation of all kinds of gurus who have a lot less pacifist ideas than the kids. We're looking for several of them wanted for fraud and homicide. There are also some escaped prisoners and army deserters we suspect have found refuge in the countless communes scattered throughout the Mojave."

"What exactly are these individuals accused of?"

"Ritual murders of farmers and drifters have been committed recently around the edge of the desert. An old lady who lived alone was murdered following a ritual. I'll spare you the details since it's always the same scene. After the Manson business there are a bunch of lunatics who have gone into action."

"Hold on. First you're talking about kids, now you're talking about wild lunatics. Which is it?"

"The drugs. A bunch of things: LSD, acid, the whole shebang... all of it messes up their heads. The youth don't know where they are anymore. They mix everything up, love with pornography, God with the Devil..."

"We're a long way from Madame Atomos."

"Except that we've found posters of Madame Atomos in some of the communes. Right next to Charles Manson and Aleister Crowley and they're store bought, Mr. Beffort. You can find them in the Haight-Ashbury in San Francisco or right here in the downtown Los Angeles. They're all banned items that we're supposed to get rid of."

"Posters of Madame Atomos? Unbelievable!"

"It's called the counterculture, Mr. Beffort, and it gets a lot worse. In the rest of the world and even in the United States some people are convinced that Madame Atomos is purely an American invention used to justify its huge military budget to finance the Vietnam War. That's only one example among many..."

"Hell, they just have to come see for themselves what she's done to our country, all the cities that are still rebuilding, all the families murdered in cold blood..."

"Some people don't travel, Mr. Beffort. There are people who never see with their own eyes what happened here and even if they did it's always easy to think the truth lies elsewhere."

"I lost my son…"

"I'm sorry. What I mean to say is that this way of thinking is part of American culture now. And people know that the worst is over, that you're destroyed the Japanese woman's bases. I even heard that she's been reduced to committing hold-ups to keep herself afloat."

"I, too, would like to believe that the worst is over…" Beffort's voice trailed off. He was staring at the wall in front of him with empty eyes.

"Don't judge our citizens too harshly, Mr. Beffort. They know what they owe you. I shouldn't have told you about the posters for sale—they're strictly prohibited and the subject of immediate prosecution. When Madame Atomos was in her heyday, such things would never have been tolerated. Now the tension is gone and they're starting to talk about the woman like it's all history, you know, like Hitler or…"

"But it's barely been a year since she's been heard from! Are people really so naïve about this?"

"They aren't naïve, they just want to have hope. You can look at these posters as a kind of exorcism. And as I told you, it's only a small minority of the population."

"Okay. So you were telling me about these lunatics in the desert?"

"I was saying that we're looking for a few individuals, but in fact it's one in particular: a psychopath by the name of Vargas, at least that's what he calls himself. He's an individual as dangerous as he is intelligent and he knows all the tricks of the desert. It was the commune where he was thought to be holed up that the events last week took place. We'd love to get our hands on him for the stash of weapons we found and the death of Sergeant Bundick under circumstances that were nothing less than shocking, the more so since it wasn't the first time."

"It wasn't the first murder?"

"We found a police officer crucified upside down less than three miles from Topanga Canyon. Bugs had eaten out his eyes. When my men pulled him down he was still alive and didn't die until two days later. His wife and two daughters were at his death bed and believe me, they're on the verge of a long stay in a psych ward. We found a second one, who's not dead, wandering around the dunes south of Temecula. The poor guy had completely lost his mind. He was going on about people living deep under the desert before he stopped talking for good. Right now he's at Gateways Hospital and I doubt he'll ever leave. Finally there's Bundick and... your nephew..."

"And the fact that he was able to escape the trap," Beffort said. "I saw Danny briefly last night and his explanation sounded very confused."

"That's the least you can say. Well, here he is now."

When Danny saw his uncle, his face lit up. He walked into the room, holding out a friendly hand.

"We were just talking about you," the sergeant said. "And your miraculous escape."

"I couldn't say much last night," Danny told Beffort. "The family should stay out of all this. And then I didn't want to get you all worked up right away at the start of your vacation."

"I'm all ears, Danny. I've been talking to the sergeant for awhile and he's told me a great deal."

"Everything happened so fast. I was with my partner, Sergeant Bundick. We'd just found the stash with all the weapons, especially those weird things I found out later were disintegrators. The sergeant went back upstairs. There was a biker gang. I didn't see their faces too well, but they were bikers were sure, the kind that just ride the highways, more like nomads. The sergeant had told me about this Vargas guy, but I don't know if he was with them or not. There was a flash and then everything happened really fast. Bundick was disintegrated right in front of me. I'm sure of it now, even if my mind refused to believe it at the time. So, I started running, straight ahead, sure that I was going to get struck down. I climbed some rocks and a whole bunch of stuff. I was going crazy. I didn't even hear the bikes. I ran and ran, straight ahead, lost all sense of time, until I passed out. Afterward they told me I was dehydrated when they found me, but nothing too serious. Everything happened so fast. I'd never been so scared in my life. I really thought I was going to die."

"And you told yourself, I'm quitting the police," Beffort joked.

"The kid was shaken up pretty bad," Wood said, "but he pulled it together quick. It's a tough family."

"What I don't understand," Danny said, "is why they let me go. Where I was, I made a perfect target."

"Maybe so you could tell your story… which seems highly improbable when you'd just found their stockpile of weapons. But the fact is that your life was spared. Did you pick up the weapons, sergeant?"

"As I said, everything was there. We kept the conventional weapons here and sent the disintegrators to the FBI."

"Is it normal to find weapons in the communes around L.A.?"

"Theoretically no. But so many weird things are happening nowadays that we're not surprised at anything anymore."

"So," Danny asked, "do you see any link with Madame Atomos?"

"None at all," Beffort confessed. "The sergeant and I talked about the possibility. The data is too flimsy to establish a link. The fact remains that your region is shaken up right now by tragic events, but they certainly have nothing to do with the diabolical Japanese. I know about human folly and it doesn't belong to only one woman. I'm afraid you're going to have your work cut out for you. Anyway, how do you figure on proceeding? Is it a matter of stepping up the patrols in the sector?"

"That won't do much good," the sergeant replied. "The Mojave Desert is huge for the uninitiated. Searching for Vargas in a traditional way would be a waste of time and we don't have the manpower. We're going to use cunning instead."

"Which means?"

"Infiltrate the communes."

"You mean you're going to send in men to mingle with desert dwellers? Don't you think cops in the commune would be a little conspicuous?"

"Not as much as you think. It'll just take a few smart, young men because the mission is dangerous, true."

"Do you have any volunteers?"

"There's one standing in front of you. Your nephew was the first one to speak up."

Chapter III

Danny got back to his beachfront apartment in Venice and packed up his things. All he had to do was contact Lori to explain to her about his long absence. The next day he was supposed to join a commune named Westridge in the Mojave near the Edwards Air Force base in a place that he did not yet know the exact location.

As for Beffort, he was hanging around Hollywood Boulevard, taking a peaceful stroll before meeting his brother Alan in Santa Monica for dinner. Alan was an insurance salesman. Recently divorced he was living with his daughter Carole who had just turned 12 and was like most kids her age.

Tonight Carole was asking her uncle a lot of questions and Alan was glad when dinner was finally over and she decided to leave the table.

"Your daughter talks a lot," Beffort said with a playful smile. "She asks relevant questions. She's interested in everything. She'll go far."

"I hope she's not too upset. Since her mother left I have the feeling that she's trying to take her place as much as possible."

"You shouldn't complain, Alan. She's big enough to be nice company."

"That's true. And what did you do this afternoon?" Alan asked as if he wanted to change the subject. "Did you visit Danny at the police station?"

"Yes. I saw Sergeant Wood and we talked about a number of things that would bore you to hear. Let's just say that everything is a little top secret. It's police business, as they say, but nothing extraordinary. So I saw Danny too and he looked good. He seems to have recovered well from his recent experience. Did he move out a long time ago?"

"No, not too long. He rented an apartment near the beach. Like that he can live his life and see his fiancée. For now it looks like he's getting off to a good start with the girl. Well, not so much a girl—she's four years older than him. Her name's Lori. Okay, I don't like her kind but I don't have much to say about it. Danny's an adult after all."

"Just this afternoon Sergeant Wood was telling me how the youth are pretty mixed up right now."

"The youth are always mixed up. We were too and I'm certainly not going to cast the first stone. Besides, I'm too wrapped up in my work to worry about that kind of stuff."

Smith Beffort saw that his brother had not understood was he was hinting at. He was obviously not informed about the recent tragic events. Danny must not talk much about his work and he was right.

"Does Danny tell you anything about his work?"

"A little. But I don't know everything. His work is top secret like you said. All I know is that he has to be away for a while, a few weeks if I understood him, but that's all he said. He just gave me the keys to his apartment so I can take care of the goldfish. That's what our relationship's come down to."

"You have a really great son," Beffort said. "And a charming daughter. You should be proud of your kids. But you have to get used to the idea that Danny's an adult. You won't see him as often as before."

"Still, taking care of the goldfish!"

"If the fish is a problem for you, I'll go and take care of it myself," Beffort joked.

"You laugh, but I'd like it if you went over there sometimes. I'm going to be very busy this week."

"Agreed, Alan. But for now I'm going to bed. Thanks for the excellent meal. Tomorrow it's my treat."

The modified Buggy swerved off the 137 and headed east on a steep, rocky path. Danny was woken up at 6 am by the French photographer, Alain Deville, who sometimes worked with the Los Angeles Police: they did little jobs for each other, quid pro quo. Danny did not like Alain Deville's attitude. He did not like his laugh or his false confidence. The Frenchman pretended that he knew everything about everything. Danny did not like being woken up at dawn either by a jumpy guy who was not from the police but who had to be his driver. The Frenchman seemed pleased with himself and pleased with his driving. Any idiot, however, could handle a Buggy on a hilly path, but the photographer was convinced that he was showing off his great control.

"A little slower," Danny shouted over the sound of the engine. "I don't have a train to catch and I don't want to end up on the side of a hill."

Deville edged his foot off the accelerator and the engine quieted down.

"Nice and easy, pal," Danny said. "Don't get worked up like that. You're abusing the car. You can drive cool."

The photographer looked at him with such a goofy smile that Danny started to wonder if he might not be a little retarded. Then the brakes screeched and the car stopped in the middle of the path. He looked at Danny sternly.

"You understand, Mr. Officer, I'm hurrying because I'd like to get there before the sun goes down. We're coming up on the property of Count Alucard, get it? Alucard... Dracula."

Deville laughed loud and hard.

The moron took some acid, Danny thought. *They sent me a driver on acid.*

"Okay, excuse me, Mr. Officer," the photographer continued after calming down. "Yes, okay, I didn't take much, but don't worry, I work for you. They told me to take you to the castle... uh, the Westridge commune. Excuse me, I'm a little stoned, it's true, but I guarantee you I know the way. And going where we're going, it's good to get in the mood, don't you think?"

"I think it'd be better if I took the wheel."

"No you don't. We'll be fine. I'm not as much of an idiot as I might seem, you know."

There was a lull. Not a word. Then the vehicle got back on its way, driven more carefully.

"Don't hold it against me," the photographer went on. "I didn't sleep last night. I ran into a pack of lunatics who made me swallow a bunch of stuff. I'm coming down slowly."

In spite of the early morning hour, warm air was already sweeping over the two men and Danny felt like it was going to be a tough day. He had to get into the Westridge commune, apparently a quiet commune but in a rather strategic location in the desert. The police had in fact observed a highly unusually amount of activity, mostly Hell's Angels type motorcycle gangs, four-wheel drives and other vehicles.

Danny was supposed to pass himself off as a Vietnam War deserter. That was the plan. So he could keep his GI crew cut. His five o'clock shadow and shabby fatigues should get him in without a problem.

Alain Deville was in charge of getting him to Westridge and picking him up two weeks later. Once there Danny would have no car and could count on nobody but himself. Only a mini-transmitter had been given to him to contact the base if he ran into any trouble.

The Buggy continued its way at almost normal speed. Concentrated on his driving the Frenchman said nothing more. It was Danny who broke the silence.

"You're a photographer? Are you planning on taking photos of the commune?"

"I've already done plenty of reporting over there. It's the kind of thing that works and the folks don't care at all. I'm bringing you there because I know two or three of them. There's Mina, you'll see, a really nice Japanese. She's the one running the commune. I'll hook you up with her and she'll help you fit in."

"Have you ever lived in a commune?"

"Lived, no. But I've spent time in them, that's for sure. Too much time. But where I'm taking you is pretty nice."

"How do they live in communes? Did Sergeant Wood explain it to you? I'm supposed to be a deserter. What do you think I'll do there all day?"

"You won't have to do much. And don't expect a big orgy. A commune is a lot different than you think."

"Are there a lot of drugs?"

"That depends on where. Like I said, where I'm taking you is pretty, I don't know how to say it... it's pretty normal. Let's just say that it's a good commune to start with. You're lucky that they're not sending you into the middle of the Mojave with the real crazy ones."

"And what are you going to do there? Are you going to stay a little while?"

"Only two or three days. I've got my Japanese girl I'm going to see. I'm retraining. I'm photographing nothing but Japanese girls now, preferably young and beautiful. My dream would be a commune of Japanese girls."

Danny thought the Frenchman was kind of a moron at first, but now that Deville seemed to be coming back down to earth he thought he was a real jerk.

Beffort woke up relatively late, noting with satisfaction that he had had a normal sleep. Alan and Carole had got up and left long before, so he had a hearty breakfast and skimmed through the morning papers. His mind was still foggy and his gaze kept wandering to the big window where he could see a stretch of the Pacific.

His morning was dedicated to a long walk along the Santa Monica Pier without knowing what to do except take advantage of the good weather that Providence was granting him. After a telephone call to Mie to assure her that all was going well, his legs carried him to Venice where he decided to check out Danny's apartment. It was not that he already needed to change the water for the goldfish, but Beffort was curious to see where the young policeman lived. Besides, his visit had been somewhat premeditated because by chance the keys to Danny's apartment were in his pocket.

The lock turn smoothly and Beffort entered a studio apartment that was bigger than he had expected. There was the main room, a kitchen and a bathroom. A quick glimpse was all it took to identify Danny's universe. A bunch of books were scattered pretty much everywhere. Sports magazines and an empty guitar case were lying on the floor. He was already regretting his intrusion into his nephew's personal life. He was about to leave when a woman's voice startled him.

"Smith Beffort?"

No one was supposed to know he was in Los Angeles. The girl who had just entered could not have been older than 30. She was pretty according to Beffort's tastes, with short, blond hair in contrast with the long hair of most young women he had seen in Los Angeles. Her jeans and t-shirt made her look much younger.

"You must be..."

"My name's Lori. Lori Adams," tossing her bag casually on the bed.

"I see I'm not the only one with a key," Beffort said.

"I got here last night. I just went out to buy some cigarettes. You didn't answer me. Are you Smith Beffort?"

"I'd be lying if I said I wasn't. And I was thinking I was incognito here. The jig's up."

"Don't fret. Danny told me a lot about you. Smith Beffort this, Smith Beffort that..."

"Speaking of Danny, did he tell you he'll be away for a while?"

"Kind of. We talked about it last night. The little cop is taking a trip to the desert."

"You don't sound like you have a very high opinion of the police. So why are you going out with Danny?"

"And whammo! Straight off the questions! Look, come into the kitchen with me. I haven't had my breakfast yet. We can try to find something to eat and I'll give you something like an answer."

Beffort followed the girl. She seemed comfortable in the kitchen, like she was at home. The coffee was ready very quickly. Lori offered him a cup and lit a cigarette after sitting down across from him.

"I don't like cops much, it's true. But Danny's different. He makes me laugh."

Beffort took a sip of coffee.

"And like they say," the girl went on, "you have to have things to do. Going out with a cop is something to do and Los Angeles is a city full of things to do."

"I haven't seen Danny in a long time," Beffort said. "Basically, I don't really know him, but I have a hard time seeing him with you. You seem to me to be very... sure of yourself..."

"I know what I want. But it's true that Danny is just a boy and by the way, I'm glad to see you because I have a thing or two I want to tell you."

"I'm listening."

"We talked about it last night and we even argued over it—why did you sent him into the desert?"

"It's a mission and it's none of your business. Neither is it mine. I'm surprised he even told you about it."

"You're crazy! I tried to talk him out it all night long, but he left in the morning."

"Well, Danny's just on an observation mission. At least that's what his boss told me. Listening to you, you'd think they were sending off to die!"

The girl jumped up, shaking with anger. "If only you knew how right you are! What do you know about Los Angeles? About this city? It's surrounded by desert and hills and people are afraid of them. They're hideouts for all the lunatics and murderers and weird sects. And you sent Danny on an observation mission out there! You're kind of out in left field!"

"Calm down. I heard there's been a little unrest there lately, that's true."

"A little unrest! What do you know about it? Los Angeles has become a city of hell. The people are scared and they have a right to be. The climate is worse than unhealthy here. Drugs are everywhere. Acid, LSD has totally ravaged the youth. At the start it came from San Francisco. The hippies and all that really started it off. Except now in San Francisco they think we're fakes. Nothing is real here. There is no scene, no place for the youth to let it all hang out. Nothing but this crappy this desert surrounding us. And then Manson came. And after him everyone started playing the Devil... But what do you know about the desert and the hills? Even the cops don't dare to go there. The last ones who went in came out raving mad. Everyone knows that here. They're still laughing about it. That's something over your head and it might just bury you."

"You're painting the picture a little black, aren't you? And Danny isn't a little boy."

The girl grabbed Beffort's sleeve and yanked him into the main room.

"Not a boy," she said, showing him a pile of books on the floor. "Look at this! Science fiction books! Danny lives in his own little world. He reads science fiction. For him there are good guys and bad guys. He's a good guy. He thinks that's how it works. Look at this book!"

She held a worn paperback four inches from his face.

"Philip K. Dick, one of his favorite authors. We went to see him the other day. He lives in Orange County, you know? Anyone can go into his house because he thinks his wife is trying to kill him. He's become paranoid and drops acid like M&M's. Danny couldn't believe his eyes. His hero getting high with a bunch of other junkies... Where was the good, where was the bad, that gave him a lot of trouble. He found a letter that Dick had written to a fellow writer that said: *There's no culture here in California, only trash. The West Coast has no tradition, no dignity, no ethics. You must work with the trash, pit it against itself.* That's what Danny read in that letter, that's what deeply upset him. I think that's what even motivated him to leave for the desert."

"In search of the truth."

"Don't give me your claptrap philosophy," the girl sobbed. "I feel like this country loves to massacre its children."

"But what do you think is going to happen to him?"

"They're going to see him coming. They're going to play with him. It'll be obvious he's a cop. The poor boy, I tried to give him advice to get by unnoticed but he didn't listen to me. I know what happened in the desert the other day. Danny told me because it really disturbed him. All his beautiful dreams came crashing down around him. And these science fiction books aren't going to change a thing."

"Stop your moaning. Instead why don't you tell me what you want me to do."

Lori shut up. Suddenly there was silence in the room.

"What do you want me to do?" Beffort repeated. "And what's in the desert that's got you so scared?"

"I told you, sects, lunatics…"

"No, I think there's something else. What's in the desert that's terrifying you so?"

She started sobbing again, quietly, while staring at Beffort.

"Go on. You were telling me about the desert. Give me some details, names… what are you afraid of?"

"Oh, I see," the girl smile weakly and dried her tears. "I talk about the Devil and you want names. You're famous in the U.S., Beffort, you know. And I see that you're still obsessed."

"A name, just one name…"

"I can't give it to you because I don't know it. I have the impression that we're not talking about the same thing."

"So is that all you want to tell me?"

Lori grabbed her bag and after a quick glance in the mirror opened the front door and turned around. "No," she said. "I want to see you again and I think I will."

Beffort waved to her slowly before she slammed the door shut, leaving him alone with the silence in Danny's universe.

Later, while walking in the streets, Lori's words kept running through his mind, repeating themselves over and over again, refusing to go away.

He took refuge in a bar and ordered a beer. A small stage crowned the back of the room, a warning that he could expect an avalanche of decibels that would rattle his brain or drive him out of the bar early. To his great surprise it was not a rock group that set up but a combo of three huge blacks who sat in front of their bongos and opened with a set of drumbeats. The sound of tom toms filled the room. The show was spectacular and fascinated Beffort. His head started spinning and his mind went into a whirlwind. The musicians watched him more and more intensely. Beffort hurried to finish his drink and rushed out of the bar. Once in the street he relaxed.

He was not in the habit of getting carried away… There was Lori, who he wanted to see again. There was this weird city, this neighborhood a stone's throw from the sea with its atmosphere, its almost physical ten-sion…

But there was also his brother whom he had to get back to. And also his vacation that had just started.

Chapter IV

Danny was looking straight ahead. The buildings were carved out on the horizon now. All around was sand and rock, nothing but sand and rock.

"You'll see," Deville said. "It's great. I'll introduce you to the Japanese girl. Let me do the talking. In case they're suspicious…"

As they got gradually closer Danny felt more and more uneasy about the look of the commune. He had imagined a huge main building but there was only a group of dingy mobile homes and run-down trailers in the middle of which stood a no less squalid building. Everything was immersed in a permanent whirlwind of dust.

"I already envy you," the photographer said as he climbed out of the Buggy after turning off the engine. "You're going to make love in a commune…"

"I don't see anybody right now," Danny said. "It looks totally empty."

"There are two possibilities," the photographer answered gravely. "Either they're all dead, gutted by Manson's brother, or they don't give a damn about our arrival and won't even bother to move. I'll bet on the latter."

Deville had barely finished speaking when a shadow came out of the building. The shadow of a young woman. It was Mina, the Japanese, who came toward them all smiles.

"Let me introduce you to Madame Atomos," Deville said. "She's the leader of the place. And she'll be in charge of your initiation."

"My initiation?"

"Peeling potatoes and cleaning toilets!"

"Don't listen to him," the Japanese said. "I've known him a long time and I've never really understood his sense of humor."

"That's normal," the photographer went on. "It's humor reserved for the initiates. Mina, this is Danny, an army deserter who just wanted to see if you might put him up for a while. Danny, this is Madame Atomos who rules over her disciples with an iron fist."

Danny forced himself to smile. The photographer's humor was, in fact, pretty hard.

The young lady offered to take them inside. It was not yet 10 am but the sun was burning hot. No sea breezes to cool the air. Danny took his bag from the Buggy and followed the two of them into the shabby, old hacienda that kept standing by God knows what miracle. The air inside the hovel was no cooler than outside.

Mina brought in a pitcher of water and three glasses and invited them to sit on the floor. What struck Danny the most was how dirty everything was. He had never imagined communes were so filthy. He thanked her for the glass of water she held out.

"You can stay here for a while," the Japanese said. "There's eight of us at the moment but a few pass through. People come and go and then some of them hang around, the regulars, the ones who never split."

"Can I put my stuff somewhere?" Danny asked.

"Look outside. We live in trailers here. There's plenty around the house. You can take the one on the left with the green roof. It belongs to Jay. I'd be surprised if he ever came back. Besides, if he does, you can leave it to him and we'll fix something else up…"

"What can I do here? I mean, can I be of any use?"

The woman looked at him thoughtfully for a moment. "You want to do something? You're on the run, if I understand correctly?"

"Yes. But what do you do with your time here?"

"Don't ask too many questions," Deville jumped in. "She'll end up thinking you're a cop."

Danny was surprised at this remark and was starting to get suspicious of the photographer, wondering what kind of work he could do for the L.A. police.

"We've got a music room. It's got an amp, two guitars and a drum set. If you want, I'll give you the keys. You can open it and close it and be responsible for the music room."

Mina and the photographer broke out laughing. Danny was completely lost, but aware that neither of them gave a damn about him. The photographer pulled a joint out of his pocket and lit it.

"We're laughing because life is hard enough here," the Japanese continued. "Strangely, we're sitting at the edge of the Mojave, so it should still be civilized, but you can already feel the desert's severity, maybe even more than anywhere else. There's no doubt why people don't stay here. See, there's a road still running right into this place. You were able to get here with no problems. But after that it's only hills."

"You mean over there?" Danny pointed at the mountains he saw through the grimy windows.

"Yes, that's right. Only the crazy ones live out there. Some nights you can hear them howling in the desert. But I've never had any problems. They know me. Manson even came by in his heyday."

"The crazy ones?" Danny asked.

"The ones living in the desert. You'll have a good lookout from here."

"Is it true that Manson was convinced that people were living under the desert?" Deville asked.

"Oh yeah? I never heard that," Mina plucked the joint from the photographer's hand.

"You're kidding me."

"Of course I'm kidding you. Everyone knows what Manson believed. Everyone knows that the Devil lives in the desert and he's going to come out very soon. I don't know if you're any good as a photographer, but as for the news you're one war behind."

Danny refused the joint that she offered him and asked to see his new digs. She motioned that the door was open, so he went out to his trailer.

The air was still, but he felt like his eyes were full of sand.

And he felt a little lost in his mission. Keep under surveillance? Keep what under surveillance? There was nothing but hostile nature around him and he heard nothing but a whistling wind that was slowly starting to rise up.

To his relief he found the inside of the trailer was not as rotten as the outside led him to believe. He stretched out on the bunk. Soon he would meet the residents of Westridge. He remembered the discussion he had had the night before with Lori. Maybe she was right after all and there was no reason for him to be here. He wanted Deville to spend a couple of nights in the commune because he had no desire to be alone. Then the Japanese lady's face appeared in his mind and he slowly repeated the name Madame Atomos. What kooky idea did the photographer have by calling her that! This woman, who was no longer so young, seemed very nice even though somewhat quirky.

He was about to fall asleep when a noise rattled him awake. Through the window he saw a black man, a very black man, in shorts, a top hat and bow tie, carrying a coffin in his arms. The man was so huge that the coffin did not even touch the ground and looked like it weighed nothing. Danny watched him pass by with a mix of awe and amazement. He would learn later that the man was one of his neighbors by the name of Hawkins and had done shows in Las Vegas nightclubs where he played the blues while coming out of a coffin dressed in a black cape. Unfortunately during a brawl after a show Hawkins broke the neck of the husband of a woman in the audience whom he was in love with. That put an end to his career and he was forced to flee into the mountains. But the madman, because that was what he was, did not forget to drag his coffin with him.

Alan's daughter, Carole, had been walking down 33rd street for a good 15 minutes. She was supposed to meet Alice, a friend who had a plan for the next three weeks, namely to moonlight in a Chinese restaurant between 8 and 11 pm. Considering her young age she did not really know whether it would be possible. But she did know that it was for a good cause: to buy a ticket to San Francisco to see the Osmond Brothers in concert and also to find a gift for her father's birthday so that he would let her go with Alice. Given her father's late hours, it should not bother him much if she worked two or three hours a night from time to time.

Carole was starting to worry that her friend would not show up when Alice suddenly appeared at the corner.

"Well?" Carole asked.

"It's all good. The boss is okay with it. You start tomorrow."

The helicopter was flying at a high altitude and Beffort was starting to get an idea of how immense the Mojave Desert was. Next to him Sergeant Wood had not spoken for more than 15 minutes, his eyes riveted on the landscape unfurling through the window, his mind lost miles and miles away.

All of a sudden he spoke to Beffort, "Look! You can see them down there, the desert dwellers, you can barely make them out. They look so lost!"

"Indeed. Supplies must be hard to get when you're so far from everything."

"They live completely cut off from the world. Even on two wheels it's impractical. But they've still got their suped-up Buggys, those damned machines that can go almost anywhere."

"Is Danny in this area?"

"Not at all. He's in a place that's a lot easier to get to. Don't worry, he's certainly with some locos but they're not too mean. We sent him there because he wanted to be of use, but I don't think he'll run into any trouble. Those shacks you see down there, on the other hand, well, I wouldn't want to live in them. You know our patrols can't come out this far. We've only got the helicopter for this."

"I understand," Beffort said.

"Set her down!" the sergeant ordered the pilot.

15 minutes later Beffort and Sergeant Wood stepped off the helicopter, leaving the pilot at the controls.

"We won't be away for more than half an hour and try to stay in sight. At the slightest sign of trouble you can contact us by radio." The pilot nodded. Sergeant Wood indicated a point in the desert and said, "We'll be heading in that direction. Let's go, Beffort."

The two men walked for a good quarter of an hour and Beffort started to realize what was before him. It was hard going with the fine sand entering their shoes.

"The rocks are eroding," the sergeant said. "You see why I brought you here? Do you understand why I talk about lunatics?"

In fact, Beffort understood. Before him, scattered over half a mile and forming, it seemed to him, a rough circle, were hundreds of wooden crosses. Each of the crosses were about the size of a man and the FBI agent could not help shivering.

"A real forest," he said. "Can you explain this to me, sergeant?"

"I've got no explanation. Except that this isn't the only one we've found. There are other crosses scattered pretty much everywhere in the desert around Los Angeles and I have the feeling that there are more and more every day."

"It's incredible. Have you found any bodies?"

"None. Only the police officer I told you about. These crosses are clean. I think they're waiting for someone."

They looked at each other without saying a word. The sun beat down hard. The long shadows of the crosses looked like snakes crawling over the sand.

Sergeant Wood finally broke the silence. "Can you believe it?"

"It's more serious than I thought. You can't plant crosses in the desert like this for no good reason. It's a lot of work, which is meaningless. Have you searched for fingerprints or traces of human activity?"

"We're not in New York here. If they are human who did this, the desert wiped out all traces long ago. If it's the Devil... the issue doesn't even arise."

"Except for humans and the Devil, who else could do this?"

The sergeant grimaced, but he did not answer.

Danny vegetated in the Westridge commune for three days, but making contact with the other members was not as easy as he had hoped. Each of them seemed to be cooped up in their trailer and there was no crowd coming to eat dinner in the main building. The young police officer was missing Deville who had stayed only one night before leaving for new adventures.

Danny had spotted three young people his own age who, like him, came and went looking like they did not really know what to do with themselves. Mina was apparently the only woman and she sometimes ate with him. She did not talk about what she did and he did not ask. Their conversations remained very superficial.

The day after Danny arrived a gang of motorcycles showed up. There were no more than a dozen and they did not bring back good memories for him. They were Hell's Angels. There was no mistaking them because the name was written on the back of their jackets. But everything seemed to go fine. The bikes knew the place and seemed to be welcome there. Mina had explained to David that they brought stuff, that they traded with the commune and that they were not the only ones. Danny preferred not to show his face around them for fear of being recognized. Even if the probability was low, it existed.

One night after a day as idle as the one before and as the uselessness of his mission was glaringly evident, alone in his trailer Danny opened a book, yawning, when Hawkins knocked on his window. Danny invited him in, but asked him to leave his coffin at the door.

"Sure thing," Hawkins said. "I don't bring my coffin everywhere. It's just for show. And I'm not as crazy as some people."

They stayed up late talking. About nothing and everything. But the young cop was surprised to Hawkins more pleasant company and less artificial than Mina. The alcohol helped and the joints as well. They ended the night with great bursts of laughter that could have woken up the whole commune. They replayed it the next night and Danny knew that he had made a real friend.

At the end of the week, when he was in Hawkins' trailer, which was bigger than his, things started looking up.

"You figure on splitting one of these days?" the officer asked.

"I'd like to. I'm a nomad, but right now I can't move on. Time is slowing down for everyone."

"How's that?"

"It's no good starting anything anymore, it's too late."

Danny thought the black was starting to babble, which happened sometimes. He would go on and on about the apocalypse and then fall over dead drunk because, as he himself said, he had decided not to sober up during the 70s. When he went a little crazy like this, sometimes making him mystical, sometimes making him sleepy, he could say interesting things if Danny managed it well.

"It's too late to do what?"

"The United States of America won't hold out for long. First Los Angeles, then the rest of the country. All the big cities wiped off the map. The time's coming, very soon."

"Who you trying to convince, Hawkins? Enough of your bull. You're totally loaded. The mix of weed and booze is doing you no good."

"Soon there will be no more weed…"

"Okay, but why are only the US cities going to be destroyed? If it's the apocalypse, it's the whole world. You gotta think big!"

"You know nothing about it. They don't even know why you're here? That's why she doesn't talk to you, Mina, I mean, or doesn't talk much. You're a deserter? You were in the war? Where's the proof?"

The conversation was taking a bad turn.

"Calm down. You were telling me about the apocalypse. It's a little over the top, don't you think? I don't know if you're giving me a line or if I can believe what you say. Would you believe a guy who's always walking around with a coffin?"

"Yes I would," Hawkins answered solemnly.

"So explain to me clearly why the apocalypse is coming."

"The apocalypse is coming because the minorities can't take it anymore. Women, yellows, blacks, all the rejects of this crappy society that rushes its kids off to get killed in a conflict that has nothing to do with them. Rebellion is rumbling. Since the pariahs of society took refuge in the desert…"

Hawkins paused to take a sip from the Jack Daniel's bottle.

"This is a bottle of Jack Daniel's," he said, "but it's not Jack Daniel's inside. It's some cheap shit alcohol. But it'll still get you smashed."

"Yes, it's true that it'll get you smashed. But you were saying the rebellion is rumbling…"

"Yeah, the rebellion… The rebellion… We need a leader… A leader for all these kids…"

He was stuttering more and more and might fall over drunk at any moment. Danny was becoming excited, feeling like he was onto something.

"Who's the leader, Hawkins? Who is it? What's his name?"

There was a moment of suspense. The black man slowly lifted his head as if he were coming around and snapping out of it.

"Oh, what's with all these questions? It's like an interrogation. You a cop or what?"

Danny had the feeling that it was all ruined, gone to pieces. Or maybe it was all just drunken babble, nothing but a meaningless conversation…

"Mina knows a lot of things and she doesn't trust you. You've got to prove yourself. I'm tired now. But don't worry. Everything in its time."

"But I'm on your side," the police officer tried a last ditch effort. "I'd really like to know this guy…"

"This guy? I never said it was a man…"

And Hawkins laughed loud and long before falling back on his bed. Danny went back to his trailer thinking that it was time to warn the sergeant. It was a moonless night and the shadows were thick. The young man felt a thousand ghosts brushing by him. The Spirits of the desert, he told himself. Without a doubt he was in the Mojave. He opened the door of his trailer with a sigh of relief.

Chapter V

It was the first time in her life that Carole was in the back of a restaurant amidst the greasy pots and piles of dirty dishes. Her work consisted in washing up for three hours on Friday evening. The boss had insisted that she come in more often but the young lady had set her conditions and had every intention of sticking to them. It was her first job and her only goal was to buy a concert ticket. She was pretty sure that she was not going to repeat the experience anytime soon. Although she was young the neighborhood was familiar to her, located only two blocks from her home. But she did not know about all nightlife since she was much too young to be hanging around the streets so late. Her father did not get home before midnight, Carole was sure. It was the same ritual every Friday night and like Cinderella she had to be home before the fatal stroke of twelve.

What a Cinderella I make, she thought with her hands in the cruddy water scrubbing the pans or taking out the garbage. The only thing that was good about it was that the boss paid in cash and she almost smiled when she pocketed the bills after work.

The toughest part was over. The Osmond concert was starting to materialize in her head. There were only five minutes left before she got home and there was no question of dragging her heels. It was not completely dark in these latter days of June. The day's heat had not dissipated and it made the slightest movement tiresome. Carole had to remain calm, but she also had to get home before her father. She had worked her three hours and only had six more before the whole thing would be over.

She was almost home when suddenly she was certain that she was being followed. It was unbelievable. She was only 50 yards from her building! This kind of thing only happened to other people… Without turning around she sped up, but the stranger's pace closed in quickly. Then Carole started running as fast as she could to cover the little distance that was left. She did not look back, but swung the door open. Now she had to cross the lobby, go through another door and then things would get complicated because she had to press a code and she was not sure she would have enough time. Her heart was pounding. The shadow got closer. She did not even try to press a single button. Her hand was still clutching the bills when she shrieked.

Danny was not in a very good mood. He had slept poorly because he kept asking himself whether he should warn the sergeant. Nothing was adding up. He had been sent on a mission to get some information, not to swallow the ramblings of an old local celebrity, a drug addict and alcoholic to boot. He went to the music room to avoid meeting Mina. He had no desire to see her this morning and chat about this and that as if nothing were wrong. On the one hand that was part of his job, but on the other he had the feeling that they did not give a damn about him, that nothing was moving forward and that Mina probably suspected that he was a cop. Well, she had the right to think whatever she wanted!

Sitting on a broken Marshall amp Danny tried to tune a Gibson lookalike. It was up to him to put more effort into his job and especially to ask the right questions. He realized that he had come here without an explicit plan and that his superiors had not clearly defined his mission. He put the guitar back on its stand after tuning it and felt a presence in the doorway. Mina was standing there motionless and watching him without making a sound.

Danny was a little startled. "Have you been there long?"

"Long enough to think you were going to make that guitar talk."

"I tuned it but it's completely whacked."

She was dressed only in jean shorts and a thin black sweater. Danny realized that she was still very beautiful and he felt trouble inside. All of a sudden he understood why Mina had come. But there was Lori whom he had left in L.A. and who was waiting for him to return. The Japanese lady smiled as if she was reading his mind and she came forward. Danny stepped back, which betrayed his fear. The situation seemed simple, but things were going too fast for him. To retreat any farther would have been ridiculous. Mina took the opportunity to get close to him.

"How would you like to make love to Madame Atomos?" she proposed.

Smith Beffort was sorry to have panicked the poor girl. He was going back to his brother's apartment and was not expecting to see her outside so late at night. Carole was completely stunned to find her uncle there.

"You have some voice!" he joked to reassure her.

The girl stammered and stuttered but nothing really coherent came out of her mouth.

"Come on, you can tell me all about it upstairs."

Once she had calmed down Carole explained her situation to Beffort, how she had found this job one night a week so she could finish certain projects. The problem facing the FBI agent right now was if he should tell his brother or let his niece continue to come and go alone. The proximity of Carole's work made him opt for the silence all the while knowing that he was taking a big risk.

"Thank you," Carole said. "That's really kind of you."

"Maybe I'm making a mistake by closing my eyes to this but I appreciate your initiative and I don't want to betray your trust. Okay, now I think it's time for you to go to bed. It's past midnight. Your father should be home any minute."

Once his niece was in bed Beffort poured himself a drink and sat in front of the big bay window in the living room. The city stretched out before him in all its nocturnal splendor. Alone with his drink his thoughts were drifting when the telephone rang. Beffort picked it up so as not to wake Carole. A female voice was on the other line.

"Hello. Smith Beffort?"

"Speaking," he answered after a short pause.

"Good evening or good morning, I'm not sure what to say at such an hour. It's Lori. Lori Adams, remember?"

He remembered.

"I know it's late but I took the liberty of calling because I saw the living room light go on."

"Where are you?"

"Downstairs. In fact, I wanted to get some news about Danny. How is he?"

"I'm not authorized to tell you. That's all police business."

"I know. But maybe you could come down? I'd like to talk about Danny. I'm worried about him."

"I'm on my way to bed. Another time perhaps…"

"Is tomorrow good for you?"

"I don't know. What exactly do you want?"

"Just to talk about Danny. I might have some things you're interested in…"

Smith Beffort thought fast. His stay in Los Angeles was nearing its end. He had nothing special to do the next day but he had no reason to meet with her. He had nothing to tell her that she did not already know.

"I'll come by tomorrow," she said. "I'll show you some areas you don't know and places you never imagined existed."

"Okay. For a tour. What time should we meet?"

"Let's say ten at Danny's apartment since we both have the key."

"Okay," he said before hanging up.

Later in bed Smith Beffort wondered whether he had made a mistake. It was not his habit to accept anything that came along. On the other hand, a meeting with this girl might change things up a bit. He had seen his brother, he had seen Sergeant Wood, he had got a little involved in the problems of the local police and now he was going to visit the city with his nephew's fiancée. He remembered that his brother did not like Lori very much. Beffort himself had been struck by their first encounter but did not see anything wrong with seeing her again.

When Danny woke up he noticed that Mina was no longer next to him. They had made love for most of the day, then most of the night and the young man was having problems getting his thoughts in order. Everything happened so fast and he had a strong feeling that he was not in control of much. This woman had made love to him with a passion that he had never known before and he was staggered. He had not thought about Lori for

even a second and was now trying, somewhat shameful-
ly, to chase away her image that was creeping up in his
mind.

Danny got up, put on his jeans and went to the window. Outside the sun was high in the sky already and
was beating down hard, but that was normal in this desert. Mina was deep in conversation with three bikers
still sitting on their hogs and listening to her as she ges-
tured excitedly as if trying to talk over the sound of the
engines. Danny put on his t-shirt and sat on the edge of
the bed.

He laughed at himself. Damn, my investigation just
took a big leap forward.

Then he tried to remember what they had spoken
about the night before. They had not just had fun, but
they had talked as well. Danny hoped that he had not let
any secrets slip out. After thinking about it he decided
no, he had not. The young man had played his role well
and in the end she had not asked too many questions.

By the time he walked outside the bikers had ridden
off. Mina was also gone. There was nothing but the usual breeze and the cream-colored trailers that looked like
permanent parts of the landscape. Hawkins' coffin was
standing next to his door, braving the hot desert wind.
Danny wondered what time it was and if the black was
still sleeping.

Mina popped up behind him. Once again he had not
seen her coming and he was starting to believe that this
woman had the ability to appear and disappear at will
like a voodoo priestess.

"It was Vargas," she said. "He just went back up
north."

Vargas! The name made his blood freeze. The last
person who pronounced this name was his partner

Bundick before being shot down in such a weird way. He hoped that he did not look too disturbed.

"Vargas? He's one of the bikers?" he managed to utter.

Mina kept watching the cloud of dust that was settling in the distance and did not answer. Then she turned to him and asked, "You told me you were looking for work?"

Danny was surprised. "Uh, yeah. Let's just say that I'm a little bored. I'd like to do something."

"It would be transporting arms and different stuff. Vargas asked me if I knew anyone reliable and trustworthy. I thought of you. It's not like I trust you completely, but we need a hand at the moment."

"That's illegal!"

"Nothing's illegal in the desert. You're not part of the world anymore. You better get that through your head right away. Things are going to change and you'll be part of it."

"Part of what?"

"Part of the elite, of those who are going to take the power. The day is coming soon. Anyway, you can't go back now. If you don't agree you'll be signing your death warrant."

Danny was speechless at her candor. Such words coming from Hawkins could be blamed on drunken babble. Could it be that Mina was crazy or on drugs? But she did appear to have a good head on her shoulders.

"You'll have to tell me a little more," Danny said cautiously. "I hear a lot of talk about the revolution but it's still just a dream. Is your thing organized? Are there many of you involved? And your Vargas, is he collecting arms just to knock off a bank?"

A hint of a smile crossed Mina's lips. "We're an outpost here," she answered. "I'm the guard and I coordinate these places. But there are hundreds of outposts. We're here to keep watch and sound the alarm in case of danger. Over there beyond the hills at the end of the world is where everything's being prepared. Do you want to be with us, Danny? You've heard about the desert dwellers, the ones living under the ground?"

Danny became aware that he should be very careful about what he said and he should especially avoid using words that spontaneously came to mind like "madmen" and "lunatics".

"Does Hawkins believe it?"

"Hawkins is constantly on hallucinogens. But it's for people like him that we're fighting for because people like him will have a place in our new society."

"But I have a practical problem: I have no vehicle. How can I transport arms?"

"Don't worry. They'll come and get you pretty soon. Your instructions won't be given here but, as I said, over the hills. You'll meet the desert people and work for them."

Danny felt his palms starting to sweat. He was moving forward but things were moving a little too fast to his liking. He stepped up to Mina but she turned around to go back to the house. Danny turned back to his trailer. He had to warn the sergeant. Everything was happening too fast. First of all the young policeman had no desire to see Vargas face to face. If he really was there at the tragedy the other day, then there was a good chance he would recognize Danny. Moreover, it all sounded like the ravings of a lunatic. It was impossible for such an organization to get set up. There were obviously wild madmen in the desert, even murderers, but it had to be disorganized. What happened with Manson and the family was an isolated case and limited to small number of people.

Danny rummaged through his bag, found his toilet kit and took out the electric razor. The base of the razor snapped off and Danny pulled out a tiny microphone that communicated with his superiors. His call was short: something was really in the works; he was going to leave and would send further messages later.

He closed up the kit and put it back in the bag. He had to see Mina and get a little more information about what his job would be.

A knock at the window made him jump but he quickly recognized the smiling, stoned face of Hawkins who must have needed some company. Danny relaxed.

"I saw you talking with the Lady," the black said. "I see she's brought you in on it. You're one of us now."

"I'm glad to know it. But really, you're a little nosey, aren't you?"

"It's because we all went through it. You arrive and Mina does the sorting. She sorts out who stays and who goes."

"And how does she sort it out?"

"It takes some time to know if we can trust someone and it's Mina who decides. She sorts and chooses."

"I'm glad to know I was accepted."

Hawkins pointed at the fridge. "See if there's any beer left, kid. I'm glad you were accepted too because I like you a lot."

"Stop. You're gonna make me cry."

"No, I swear it, it didn't look good at the start. They were really suspicious of you. And then the Lady had her way with you and she knew everything about you."

Danny felt a knot in this throat. "What do you mean? A night with her is like a lie detector?"

The black man got up and motioned to Danny to follow him. Behind the building Hawkins opened a trap door in the ground. There were stone stairs leading down into a basement.

"Come on, pal. Since you're one of us now. You'll see, it's cool inside, real nice."

Danny followed Hawkins down the stairs. Curiously he was not scared now that he was part of the great brotherhood of lunatics.

"It's true that it feels good," he said.

They were in a big, empty room, which indeed was a few degrees cooler than outside. A dim light filtered through the trapdoor left open to give some light.

"There's nothing here. This room is totally empty. What did you want to show me?"

"We got here too late," Hawkins said. "I wanted to show you the body."

"What body?" Danny asked, wavering between fear and bewilderment.

"The body of the photographer. The bastard was working for the cops and he came poking around here a few times. I just wanted to show you how they settled his score. But they must have taken the body away this morning. Mina's disinfected everything. It smells like roses now. It was not a pretty sight, I can tell you. They must have buried him in the desert. Right now he's probably got a mouth full of sand."

Chapter VI

Lori Adams had not lied in promising to show Beffort the weird parts of the city. It started with a descent into the clubs around Sunset Boulevard, the Hullabaloo, the Whisky a Go Go, tiny, smoky places that distilled the same dull music.

"I know what you're thinking," Lori said. "It's just noise, sonic mush…"

"I'm no expert on music. But the fact is we haven't found a quiet place to talk."

"That's true. Well, I know a place…"

"If it's all the same to you, I'll choose this time."

Half an hour later Smith Beffort and Lori Adams were sitting in a place without any noise but the sounds coming from the busy street. Beffort was in a rather bad mood because the girl was wasting his time. He was on vacation and needed to clear his head, not fill it with distorted music and sterile conversations. Soon he would be back with Mie. Soon he would once again cross paths with Madame Atomos. He knew that he was inescapably bound to her and he did not believe she had disappeared. As for me Mie, he needed her. They had lived through too many things together, suffered too much as well. Their son, who had been taken away from them by Madame Atomos, had left a permanent scar on their existence.

The vacation in Los Angeles was almost over. Tomorrow he would be back with his wife. He would try to keep in regular touch with his brother, Carole and Danny, too, whose mission he hoped was not too dangerous and would soon be over.

Lori had tried to interest him in the music being made in Los Angeles in answer to the British invasion, all the Beatles clones wanting their hour of glory. Beffort listened politely. Then he realized that mentioning the youth and their music systematically went back to the theme of revolt, communes, the Vietnam War. It was a dead end. Always the same subjects. He had been in L.A. for a week now and he felt a very distinct tension from the day he arrived, a tension that he had never felt in any other city. He knew all about fear, the panic that the acts of Madame Atomos gave rise to, but he had never before experienced the kind of tension lingering over L.A.

The people here seemed sick; it was high time he left. He had mentioned this to his brother who replied that they were all leading a crazy life, that it was not easy for anyone here and that he too was nervous because of his job. So, when he looked at Lori, in spite of her eyes and her beauty, he felt an anxiety that he could not identify.

"I'm boring you," the girl said.

"No, I'm sorry, it's Los Angeles that's boring me."

"You feel it, too. It's in the air. The cynics say there are only two forms of transportation in this city: the car and the ambulance."

"You could add the hearse," he said as he stood up. "Sorry, it's not funny. Thank you for the evening, Lori, but it's time I got back. I'm leaving tomorrow and I have to pack my bags."

The young lady remained silent.

"Don't worry about Danny," Beffort continued. "He's a big boy and he's a professional. Besides, there's not much to fear in the place he's at."

"How do you know?"

"His superiors assured me."

"His superiors! Don't make me laugh. What do they know about the desert? They've barely even patrolled the quiet areas. It's been a long time since the cops gave up trying to venture into the heart of the Mojave. Sit down, I have something to tell you."

Beffort was surprised by the authoritative tone the girl had taken and by her sudden arrogance.

"I'm not in the habit of being spoken to like that," he said. "So far I've found you very nice. Don't go and spoil everything."

"Please, sit down."

"Give me one good reason to sit back down and I'll stay five more minutes to humor you. What exactly are you looking for? I'm too old for you, so go to a club and have some fun."

"I still have things to tell you."

"Okay, go on. I'm in a hurry."

"Did you see the crosses in the desert?"

Smith Beffort was bowled over. The police made sure that this information would not get out. No one knew about the existence of the crosses. They were far away from any homes and the press had not been informed. Even if there had been a leak, the discovery was too recent to spread through the public. He sat down."

"What do you know about the crosses?"

"That's the whole problem with cops and with adults in general: no communication. You think we're little kids. You believe that we don't know anything or that we're blind and deaf. But there's an underground life in L.A., a parallel life. The youth are moving around. We know. Sometimes better than the cops."

"No offense but you're not as young as that. Don't try to pass yourself off as a teenager in the lurch. You're older than Danny who's 25. What do you know about those crosses? And how could you know?"

"I know that the crosses surround L.A. and they're getting closer. I also know that very soon it'll be impossible not to see them and that there's one for every inhabitant of this goddamn city."

"A cross for every inhabitant?"

"That's what I said, Mr. Beffort."

"But who says so? Who told you that?"

"Everyone knows it, everyone. It's only the cops who think it's a secret. The hippies started preaching love years ago but everything got all twisted. Satan ensnared us and if he's hiding in the desert it's in order to better prepare his troops to charge into Los Angeles."

"So, except for these rumors that I've been bombarded with, you don't anything more concrete to tell me?"

"Yes. You have to save Danny."

"I'll tell you again, Danny's not in danger."

"And I'm telling you he is! And you don't even realize how deep he's in because you and the other cops are so far off the mark."

"Right, okay. Let's not get upset. Is there anyone who can tell me what's going on? I mean, if the cops can't tell me, who can?"

"You have to go there yourself."

"Excuse me?"

"You and me. We'll go get Danny."

"That's impossible. My plane takes off tomorrow."

"We're talking about your nephew. If you don't try to help him, you sign his warrant. It might already be too late."

"I'm leaving tomorrow. I'm sorry."

"More than you know. Please, think about it. In case you change your mind, I'm living at Danny's."

"Goodbye Lori."

This time he left her for good. He left with an uneasy feeling that kept growing and without knowing who or what, the girl or the city, was the real cause. He was leaving tomorrow, which calmed him down a little.

There was no turning back. Things were clear now and Danny never felt so alone. The Westridge commune was like a cemetery in his view. He was hoping that his messages would arrive at their destination. It was still hard for him to believe that Alain Deville was dead, wondering whether they were playing some huge, macabre trick on him. When he looked at Mina and Hawkins, he could not picture either one as a cold-blooded killer of another human being. Life seemed to go on here as if everything that happened was perfectly normal. Sometimes Danny had doubts and thought that they all knew that he was a cop and were playing with him. He went back to the music room but his trembling hands could no longer pluck any audible sounds from a guitar.

A few bikers came by in the afternoon but did not talk to anyone. Mina seemed to have disappeared. Hawkins was sitting alone on the front steps of his trailer listening to a blues record that was playing on top of his wooden coffin. The sky above was still an intense blue and the sun still blazing, but Danny did not feel the heat. His body had stopped talking to him, sending only the information that was necessary for him to survive under such circumstances. He was swamped in fear.

"Hey, kid! You look nervous all of a sudden," Hawkins said as Danny crossed the deserted courtyard in front of him.

He could not hide it. He knew that his attitude and his anxiety were betraying him. "What you showed me gave me the chills."

"That's normal. It's always like that the first time. It's because you didn't see anything. You're just imagining it. Where'd you meet that guy anyway?"

"He picked me up in New Mexico, I don't know where exactly. I never thought he could be working for the cops."

Danny realized how fake he sounded. He tried to patch it up.

"But what did you mean by 'working for the cops'? Was the guy a snitch or something like that?"

"That very well could be. Something like that."

"Where's he buried? Over there?" He pointed to the desert that looked endless and realized how ridiculous his question was. Hawkins did not answer. He flipped the record over after it started crackling.

They could not know that Danny was a policeman; they were just messing with him. The young man calculated his odds of escaping the place, but the conclusion was self-evident: not a chance in hell. When he looked up and his eyes met Hawkins' he felt like the black man was reading his mind.

With majestic slowness Hawkins let the needle down onto the vinyl. Another dark blues came out and got lost in the desert wind. "You won't have long to wait now," he said.

Danny followed his gaze. A cloud of dust was rising in the north, coming from the hills. Danny had seen plenty of them lately, every time some bikers arrived, but this cloud looked bigger than the others.

"I know what you're thinking, kid. You telling yourself you've never seen such a big trail of dust before and you're right. I've learned to read the signs of the desert. I can tell you what's coming by how high the vehicles are kicking shit up. That there is one hell of a pack coming from the north. No doubt about it, it's Vargas and his gang. You're lucky, your initiation is about to begin."

Sergeant Ross was at the wheel of his unmarked car near the intersection of Hollywood and Vine. It was one of his favorite lookouts and he always insisted on getting the same sector, especially after the attack on his colleague. He parked right behind the Capitol Records building. For some unknown reason the car radio was constantly scrambled in this spot. The sergeant always received channel 33 clearly but when he turned to channel 36 the radio started to pour out a river of 50s rock 'n' roll and Sergeant Ross was a big fan, contrary to the music that the teenagers liked and that he himself called druggie music.

Therefore, on this beautiful afternoon in June, when nothing seemed likely to interrupt this rock 'n' roll moment as the first chords of High School Confidential echoed in the car and while Sergeant Ross leaned over to turn up the volume—all the way, rock 'n' roll is all the way, he often told his wife—at that moment, then, he noticed a vague commotion outside. He did not understand right away. Of course, he could only watch because the sounds were drowned out by the voice of Jerry Lee Lewis. But he ended up realizing that a fight had broken out right across the street.

At first, Sergeant Ross had only seen a few excited pedestrians, then a whole crowd, and finally he saw the scene clearly. A long-haired youth was being held down and beaten up by some adults. The kid, because he could not have been older than 18, maybe even a lot younger, was on the ground and three men were raining blows down on him. He was covering his head but his face was still bloody and the rest of his body was being kicked.

Sergeant Ross thought the scene was a perfect fit with the music and even pretty cheerful. He lit a cigarette and lowered the window. The sound from outside was distorted by the song but he could still hear the teenager bawling. Other men arrived and he could not see much. No doubt the long-haired kid was having a hard 15 minutes and was sorry he had left his parents house. Sergeant Ross picked up his magazine and swore when he saw that the mayonnaise from his sandwich was spread all over the cover. It was getting harder and harder to stake out this sector; he could not do 36 things at the same time. But it could have been worse: if his idiot co-worker hadn't been sick, he wouldn't be eating sandwiches and reading Playboy.

He did a little cleaning inside the car. He threw away the rest of the bread, tore off the cover of the magazine, rolled it into a ball and tossed it out the window. When his gaze fell inadvertently on the sight of the incident, the young man was still on the ground and, as far as he could see, was not moving very much. A man approached with something in his hand. The sergeant recognized the bright glare of a metal saw. Good God, they were going to scalp him!

Sergeant Ross thought that this kind of thing did not happen in the United States. You could have a little laugh but the murder of another human being was forbidden. So, he bucked up his courage and opened the door to wrestle his 240 pounds out of the car. On his way over he saw the Playboy covered balled up and kicked it into the gutter, making the streets a little cleaner that way. Then he headed toward the group of men who looked like they were having a ball.

"Okay, that's enough, boys," he said. "Stop this nonsense right now or I'm bringing you in."

The group froze. In truth there were only three really doing anything, but the one holding the saw, who unfortunately did not have time to start his work, looked terribly annoyed. The sergeant stepped up to the motionless body on the sidewalk.

"You're not very smart, boys. Would one of you at least call an ambulance…"

"But there's no need, officer," the guy with the saw said. "He's dead. You didn't think we were going to scalp him alive, did you? We're not savages!"

The remark made the sergeant smile, but he tried hard not to show it. His hands were clammy, so he looked for a newspaper to dry them. He reflected that he would never again eat a tuna sandwich with mayonnaise while on duty.

Chapter VII

Mie was expecting Beffort at any moment. Her husband was coming back from Los Angeles and should take a very specific route, known only to a few, in order to keep their residence a secret. All these complications made her smirk. Madame Atomos would have no problem finding them if she wanted to because she always got her way. However, it made Beffort feel better thinking that his family was protected, even if in Mie's eyes the protection was laughable.

They spent the evening forcing themselves to appear calm and serene, but neither of them were fooled and sometimes when their eyes met it was a little awkward. They were aware that this situation could not last forever.

"We can't live a normal life until this damned Japanese woman is gone for good," Mie said.

"For now we have to try to make do."

"So tell me about your stay in L.A. Was it interesting or only a vacation? And how are Alan and his children?"

"I saw some unbelievable things," Beffort started. "So unbelievable that it's hard for me to talk about them. But you're the only one I can tell who won't think I'm crazy."

And he told her everything. He talked about Alan and Danny, Sergeant Bundick and the investigation into his death, and also about his discoveries in the Mojave Desert. He told her that Danny had grown up, that he would probably not have recognized him if he ran into him on the street and that it was a young man who knew what he wanted and was currently on a mission in a commune.

"Los Angeles is getting weird," he went on. "It's not the first time I was there. I had some long stays there in the past. But today there's something in the air…"

"Like what?"

"I don't know… Call it a tension in the people that I've never felt anywhere else."

"I think I believe you. You seem extremely nervous since you got back."

"That doesn't surprise me. It really rubbed me the wrong way."

"And your brother? Was he nervous too?"

"Of course, like everyone."

"People who live in those big California cities are more and more susceptible to tension, that's just modern life. The next time you should go to the country."

Beffort smiled. He complimented Mie on her cooking, which was always excellent, and tried to relax by changing the conversation. But he was, in fact, becoming more and more anxious. Mie felt like he had something to say but it would not come out.

"Is there something else you're not telling me? You said I'm the only one who would understand but nothing you've said so far is very extraordinary."

"That's true. I haven't told you everything. But first I want to ask you a question."

"Yes?"

"Do you believe in woman's intuition?"

"Yes, of course. Well, maybe. That's a funny question."

"And for men?"

"You mean men's intuition?'

"Look, if I tell you a truth... not just an assertion... let's say a certainty but I have no proof... Would you believe me?"

"If you've got no proof, I can't believe you 100 per cent. But since I know you, I think there's little chance that it would be false."

"There's always being crazy," Beffort said.

"What? You want to tell me something but you're wondering whether you're crazy?"

"No. I want to share with you a conviction I have that might make me sound crazy. You're the only one who might believe me."

"Go on."

"In Los Angeles I had dinner with Madame Atomos."

The dust cloud had taken on a human face. *The way Satan transforms himself.* At least that is what Danny thought when he saw the pack of lunar vehicles approaching out of nowhere. As always the suped-up Buggys, the best thing for a desert excursion. There were five cars followed by three motorcycles.

The unusual sight relaxed the young policeman somewhat. It was a little over the top, borderline ridiculous, and it reduced the gang's credibility. When the first bikers got off their Harleys, the effect was even more ludicrous. It was like a spaghetti western and Danny wondered if he was not just surrounded by a bunch of morons. It was the best explanation. All of them morons. First this black guy with his coffin who was just a showman and now these guys!

As far as Alain Deville, the so-called dead man in the cellar, he was ready to laugh at it right now. A great big farce. They had to have their fun every now and again, the freaks. It's true that the first guys who came up to Danny were not especially comforting. Bikers! But he knew bikers; California was full of them. Some of them even worked at the bank or as insurance salesmen during the week. None of this meant very much.

They were all on their feet now, around 20 men more worried about striking a pose than paying attention to him. They were all mountain men, wide shoulders and scruffy beards and dirty. There were bound to be some Nazi insignia too, the Hell's Angels were wild about that kind of thing.

Danny glanced quickly at Hawkins who sat calmly on his makeshift stool and did not bother to change the record. Then he looked back at the group.

And he was really shocked to see who seemed to be hiding behind the others because he was so tiny and fragile compared to the bikers. But his eyes were so intense that Danny knew right away that it had to be Vargas. He also knew how he could lead all these guys, how he could be a guru for a hundred people. The difference. A difference and an extraordinary charisma emanated from the frail-looking man. His appearance was bafflingly simple, but it was clever thinking. A ratty military jacket over a dirty t-shirt and a shaved head and face. A shaved head among all these guys. And the piercing eyes in his lifeless face, the contrast was striking.

Vargas (Danny had no doubt it was him) stepped away from the group and came toward him. The young police officer tried to look cool and to be careful that his first words were not too stupid. He, too, had short hair, which he could explain as being a deserter. And he, too, was wearing an army jacket. That gave him at least two points in common with Vargas.

As Vargas came closer, Danny became aware of how exceptional the man was, even before he spoke one word.

It was Mina who broke the silence. Coming out of who knows where, she scuttled over to Vargas with a big smile on her face. *She looks radiant*, Danny thought having never seen her like this before, even during the night they spent together.

Not the slightest change in Vargas' face, but his eyes spoke for him. Mina, still smiling, took his arm and they disappeared into the building.

To pass the time, some of Vargas' men went over to talk with Hawkins; the others napped in the sun. Danny had been called to join Mina and Vargas in the house and the three of them sat at the kitchen table in front of beers.

"It'd be nice if you'd tell one of your men to take a look at the generator," Mina said. "It stopped working a few times this month and it might leave us without electricity for good."

Vargas did not answer; he just drank and let his eyes wander between the beer can and the window.

She continued, "I'm saying this so you can always have a cold beer when you come by."

A furtive smile flashed across Vargas' face. "You're cute, Mina," he said. "We certainly can't let your fridge go on the blink. You know, I've always made sure that you have everything you need here and I will continue to do so. You're like my little guard girl, the guard for all of us. I'll tell Peto to help you out before we leave."

Vargas left the kitchen to give his orders. When he came back Mina and Danny had still not spoken a word to each other as if they were under orders to stay silent. Vargas sat across the table from Danny.

"So you're the one I'm taking today. Mina, it seems, trusts you. completely"

"I'm glad."

"I'm taking you into the hills. This here is only a way station. Mina must have told you all this."

"To tell you the truth, no. I haven't been told much at all except there's an initiation or something like that. I'm just looking for a cool place where I can chill out. I'm not looking to be initiated into anything."

"It's more like truth seeking than a real initiation."

They were there! They were going to give him the "truth seeking" bit. It was starting to sound old hat. Danny was about to ask what they had done with the photographer, but he finally decided not to ask any question.

"Yeah, but that's still a little vague. You all talk in enigmas. I think it's all kind of... superficial."

"What do you want me to prove to you? Starting right now, since you're here and you've met me, you can stop searching and stop asking your damn questions. Let yourself be led, you just have to listen to me and do what I say. You've been chosen among all the others to participate in a great adventure. Don't spoil your luck with stupid thoughts."

There was a pause during which Vargas slowly crushed his empty can in the palm of his hand. Danny noticed that he tried to show a particular intensity in this gesture.

Vargas continued, "Don't switch roles. It's not for you to ask if I'm a clown or not. It's me who's asking who I'm dealing with here. Are you really a deserter? Or are you a cop?"

"I..."

"No need to answer. Mina's already answered and I trust Mina. Since things are clear," his voice rose with astonishing speed, "I won't ask if you're a cop and you stop asking your stupid questions!"

Danny was not happy that Vargas might be accusing him of being a cop. He did not know what to think. Was it a bad joke turning into a tragedy or the opposite. When he had offered to infiltrate the commune, he had no idea that things would turn out like this. In truth he had not thought much about it at all. Maybe today was his chance, his chance to fully investigate the situation. Danny knew that Vargas was sizing him up, trying to evaluate what kind of edge he could have on him. He could not let himself be shaken up.

"Okay. You don't have to get upset. I won't ask any more questions. I'll go truth seeking with you."

He tried to sound casual to mask his nervousness. If this guy was crazy, Danny knew that it was a mistake to act like this: you don't confront madmen and you don't mock them. But he had to swagger because it was the only way he could stay a little balanced, all the while knowing that things could turn ugly at any moment.

"It's true that you're different than the others," Vargas said in a softer voice. "I know that you don't trust me but I won't hold it against you. What you're going to see in the hills will change your life and your ideas about things so much that I'm already laughing at the thought of seeing your face. Okay, let's get going."

"Aren't we going to wait for the guy who's fixing the generator?"

"First you and I are going to take a little tour of the desert. It won't take long."

"What's this about?"

"Let's call it part of your initiation."

Vargas made a sign to two bearded bikers lounging in the shade against the wall of the house. The four of them headed for the first Buggy. Danny and Vargas sat in the back. The biker at the wheel turned the ignition and then revved the engine. Danny wondered what they would do in the desert but did not dare to ask any questions. He quickly pushed the idea out of his mind that his life was at stake.

The Buggy sped off and the house became a black dot on their left. They drove east, parallel to the hills. There was no road to be seen but the driver seemed to know where he was going.

After 15 minutes, which felt like an eternity to Danny, the buggy slowed down. None of the four men spoke. They had arrived in front of a low wall that must have been part of an old building. The vehicle came to a complete stop and the driver cut the engine. Danny saw some crosses. Their destination was a cemetery.

"It's an old cemetery," Vargas confirmed. "It wasn't used by an old Indian tribe or by drifters. No, it's a real cemetery for real Americans. There was a whole colony here once. They had houses, shops and even a place to bury their dead. But hey, I didn't bring you here to give you a history lesson."

There were no more than a dozen crosses tilted by time but still standing, more than the stone buildings at any rate that were practically in ruin.

"I should congratulate you," Vargas said. "You didn't ask a single question coming here. And yet you're afraid, you're wondering what's going to happen. But you didn't say a thing. That's good, very brave. An essential quality to survive in the desert."

The two bikers stayed in the Buggy staring straight ahead as if none of this concerned them. On Vargas' order one of them finally got out, lifted the tarp in back and took out a shovel.

"First step of the initiation," Vargas said. "Take the shovel and dig."

Danny took the shovel being held out of him. "Hold on. Is this a joke? You're not really going to make me dig… what's going on here?"

"You disappoint me. You've been so good so far. Don't mess things up now."

"Okay. And where do you want me to dig? What kind of hole? Big enough for a man?"

"Don't worry. I'm not asking you to dig your own grave. I told you, you came here to start your initiation. Initiation is life, not death. Go see Pete. He'll tell you where to dig. Pete, show him!"

The bearded biker pointed to a small plot of sandy soil that looked like it had recently been loosened up and Danny began his tiresome work. After a short time, he hit something soft but solid. The young policeman stopped digging, overcome by horror, full of dread. He brushed away the dirt around the object with his hands so that he would not damage it. At first he thought it was a pile of dirty laundry. It was an absurd thought but his mind refused to admit that the shovel had scraped a human belly and he was looking at a shirt.

"Okay, you can stop," Vargas said. "You're going to mess up all Pete's hard work. Just look at the face, I think you'll recognize it."

"I can't," Danny said. "I know who it is."

"I told you to look. Look at his eyes if they haven't been eaten by worms yet. Maybe they have something to tell you."

Danny obeyed. He delicately wiped the sand off the corpse's head. He was hoping that the eyelids were closed but it was certainly not his lucky day because Alain Deville's eyes, once they were uncovered, were staring at him intently as if they were staring into eternity. The photographer could not have been dead long because his face showed no sign of decay; it look like a wax statue. But the stench that suddenly raided his nostrils assured him that the poor man was really dead.

"Impressive, isn't it?" Vargas murmured. "Looks like he wasn't as lucky as you. But don't feel guilty. Not everyone can pick the winning number."

Chapter VIII

"It's very troubling," Mie told Beffort, "this certainty you have that the woman is Madame Atomos. What do you plan to do?"

"I have to go back to Los Angeles."

"And then?"

"I've got a million ways to kill her. All I need is one bullet to take her down. But that seems to simple. It's obvious that she wants to play with me. The question is whether she knows that I know her identity."

"No. The question is whether she's really Madame Atomos. That seems to me by far the most important point. You have absolutely no proof, nothing but your intuition. A bullet between the eyes might be the simplest solution but it's also the most dangerous for your future."

"That's what I'm trying to explain to you. I think you're the only one I can talk to. But even you are doubtful. But I'm sure it's her."

"It's true that Madame Atomos often sheds her skin, but until we have proof to the contrary she has never changed her race. This girl you're talking about is of European descent?"

"So what? We shouldn't be surprised at this Japanese woman anymore. We have to expect anything from her."

"That's true, but it's this apparent certainty that bothers me. How can you be so sure?"

"I can't explain it to you. I believe it's her eyes. Madame Atomos can shed her skin, change her hair and age, but she'll always be Madame Atomos. And if the eyes are the window to the soul, then I'm sure it's her."

"That sounds hard to believe. I don't know what to think."

"I do. I'm sure of what I'm saying. Mie, you've always trusted me!"

"Of course, but that's not the question. To go from there to killing someone in cold blood! Can't we first find out about this girl, look into her life, her parents, her family?"

"Of course, but I can assure you that her cover is bound to be perfect. Madame Atomos leaves nothing to chance. Plus, we've run out of time. If she's in L.A. it's to prepare something and Danny is in the thick of it."

"To think that you were going to relax in L.A. and you happened to pick the one city where we can suspect she's planning an attack!"

"No, Mie, I went there because Alan asked me to. It's his son and the L.A. police who first made the connection with her. I didn't want to believe them. The connection is too shaky and we get a lot of false alarms. But after meeting that girl, I know that Madame Atomos is behind it all. I don't know what she's planning but I'm sure that in the near future some serious crisis is going to hit the west coast."

"If you go back, I'm coming with you."

"I'd rather you didn't. I've finally got a chance to be alone with her and settle the score."

"It's almost like you're enjoying this."

Beffort was surprised by Mie's observation. He had to admit that he had been feeling terribly nervous since his face-to-face with Danny's fiancée.

"Mie, I'd hate it if she disappeared too quickly. Even if she doesn't manage to kill us, she's already destroyed us. It seems the least we can do is get an explanation out of her."

"In my opinion it'll be too hard. When she finds out that she's been discovered, she won't be sitting down for a friendly conversation."

"I've already thought of that and I'm going to think about it some more. But I consider this an opportunity that I can't pass up. She asked me to go into the desert with her to save Danny, according to her. It'll be just the two of us."

"And what if it's a trap?"

"It certainly is. I just have to get the jump on her."

"You're scaring me a little," Mie stared hard into her husband's eyes. "I've never seen you so wound up. Are you sure you want to leave tomorrow?"

"It's our chance, I tell you. If we want to win, quick action is the only way."

"The fastest draw, is that it?"

"Exactly, Mie. It's exactly that."

Carole spent more and more time window-shopping. Looking for a special present for her father was becoming a daily obsession. The stakes were high; this present was going to determine the time she wanted to enjoy in San Francisco in less than two weeks. She had to see those guys no matter what. No matter what, her father had to let her make the trip. These musicians were gods and he could not refuse her. He had no right. Therefore, she needed an appropriate gift. She looked in vain at the typical men's products and they were always the same junk. And then one day she saw the perfect gift and thought it was such a great idea that she wondered why she had not thought if it before.

She entered a small bookstore after seeing the stack of *Famous Monsters of Filmland* in the window. There must have been 20 of them. Her father was a big fan of this magazine. Carole remembered the day he lost his entire collection when they moved. He did not sleep that night after realizing it. So, she was sure that buying the copies in the bookstore was perfect because he did not have any left. All she had to do was get the price and maybe negotiate skillfully.

The shopkeeper did not remember that he had the abandoned copies in the corner of his window so the young lady got them all for less than 20 dollars. Exactly 26 issues from the early collection and even though the mythic issue 1 was missing, she got a good deal. Her ticket to San Francisco was in the bag.

At the station Sergeant Wood was, as usual, shuffling the morning paperwork. The various administrative formalities tended to get worse and worse every day. The lieutenant came by for a surprise visit, like he did every Monday, and commented on the cleanliness of the premises, which did not put the sergeant in a very good mood. Nevertheless, Wood had other fish to fry, especially since a phone call had notified him of the strange behavior of a colleague. A youth beaten to death on the street in broad daylight by supposedly upstanding citizens and an officer on duty just looked on without batting an eyelid. Wood could not get over it. What really bothered him was that Sergeant Ross did not even try to make excuses but stated that the youth are more and more out of control, that they are lazier and lazier and that the unfortunate incident might teach them a lesson.

The lieutenant did not mention the incident. Although incident is a funny word to use for a lynching.

The lieutenant was only concerned with trivial matters. It was true that with less than one year to go for retirement you prefer to worry more about litter than murder.

Sergeant Wood was anxious for the day to end so he could go home and thank heaven that he did not live in this lunatic city. He and his family lived outside of L.A. and he wanted to retain this privilege for as long as possible.

Smith Beffort left the airport and his taxi headed for the Western Division office. Maybe he was leaping into a trap as Mie led him to believe but he could not turn back now. It was an opportunity he could not refuse.

When he arrived at the police station Sergeant Wood told him about the events over the last 24 hours.

"I got a call from Danny late in the morning. Things are moving and moving fast. He told me that a large-scale action was being planned."

"Did he give any details?"

"For the moment, not much, except that the target was Los Angeles. By the sound of his voice he was a little panicky. In my opinion he's really onto something. All he needs now is the date of the operation. He won't be using his transmitter anymore because it's too dangerous. His next message will be in Morse code. Danny's got a small device that he can use to contact us in case of emergency and the operator will decipher everything."

"Does he feel like he's in immediate danger?"

"Apparently your nephew is leaving the commune for an unknown location. He didn't say anything about personal danger for him."

"What measures are you taking, sergeant?"

"I'm going to alert the other stations and we'll beef up our patrols in the desert, raid some of the suspicious communes and push farther into the Mojave if we have to. It all depends on Danny's next message. We need something more concrete."

"And you, personally, do you really believe that a large-scale action can be planned by these kids?"

"I do think they lack organization, unless, of course, they're getting help. You know what I think, Mr. Beffort? It's the reason you're here…"

"You think Madame Atomos might be behind all this?"

"It's a possibility. A slim chance but we have to consider it. However, I can't send the whole L.A. police force into the Mojave. It's not my decision. I have superiors, Mr. Beffort.. So if the FBI decides to do something, I see nothing wrong with it."

"You're right, sergeant. Madame Atomos is behind all this, I'm certain of it."

"And you have proof?"

"It would be too long to explain it to you but in fact we have to alert your superiors. I'll take care of doing it with the FBI and we can lead the operation together."

"Hold on. You have to explain, Beffort. What do you have?"

"Not much, I'm afraid, and that's the problem. It's true we need something more solid. We'll have to wait. Wait but be on guard."

Beffort did not want to talk about his suspicions, or rather his conviction, about the connection he had made between Lori Adams and Madame Atomos. Nor did he desire to hide anything from the police. He simply wanted to take care of what he considered personal business.

"Wait?" the sergeant questioned.

"Well, like you said, to increase the patrols and stay on the lookout, search the Mojave in a helicopter for any suspicious activity."

"Do you have any idea of what to look for exactly?"

"Maybe weapons, guns or a giant laser concealed in the desert. Anything at all out of the ordinary…"

"We already found the crosses."

"By the way, sergeant, have you ever heard the theory that every one of those crosses are reserved for an inhabitant of Los Angeles?"

"My God, no! That's a pretty morbid idea and completely outrageous. Besides, we haven't found so many of them. Who told you that?"

"It seems it's making the rounds in the city, sergeant. People are more and more paranoid. But if Madame Atomos is around, I wouldn't blame them."

"It's true that our fellow citizens seem to going raving mad more and more often. Sometimes the kids are attacked by overexcited adults and…"

"The people feel a presence," Beffort said. "I don't know how, but they feel it, I'm sure, and in some way they're being stirred up by it… There's a force up there in the mountains and what we need to find out is when it's going to strike."

"I'm at your disposal, Beffort. I trust your judgment implicitly. I'll alert my superiors immediately."

"In fact, sergeant, I will need your help. I figure on going myself to check things out in the hills. A good map and some advice would be welcome since you know the terrain better than I."

"You're planning on venturing out into the Mojave?"

"Yes. And doing more than just sightseeing. I'd like to go to Danny's commune. Westridge, I think?"

"He's gone. You won't find much there."

"I have to do something, sergeant. Could you get me what I need on the double?"

"A map is not too hard, but maps of the Mojave are pretty limited, they can't cover the whole territory. As for advice... bring lots of water and watch out for snakes. Are you going alone?"

"I'm going with Danny's fiancée. In fact, she's the one who asked me to go with her."

Beffort saw no reaction, no particular sign of anything at all on Sergeant Wood's face. Maybe he did not know the young lady.

"The Mojave is not really a place for a woman. But, hey, they do what they want. Come on, I'll get you that map."

On leaving the police station Beffort found himself blinded by the Californian sun on a deserted street ravaged by the heat. He had informed the local authorities of a probable attack by the terrible Japanese woman. Now he just had to accomplish the second part of his mission. In order to stay in contact and continue to stay in touch Sergeant Wood had given him a transmitter. Beffort was certain that at any moment something would happen.

He started walking towards Danny's apartment. Going along the beach he thought of all the people enjoying their vacation. He had work to do: find Lori, pretend like nothing happened although perhaps she knew everything, play cat and mouse without knowing who was the real hunter and who the prey. Maybe she would not be at Danny's in spite of what she had said. He wondered whether he wanted to see her again when all was said and done.

But Beffort was fooling himself. Lori was there. She seemed to be waiting patiently for him, sitting on the couch, as if she had been in the room for only a few hours.

Well, well, Beffort told himself, *I better not fool myself too often.*

Then he smiled at the young lady.

Chapter IX

"I knew you'd be back," she said. "At least I hoped so."

This new meeting with her, barely two days after the first, was far more difficult. Smith had made up his mind not to stare at her too much. Lori Adams was a beautiful young woman but he already considered her as less than human. Was there a real Lori who had been eliminated? For how long did Danny know her? Beffort would have loved to have Mie there to see this woman in person. She would have understood that there was no mistaking her. It was proof; he only had to look into her eyes. Such eyes that Beffort had seen only once in his life and they could belong to only one person.

"I'm ready to go with you to look for Danny but it won't be easy. Danny isn't in Westridge anymore. Apparently things are moving fast."

"I told you. Every minute counts and we've already lost precious time. When can we leave?"

"Tomorrow morning. I have a few things to take care of. I'll come by to pick you up early. Do you have the time?"

"I'm totally free."

"I ought to warn you that it could be a long and dangerous trek."

"I know. And I know the desert as well as any cop. With the two of us there's a better chance of finding Danny."

"Okay, tomorrow we head out for Westridge."

"Why Westridge? You just said Danny wasn't there. Let's go directly into the hills where Vargas has his lair."

"Are you absolutely certain that Danny is there?"

"Absolutely. Certain too that they'll smell a cop a mile away. Why not leave tonight? It could be that Danny's already dead and the longer we wait…"

"Calm down. I wouldn't have come."

"Yes, but you're here."

He came up with the quick excuse that he had business to take care of for the trip, which was not completely a lie. Over the course of the conversation he felt more certain and was glad to have got back in touch with her. But he had no desire to drag it out.

"I hope your car isn't a piece of junk. You don't go driving around the desert in any old heap."

He nodded his head and disappeared.

Sergeant Wood had lent Beffort a jacked up Ford that was solid enough to cross a hostile environment. Beffort had checked all his material, loaded his .38 special and double-checked all the points where they could get gas. He hoped that the Ford could reach, if it was possible, the place where the crosses were standing. That would make a good start. Then maybe his partner would take off her mask, but if not, he knew how to force her.

And it was of vital importance to get Danny out of his tight spot.

He was putting Madame Atomos on a cross in front of his FBI colleagues who were applauding wildly. It was like a scene from the Spanish Inquisition and Beffort was in no way bothered by the ghosts of the desert who were whirling around him. Sergeant Wood held out the matches and Danny was smiling at him.

He woke up sweating but his dream had fulfilled him in a way. He was just disappointed that he did not see the end.

He parked the gray and red Ford in front of Danny's building. It was just past 7 am. Lori did not make him wait, a smile on her face and in a good mood, which was a nice change.

"Sorry Smith, I misjudged you yesterday. I didn't think you'd dig up such a neat car."

The sudden change in her attitude puzzled Beffort. He wondered what kind of woman she was to go from her usual melodrama to this superficial prattle about a car when they were off to save her fiancé. A doubt crept up in his mind about her being Madame Atomos. But he knew how smart the Japanese woman was and that she was never where you expected her to be.

The sheriff and Chief Cunha were presiding over the meeting being held at the L.A. police headquarters. Several high-ranking officers were there along with Sergeant Wood who recognized three Lieutenants and General Fred Sears. Sergeant Wood had almost arrived late. He would take the floor very soon and he already knew what he was going to say. They needed the support of the army, even if it was busy elsewhere in another conflict. The army, however, was not to blame and had already paid dearly in the fight against Madame Atomos. Nevertheless once again it had to be on war footing.

"Several undercover agents in my sector confirmed the proliferation of all kinds of heavy weapons in different communes, especially in the west of the Mojave.

That's my business. But the other stations have observed the same phenomenon so that for several months now we've suspected the preparation of attacks against L.A. Officer Danny Beffort, after infiltrating the Westridge commune in the North of the Mojave, has confirmed our suspicions. It's a proven fact and on a major scale."

"What details of the threat did Officer Beffort provide, sergeant?"

"Weapons of mass destruction are set up all around Los Angeles, pointed at the city. Moreover, a revolution is in the works, also focused on our city. That's why we're asking for the army's cooperation."

"It's far too vague. It won't be enough. Whose revolution? Weapons of mass destruction aimed at what by whom?"

"We don't know where or when but the fact is that we're going to be facing some pretty heavy firepower."

"It won't be enough to bring the army in; they've got too much going on elsewhere. Still, I grant you that some troubling things have been happening in all sectors. Therefore, we'll step up the raids in the communes in question, arrest the ringleaders, you know, show them who's boss. By the way, have you finally got hold of that Vargas guy?"

"We have no case against him, chief. Plus, he lives in the desert. He's one of the many gangs that come and go in the Mojave. It won't be easy to get our hands on him. But if we act hard and fast, we'll have a better chance of collaring him and getting hold of something to charge him with."

"Yes. We'll put in more men and better tactics. You can't fight against the forces of order and get away with it. What have you heard from the FBI agent Smith Beffort?"

"I've been keeping him abreast of the situation because we thought there might be connection with Madame Atomos. He's the one who asked me to get you to speed up our risk prevention operations. Agent Beffort is sure that the Japanese woman is behind everything and for his part he's going to inform his superiors and get some more forces."

"The Green Dragon Force? I think he's jumping the gun. Even if we can't leave any stone unturned... Smith Beffort's advice is usually not to be taken lightly. Why isn't he here with us?"

"He's already on the ground. Right now he's on his way to the Westridge commune."

Beffort had to put his foot down to drive the vehicle. Lori was adamant about taking the wheel, claiming she knew the area better and she wanted to handle the funky car. The Ford seemed to defy the laws of gravity thanks to its oversized tires, which the girl thought was cool. But that did not work on Beffort as he watched her pretend to be surprised. The young woman was playing the little girl but she was a bad actress and he could not understand why she was making such a show of it. Anyway, the game was unbearable and did not last long.

He felt the weight of his gun against his thigh and its presence reassured him. *Whoever shoots first wins*, Mie had said and she was absolutely right.

The car had been driving for more than an hour on the last real road before the desert, even though the desolate landscape made you believe that you were already there. The road had long before turned to gravel and dirt as the Ford bounced through the ruts.

"Drive faster, Smith! Let's have a little fun..."

"I don't plan to wreck a car that doesn't belong to me."

"Loosen up and crack a smile. You're always so gloomy!"

"I'm in a hurry to get there. I'm in a hurry to get this all over with."

"I think you look really nervous, Mr. Policeman."

"You should be, too. After all it's your fiancé and you're the one who asked to go look for him. From what you said he's got himself in a real bind, so I see no reason to be smiling."

Lori did not look like she heard a word. "We're going to turn off here, Beffort. Go left and we'll be headed straight for Westridge."

"Is it much farther?"

"A good two hours more. You know, there's one final civilized place near here. You know what I mean?"

"A truck stop?"

"Exactly. The last one before the boondocks. The last chance saloon, as old Jack would say. You want to stop? I'm starting to get really thirsty."

"That's not a bad idea. I'll buy you a beer."

"I think we're relaxing, Mr. Policeman. Watch out or you'll end up flirting with me."

"I really have no idea what Danny was doing with you."

"Why *was*? He's not dead yet, I think, at least not before we've found him."

The Vip Vop was the last stop before the vastness of the Mojave. Beffort parked the Ford in the lot, which was almost deserted except for a few big motorcycles. The sun was beating down hard, so the FBI agent did not grumble about taking a little break. Inside the building was clean and surprisingly refreshing. Three bikers were drinking at the counter. From the looks of them they were probably Hell's Angels.

"You have no idea how lucky you are to be traveling with me," Lori said after downing half her beer in one gulf.

"Why's that?"

"It's very simple. Starting right now you're entering an area that cops usually don't dare go into. There are too many codes, too many rituals that you don't know about. You need information and no one will give it to you because you look too much like a cop. You need me with you to help you. Without me you'd get nothing."

"I'm glad to know that. What do you propose?"

"You see those guys at the bar? They're Hell's Angels. I'm sure that despite your fancy car they already know you're a cop. Any second now they could take you down and make your corpse disappear in the Mojave. But I can keep them from doing this."

"How so?"

"Just because we know each other. They know I'm cool. They know who I am and they won't touch me."

"You're all one big happy family and I'm very lucky to be with you, that's for sure."

"You laugh, but one word from me and you disappear under the ground."

Beffort was constantly astonished at the girl's sudden mood swings. Lori Adams went from joy to anger in a flash and always with latent violence.

"And Madame Atomos," he asked, "what do you think of her?"

There was sudden silence that the young lady broke after a few seconds.

"I don't see the connection. What does Madame Atomos have to do with this?"

"You know who I am. I'm Smith Beffort. And your boyfriend is a police officer, meaning a representative of law and order, in case you didn't understand that. So, what's your game? What do you really want?"

"I told you. I want to find Danny."

"Then why are you telling me about these guys who you could order to bury me in the desert?"

"It was just to warn you that it won't be easy."

"Oh come on! But you didn't answer, what do you think of Madame Atomos?"

Smith Beffort knew that he was playing with fire but he could not help this obvious and completely useless provocation.

"What do you want me to say? I don't give a damn. Hold on, you think she's behind all this! You're still looking for the crazy woman?"

"It's my job. I look at all possibilities. Danny saw the possibility, too, that Madame Atomos was mixed up in everything going on here. You should know that because he told you everything, right?"

"Danny never talked about his work. And anyway I don't care. Okay, you're going to finish your beer and we'll get out of here, Beffort. We have work to do."

"Did I hit a nerve? Beffort smiled.

Lori shrugged and stood up.

After a long, chaotic drive he finally spotted the Westridge commune in the distance. They had driven two hours in heavy silence. Arriving at their destination quickly lightened the mood.

Everything looked calm at Westridge. Beffort parked the car near a trailer and the two of them climbed out to inspect the grounds. They figured out pretty quickly that there was not a soul in sight, so they made a methodical search everywhere: in the house, the basement, each of the trailers. The place was completely deserted.

"That's weird," Lori said. "It makes me think of the *Mary Celeste*. It looks like they jumped ship in a hurry."

"You're right," Beffort responded. "But they haven't been gone for long."

Near the door of one of the trailers Lori found an empty coffin with a turntable on it, still crackling.

"Look, the record player is still on. Like the *Mary Celeste*..."

Beffort lifted the tone arm and gently put it back on its stand, a habitual gesture to make sure he was not dreaming.

"Since you know all the secrets of the desert," Beffort asked, "can you explain this?"

"They all left with Danny. We have to move on. There's nothing but ghosts here."

"Yes. Let's check out the hills."

Beffort was opening the car door when he saw Lori pull a gun out of her pocket and aim it at him. She was too far for him to identify the small gun although he thought it might be a disintegrator. He kicked himself for letting his guard down but it was too late for regrets now. One shot told him that it was a regular gun with regular bullets, one of which caused a sharp pain to run through his body.

Chapter X

"I don't want to go this time," the younger one said. "He gives me the creeps!"

The guard on duty took the tray, placed it on the desk and said, "I don't see what the problem is. Manson is locked up good. He's been here three years without an incident. Sure, he shouts his head off sometimes but he's just a first-class lunatic."

"Exactly. This lunatic scares me."

"You're starting to tick me off. I'll bring him his grub but never again. Get another job or get transferred."

"Listen, it's the first time I've asked for your help. I've got a bad feeling."

The guard snapped up the tray and barked, "Unlock it. I'm going but like I said, never again."

He barely finished speaking when a shriek, followed by grotesque laughter echoed through Manson's cell. The prisoner was in solitary confinement on a lower floor but to hear his laughter, in spite of the distance, would make your skin crawl.

"Okay, you're right," the senior guard said. "It sounds like this fit is worse than usual. I'll check it out." Straightaway he puts the tray down and rushes down the stairs. The laughter gave way to an even more agonizing silence.

Manson was sitting on the only chair in the cell and staring at the guard as he entered cautiously. His face did not change, his eyes remained fixed and intense.

"What's going on?" the guard asked. "You're going to give us a hard time today?"

Manson's only answer was a loud guffaw that filled the space of his dementia. Then he calmed down and started gulping slowly, trying to talk but the words would not come out.

"They've left," he finally struggled out.

"Who left? What are you talking about, Manson?"

"The desert dwellers who live in the bowels of the earth."

"That's right, I forgot," the guard snickered. "Since it's all you talk about, I should have guessed."

Able to talk normally now Manson continued calmly. "What's unbelievable is that you don't believe me. I could get upset, I could jump you and gouge out your eyes. But I'm calm because I know that others will do it for me and I ask for nothing more."

"Don't push me, Manson. I'll play nice with you but don't push me."

"Right now they're already on their way. California will soon be bloody havoc. I hope I'm still alive when they rip your guts out. Shh! Listen, do you hear that? They're here!"

Instinctively the guard pricked up his ears as if he might hear something. It's always the same when you listen to the ramblings of a lunatic. Then he loosened up for a moment, dropping his guard.

And Manson took that brief instant to rush at him, letting loose an ear-splitting shriek. All the weight of the prisoner slammed into the bars. Luckily the door was closed and the guard congratulated himself for not being reckless. He was starting to know this maniac's tricks. Unfortunately he did not dodge the pencil aimed at his eye. In truth he did not even see it. He just felt a slight snap when the sharpened lead pierced his eye and then an awful pain when it stabbed through his eyeball.

Manson laughed and screamed like a damned soul. The guard was double over, twisting in pain but luckily on the safe side of the bars.

Chris was waiting for them to pass him the joint and he was really starting to get impatient. Even though he was stoned, he knew that they had passed him by twice. He was not going to stay here for long. The others were starting to get on his nerves. These guys were turning into wrecks, in fact. Chris had had a job in the city before. A good job that he figured he could get back. Get back to work and a normal life. To hell with all this crap. He would let this bunch of weirdoes change society by themselves! Change society? What a joke! Okay, but the joint?

There were ten of them in the room, sitting cross-legged and all them heard the engine at the same time. Okay, since they had smoked they might believe that their perception was slightly distorted, but this was not the kind of thing that they were used to hearing on their trips. This time it was serious. An LAPD helicopter just for them had landed on the happy ranch. Some of them laughed stupidly. It was a raid and the cops looked like they were not messing around.

In less than 30 seconds the ranch was surrounded. The LAPD abruptly searched the people and the buildings from top to bottom. The operation lasted no more than 30 minutes before the helicopter took off without finding anything but a few joints. But there were plenty of other communes to visit. The hippies did not even have time to be scared. It was a well-done job.

Everything happened too fast. Beffort had first believed that the pain came from the bullet that Lori had shot at him. In fact, the bullet did not hit him. It was meant for the snake that was at his feet and that had bitten him with lightning speed. Lori made him sit down, used her scarf as a tourniquet and cut the wound with a knife to suck out as much poison as possible. Then she disinfected it with the car's cigarette lighter. The pain was intense. But it was professional work, quick and faultless, so that only a tiny amount of venom was still circulating in Beffort's veins, which made him a heavy burden.

He was only semi-conscious when he realized that Lori had taken the wheel. He was lying on the backseat and drifting off again into a sweet sleep when his mind lit up. Madame Atomos had saved his life. It was inconceivable. Or else it was another diabolical plan. Cat and mouse, whoever shoots first. Too diabolical. He was lulled to sleep as the car bumped gently over the gravelly path.

"Wake up, Smith! You're out of danger."

Beffort was in a small room decorated with a hodgepodge of objects. The sun shone through a small window, flooding the space with its heat and light. Beffort realized how hot and thirsty he was.

"Don't get up," Lori said. "You're out of danger but still very weak. Drink this glass of water, you have to rehydrate."

"Where are we?"

"At a friend's place who's not here unfortunately. This old shack belongs to Tony, an old Indian who earns his living giving tattoos. I stopped here so you could get some strength back."

"I'd never guess that you knew so many people in the desert."

"Everyone knows Tony. Everyone, at some time, has come into the tattooist's place, one of the last civilized spots around, a little like the bar this morning. Tony's kind of like the guardian of the Mojave."

"And your friend Tony isn't here?"

"His body's here, but apparently not his spirit."

"He's dead?"

"No, he's alive. But it's like he's lost his mind."

Beffort looked around and saw an old man, small in stature, bronze skinned, smiling and blank-eyed.

"I don't know what happened to him," Lori continued. "He doesn't recognize me, doesn't answer me. I can't get anything out of him."

"Too much loneliness maybe."

"I don't think so. I think he had a shock or he saw something. He's not called the guardian of the desert for nothing. Evil spirits have woken up and Toni couldn't deal with it."

But it was not Tony's fate that worried Beffort. No, what worried him was that Lori had a gun. She had taken care of him but she was armed and he felt a little powerless stuck in this strange place in the middle of the desert with nobody but an old Indian who had lost his mind and a woman who was talking about evil spirits. Maybe she had saved his life but he was still clear-headed. He would not be manipulated so easily. He would not hesitate to bring her down if necessary.

"So what do we do now?" he asked.

"We stay here and get a little rest. Unless you want to call your colleagues on your transmitter first. It's in the car."

"I think I'll stay with you and get some rest."

"That's the better plan. We've had enough excitement for the day. We'll see what's in store tomorrow."

Danny was not expecting such an organization in the desert. Around ten huge, khaki tents were planted in the rocky ground. Some men in the camp were busy co-ordinating their movements with military precision.

"You'll be staying here," Vargas pointed to one of the tents. "You can leave all your stuff, get washed up and then I'll come see you later."

Danny did not need to be asked twice. He was tired from the trip and long overdue for sleep, but he also had to warn Sergeant Wood now that he knew the exact date of the offensive. Vargas had seen no reason to be wary of a man at his mercy and had blurted out July 4, Inde-pendence Day, less than a week away. Less than a week to foil the plans of this well-equipped commando team.

When he was finally alone Danny lost no time sending a coded message. The future of Los Angeles depended on him now. After that he arranged the few things he had brought, lit a cigarette and tried to relax. Then he laid down on the cot and stared at the canvas ceiling, daydreaming. He was nearing the end: he knew the when but not the how. It was unbelievable. A para-military organization! This was a long way from "Peace and Love"!

He was about to fall asleep when Vargas entered the tent. Danny was startled and almost jumped up to block a blow but Vargas waved him down.

"Calm down. I just came to see if everything was all right."

"Right enough," Danny said. "But I never imagined such an organized set-up. I'm impressed."

"You haven't seen anything yet. Just a few tents in the desert. Soon you'll see the organization's bases and that too you'll never imagine…"

"What's my role in all this?"

"The role you're playing. The role of cop."

This time Danny did jump up but Vargas was faster and put a pistol to his head.

"Don't get all worked up. I'm armed and you're not. We weren't fooled for a minute. We've known who you are for a long time, so don't do anything stupid."

Danny felt big beads of sweat roll down his forehead.

"We left you alone because that's what the boss wanted. If it was up to me, you'd be vulture food in the Mojave, but orders come from above. At least now we know that you're still in contact with your superiors."

"What do you want from me? Who's your boss?" Danny asked vacantly.

"You haven't guessed? Come with me, I'm going to show you something."

Vargas crooked his finger at the policeman and they walked out of the tent into the blazing sunlight. There was nothing but desert stretching unto infinity. Danny wondered if he was marching to his execution.

Then the ground started trembling. At first it was a small, seismic tremor with a muffled sound, then two panels of ground slid open. A 15-foot square in the earth revealed a wide staircase leading into darkness.

"It's one of the service entrances," Vargas snickered. "Come on, we're going down."

It looked like a subway entrance in the middle of the desert. Neon lights ran along the side of the stairs and Danny could hear the dull sound of a generator, unless it was some kind of power station. At the bottom of the stairs they came into a brightly lit tunnel.

"I told you there were more surprises in store. Except now you can't tell your superiors about it."

"You don't like me much," Lori stated.

Beffort was not surprised by the remark. Besides, nothing would surprise him now. His ankle was almost back to normal size and except for a lingering drowsiness the effects of the venom had practically disappeared.

"I don't know what to think," he lied. "I owe you my life, so please excuse my attitude if I seem ungrateful."

"Enough with the courtesies, it was just a statement. I know we live in different worlds. You're wondering what I'm doing with your nephew, if I'm not squeezing him for information from the police. You're wrong. I just like him. The cop and the rebel, it's an old story."

"You can love the uniform and object to the society."

"I don't love the uniform. You are wrong again."

"It's strange that you're polite to me when you're angry."

"That's some cop psychology for you!"

"No, that, too, is just a statement." Beffort held back from asking why she was carrying a gun. The old Indian kept staring absently at them. "We can't leave him here. We have to do something for him."

"He's not going anywhere. He's at home. Even if his soul is flying with the spirits of the desert, it'll probably come back some day."

"You can't be serious!"

"What do you know about it? Anyway, it's not your world here."

"Exactly. And you're supposed to help me. We're looking for the same person, so maybe it would be wise not to sit around here for too long."

"If you're feeling up to it, we can go. But I'm driving."

Beffort nodded, then got his stuff. His weapon was gone but a quick glance spotted his bag on the table.

"Don't worry," Lori said, "I put everything inside. Your gun, bullets, everything's there. In the state you were in I had to do something, so I cleaned you up a little."

"Thanks. I think we can go."

Beffort stood up without difficulty. He felt better. He let Lori keep the keys to the Ford. They waved goodbye to the old Indian but he gave no response.

"Wait," Beffort said. "Before leaving we should get some water. I think I saw a well…"

"What do you think I did while you were sleeping? Come on, we can go, there's plenty of water."

On the road Beffort glanced at the gas gauge. That, too, was full and they even had 20 extra gallons in the trunk. Enough gas for any emergency. However, he knew that the fuel would not last forever and their stay in the desert was limited. He had to find Danny and fast.

"Do you know where you're going?" Beffort asked.

"We're headed due east, into the hills. That's where they brought him."

"You're sure about that?"

"Absolutely. I know where I'm going."

There was no longer a road, not even a path. The hills gradually got closer as the desert seemed to change and the sky became darker even though there were no clouds.

Beffort was doing better. He had recovered his health and his gun, which made him feel safer. Now he had to do something. To make a decision. He had to take control of the situation. Otherwise he would continue being led around and that would inevitably be fatal.

Chapter XI

Carole could not turn back. The tickets were bought and her father had to let her go to San Francisco to see the Osmond Brothers. The trip was all planned. She would only stay one night. Her father's birthday was in five days and the concert one week later. Carole thought that the fact that he was born on the fourth of July was a good omen for her. Carole was still young.

She had just finished wrapping her present—the 19 issues of *Famous Monsters* with a loving note. She hid it in the bottom drawer of her dresser. Her father was going to flip when he saw the present.

Sergeant Wood called the station and asked for Chief Cunha urgently.

"We got it!" he said excitedly. "I just got a message from Danny Beffort. He gave me the date of the operation: July 4, Independence Day."

"Thanks for reminding me that July 4 is Independence Day," the chief scoffed. "In case I forgot."

"It's no joke. A lot of our men will be on duty but a surprise attack will throw them into confusion."

"But what kind of surprise attack, sergeant? I recall that you've already stepped up patrols. Any reports to confirm preparations?"

"Not yet, chief. But it won't be long."

"And if nothing turns up?"

"That can't be. Officer Beffort is a crucial factor and my men are out there every day. Los Angeles is wound up like you wouldn't believe."

"Nothing proves that the tension in the city is connected with what's happening in the desert. A lot of men should be on duty for July 4 but I've made an exception for you and sent a quarter of them to watch the communes. Only because I'm not taking your word lightly. But get this, I can't send all my men after a bunch of dirty tramps."

The sergeant almost asked him if he had bought the latest Grateful Dead album but thought better of it. "Thank you, chief. We'll intensify our search."

"And keep me informed of anything you find."

The sergeant hung up feeling like mayhem was in store. Something that would go down in the annals of Los Angeles and that would make him one of its first victims.

"Tell me about your parents," Beffort said. "I know so little about you."

"I don't want to sound like I take everything you say in the wrong way, but I really feel like every conversation with you turns into an interrogation. Maybe you should stop treating me like an idiot. What do my parents matter?"

She had barely finished speaking when the car swerved suddenly. Lori tried to straighten it out but the front left tire had hit a big hole and the girl lost control. Beffort jumped on the wheel but was too late. The tires left the ground and the Ford flipped over twice.

Beffort and Lori were both thrown from the car. The FBI agent landed in the sand, the gas cans flying through the air above him. Then the Ford crashed down on its roof making a terrible racket.

Everything happened very quickly and Beffort got off pretty easily. He was conscious and barely had a scratch. He ran to Lori who looked worse off. She had lost consciousness but luckily was uninjured. She would come out of it soon. Beffort sized up the damage. One of the gas cans was leaking its precious liquid. The other was intact but of no use for the moment seeing that the Ford's tires were spinning in the air.

As she woke up Lori gradually realized what had happened. Driving fast in such a place put all the blame on her. She tried to get up but something was preventing her. Her right wrist refused to move. She tried again and felt a sharp pain. That was when she saw the handcuffs. The other end was attached to the Ford.

Beffort squatted in front of her. "We have some things to talk about," he said. "I know who you are. Tell me your name is Lori Adams one more time and I'll kill you on the spot."

The helicopter was flying over the Mojave and the day was turning out like the previous: miles and miles searched and nothing but desert. It was not a transport vehicle but a patrol craft, which meant that there was only the pilot and the officer in charge of checking the radar on board. In other words, the two men were bored stiff. Deskwork. The pilot was having a hard time not dozing off, which was a real hoot to his partner.

"It's not my fault! Come on, we're almost done for the day."

"What kind of info you got?"

"Sectors A-Z-3 and A-Z-4 from NNW were checked this afternoon with nothing to report."

"Another super day. Are there any beers left?"

"One and it's all mine."

"Don't throw the can out the window in case it lands on one of those long-haired skulls."

The two men laughed like hyenas. Laughs that stopped abruptly when they saw a huge satellite dish a few hundred yards before them.

"What's that thing? It's got to be over 300 feet high!"

"We hit the jackpot! Call headquarters quick, we've got something here!"

The co-pilot grabbed the radio with a trembling hand. "4A72 calling. 4A72 calling."

"Go ahead 4A72."

"We've just spotted something weird in sector B-Z-1."

"Be more precise 4A72."

"A satellite dish bigger than I've ever seen. Wait, something's happening…"

The two men saw the same thing: the satellite dish started sinking slowly into the rocky desert land. The helicopter circled around the phenomenon long enough for the men to know they were not dreaming. It had really disappeared under the earth.

"What's happening? Come in 4A72. What's going on?"

The officer was still holding the mic in his hand. "We've just witnessed an unbelievable event. The dish disappeared. We're coming back to base. Over and out."

The helicopter turned around and headed for Los Angeles.

The police stations were abuzz. A rumor was making the rounds but they did not really know how well-founded it was. Still, several reports were telling of various events in the Mojave. The most surprising was the discovery of strange machines, huge satellite dishes that looked like powerful disintegrators pointed at the city of

Los Angeles. Sergeant Wood was swamped by phone calls, this time coming from the chief of police.

"What exactly is happening, sergeant? You were supposed to keep me informed."

"Some machines were spotted, chief. All four helicopters reported these huge antennas rising up or sinking into the ground. In any case, they're movable machines."

"Lasers! Did you think about lasers?"

"It's still too early to make any kind of statement. No verification can be made."

"Are you still thinking of the hippies?"

"No. I think we're a long way from the student protests against the Vietnam War. If it turns out that the devices really are weapons, then Los Angeles could be wiped off the map."

"Are you thinking of Madame Atomos?"

"That's the most probable hypothesis, chief."

"I'll inform the army. We're going to mobilize all available troops."

"I'm glad to hear you say that, chief."

"Beffort, you're a sicko."

Lori Adams was calm now. She had already told him this over and over. Beffort was unmoved. He had slapped the end of the handcuffs to his own wrist and the two of them were now walking through the hostile desert, chained together.

"This way I can be sure you won't escape."

"You're completely whacked out. Why don't you throw the key away while you're at it. What's the point Beffort? You want to kill us both?"

"I know who you are. I've been hunting you for years. You kept getting weaker because we destroyed your bases but you never died. You changed your body,

116

changed your face to look like whomever you wanted, but your eyes don't lie. You killed my son and you're going to pay for it today."

Lori started sobbing as Beffort marched toward the hills dragging her along by the wrist.

"Think about it," she begged. "We have no more car and no more water. In this heat we'll be dead in no time."

"You'll die before me."

"There's a big problem with this whole thing, Beffort. If I were Madame Atomos, why not kill me right away? You have the will and the means."

"I want to find Danny. I know that he's over these hills and you're going to take me to him because you've lost this round for good."

The two shadows progressed slowly in the immensity of the desert. Beffort was holding up well. He was sure that she would end up cracking and reveal to him her true identity. He knew that he would be lost in this hostile territory if he did not find Danny in time. If worse came to worst at least he would have the satisfaction of putting a bullet in the head of his enemy.

After what seemed an eternity, just as they reached a wide canyon, they stumbled upon a range of hundreds of crosses in the sand and Beffort remembered his helicopter tour with Sergeant Wood. They had now entered the forbidden area whence the apocalypse was supposed to come. Lies, all of it! It was just a show to hide the truth.

And the truth was that Madame Atomos, this formidable enemy, was now in his power. How could she unleash the fires of hell while she was chained to him? Beffort smiled at this thought. However, the blazing sun called him back to reality. He had to figure something out quickly or he would collapse. Madame Atomos was in handcuffs but ready to pounce. He knew that this game was dangerous, so he gripped his gun tightly in his hand and hit her hard on the head. She collapsed without a sound.

General Sears did not look kindly on the excitement of the police. "There are things that the different departments in Los Angeles have no clue about, especially when it comes to the Army's experience with drugs. No bureaucrats are going to screw up this project and I think this needs to be known."

Chief of Police Cunha was standing before him, impressed that a man who looked so sickly and weak could be at the head of more than one third of the country's military force.

"You see," General Sears continued, "the army's in close contact with the hippies, I'm talking about the rebels and draft dodgers, all the kids who hate the war..."

"I don't understand. Is this a joke?"

"I'm not the kind of man to joke. I'm going to tell you about the experiments, chief. In collaboration with the FBI we've got a program to spread LSD and observe its effects as a weapon of war."

"I've never heard about this project."

"Of course you've never heard of it. It's not your job. We sprayed loads of LSD before the attacks in Vietnam. We also got LSD onto the streets of San Francisco and some of the communes in L.A. are under our control. We use these crazy hippies as guinea pigs. So I hope you're not going to screw everything up now. The army has organized an experiment that's got to stay under control."

"You said the FBI knows about it, but how about Smith Beffort?"

"Beffort takes care of Madame Atomos. To each his own."

"Exactly. There might be a connection between Madame Atomos and what's happening right now."

"That's why we're going to intervene, even if it's too early to know for sure. I'm not going to let a bunch degenerates, high on LSD or anything else, stir shit up in your charming city. The same goes for a Japanese woman who's got a score to settle with Uncle Sam."

"We'll have to coordinate out actions."

"We'll take care of that. I've already got some men on the ground, chief. We're going to replay the landing at Normandy in the Mojave."

The chief was becoming more and more distrustful of this little man who reminded him vaguely of Joseph Goebbels.

After knocking her out Beffort had dragged the young lady by her arms. Lori was still unconscious. Beffort knew he had acted madly. He was thirsty and felt beaten down by the desert heat. His apparent madness had to have a reason, a goal. And this goal was right in front of him. It was the crosses. The crosses that he had already seen with Sergeant Wood and that showed up here as if by magic.

The situation had already got out of hand for a while. To be chained to Madame Atomos was more than a symbol for Beffort. It was a vengeance that he wanted to make last because he would never have another chance. She was at his mercy. He could kill her whenever he wanted. Plant his gun between her eyes. So perfect that he refused to do it. Beffort knew that there was a little madness in him but certainly no sadism. Especially since he had questions that needed answers for years and years, that there was Mie, there had been their son and even the dead were waiting for answers.

It was not too hard to reach the first cross with his human package. He took off his handcuff and tried to wrap it around the left beam but the chain was too short. Madame Atomos was waking up. Beffort wanted her to be well restrained so he could question her while keeping his hands free. So, he grabbed his gun and knocked her out again. Blood flowed out of the wound on her forehead. Beffort took the opportunity to take off her jeans and tie her feet together.

When she came to a sticky liquid was oozing over eyes. She did not realize it at first but it was blood veiling her sight. There was something else wrong. She was tied to a cross and in a weird way: she was attached by her feet with her head down. In her field of vision was a small part of the sky that was slowly darkening, but what she mostly saw was the upside-down face of the policeman watching her with a strange expression on his face.

Chapter XII

An incredibly modern and cozy place is all that Danny could think of to describe the room where Vargas had left him. From what he could tell by their descent this place, which he could call a room and not a cell because it had a big bed, was built deep underground. It was lit by a warm bluish neon light coming from the corners. Danny felt like he was in a luxury hotel, as he imagined one since he had never set foot in such a place. All he was missing was a suitcase to look like a traveling businessman.

Exhausted, Danny sat on the bed. In fact, the room was really a gilded cell that did not promise a very bright future. He felt trapped. These guys had never been fooled by his cover any more than Hawkins and Mina. Moreover, Mina might even be Madame Atomos. Anyway, there was no more doubt—an underground base like this could only be the work of the diabolical Japanese woman. He had heard of her secret bases that everyone thought had been destroyed. However, today he was underground somewhere in the Mojave in an ultra-sophisticated complex. How much power did Madame Atomos have to be able to build such a thing in the desert?

An electric door slid open and Vargas stood there, giving off a different appearance depending on where he was: a biker outside but here second in command of Madame Atomos' troops. For, she was certainly in command of the place, as Vargas quickly confirmed.

"There are hundreds, even thousands of us waiting for this moment. Madame Atomos is going to help us in our revolution. Thanks to her we'll have the technological means to destroy this country."

Danny did not quite understand his reasoning. He knew of life in Los Angeles and the counter culture with its music and paradoxes. He was engaged to a girl who did not always share the same ideas as him but he loved her. He could not picture a bunch of rebels marching through the streets of L.A. It just did not add up. Or maybe the Japanese woman had lobotomized the youth with her famous motor brains and was going to command them from a distance like zombies.

"There are very few of us living here," Vargas continued. "Ten or so in this underground complex. And a hundred outside in tents. A real small army. We're the spearhead of those who are going to conquer the United States."

"But what's the point? What's your goal?"

"The destruction of the old world. The adults have cheated us for too long. They won't be using us anymore. Now we're going to get our revenge."

"You're not so young, Vargas. I'm at least ten years younger than you and I don't want to rule the world."

"Yeah, of course not, you're a cop. Age is not the only factor. Society has to change. And that's something you can't understand."

"What are you planning to do with me?"

"Madame Atomos wants to see you because you're Smith Beffort's nephew. It seems she has a score to settle with your family."

With these words Danny knew his end was near.

Vargas went on. "It's almost time. On July 4 our weapons will attack. High-powered disintegrators hidden in strategic locations in the Mojave will strike Los Angeles. Then we'll march in when L.A. lies in ashes. We'll free Manson and build a new church on the ruins of your corrupt society."

Danny thought Vargas was boasting a little too much, which made him look slightly deranged.

"Madame Atomos is not here right now," Vargas spoke more calmly. "When she gets here she'll want to see you, so I'll come get you. In the meantime, make yourself comfortable. It won't be long."

Left alone Danny lit a cigarette, wondering if such an action was dangerous underground, if he would set off an alarm or use up too much oxygen. Then to his surprise he realized that he could still worry about such details in his situation.

On July 3 General Sears' troops were stationed on the military base ready for action and the forces of the police were moving in on the communes to get a full count of the individuals and dwellings as well as all motorized vehicles. Everything looked calm and no hint of a future attack was observed. The four giant satellite dishes vanished under the earth. Men had booby trapped the land to blow them up at their first appearance and helicopters were flying over the area. All the forces in Los Angeles County were synchronized with the army for a wide-scale action.

"It seems clear that these dishes are really disintegrators," General Sears said. "My men are on alert and will take care of them when they reappear."

"And Beffort is still missing. Did you contact the FBI?" the Chief of Police asked.

"The FBI is working with the Green Dragon Force, who should be show up here anytime now to give you more support on the ground. It looks like Beffort is somewhere in the Mojave but we've had no news from him."

"All the communes have been thoroughly searched and except for a few upstarts we're familiar with, we haven't met with any hostility or found anything suggestive of an attack."

"It could be a problem of interpretation of information. The fact is that these machines could not have been built by bums, no matter how brainy. They're the work of an organization with no other name but Atomos."

Many military vehicles, especially Jeeps and tanks, were ceaselessly roaming through the Mojave. The communes and also all the habitable places were meticulously searched. Since ground vehicles could not cover the whole desert helicopters and a few patrol planes were flying over the territory.

"We just have to wait," the general said. "Our men are good and ready for any attack."

Beffort looked up at the sky. The crossing airplanes were becoming more and more frequent but they were flying too high to see him. Moreover, they were keeping at a distance, not flying directly over him. He wondered whether all these crosses could be seen from up there.

He glanced at the girl still in handcuffs and bound by her ankles with the torn jeans. She wore her dirty white t-shirt that had yet to be stained by the blood dripping from her forehead over part of her face.

Beffort stepped back to get a better look at the scene. It was like a medieval painting with a dose of religious madness under a blazing sun. A sun that would destroy both of them, him and Madame Atomos. He knew that help from a helicopter was still possible but since the accident he had lost the transmitter and therefore alone with his prisoner. He would make sure that she did not die, which would be a pity. She would have to know what was happening to her.

The girl's body sometimes shook with slight jolts. Then the agent put his face up to hers and murmured in her ear, "You've lost, Madame Atomos. We're going to die but your death throes will last much longer than mine."

"Please," the girl pleaded, "I'm not Madame Atomos. You're wrong. Untie me."

Lori's wound had stopped bleeding. The blood was dried on her face, sealing shut her eyelids. The picture was totally surrealistic.

Damn, I'm going crazy, Beffort thought. *I have to figure out how to get us out of here.*

Around him all he saw were the crosses, the sand and the infernal sun. But since Madame Atomos was with him she could not hurt him. Thus the nightmare for mankind would be over and if he did not get the answers he was looking for, at least the earth would be rid of a monster.

He sat down, resigned. The planes had lost interest in their zone and no helicopter was in sight. He leaned his head against the cross opposite the hanging girl so that he could talk to her in a relatively comfortable position. Lori's body shaded him and she suffered the sunlight more.

"This had to end someday," he whispered.

"Untie me. Please. The sun is burning me up."

"Confess that you're Madame Atomos."

"Why? Why do you want me to say it if you already know it."

"I want to hear it from your own lips."

"And after you'll untie me?"

"After I'll untie you."

"Okay, I'm her."

"Who?"

"Madame Atomos."

Beffort untied the girl and laid her body gently on the ground. She was dehydrated. Beffort watched her struggle to unglue her eyelids, then two eyes opened in the bloody face.

"Look," Lori said.

Beffort looked up and saw the sky darken behind him in a weird way. It was not clouds but a huge shadow rising over them, followed by a deafening noise.

"Let's get out of here," Lori spurted. "It's an earthquake."

Too many things were happening simultaneously to be understood. The shadow, the ground sliding, the thundering drone... they were too close to understand. But something was rising up out of the ground, a gigantic, silvery white machine that towered over the field of devastated crosses. If Beffort had been far enough back he would have seen a huge satellite dish over 600 feet high.

At the end of the day the men stationed at the edge of the desert were burning to fight it out with the invisible enemy. At five past midnight they were all at the ready waiting for a grand offensive but the Mojave remained calm. At 8 am General Sears, who had not slept the night before, was still talking with his subordinates.

"We should probably expect a real war. Madame Atomos' disintegrators will definitely show up today. The question is whether our weapons are powerful enough to destroy them before they cause too much damage."

"General, Sergeant Wood is on the phone. He's with some FBI guys and the Green Dragon Force. He wants to talk to you."

"Thanks, put him through. Hello, sergeant."

"How are things going there, general?"

"We're waiting for the damn disintegrators to pop up and we're shooting at them."

"Have you spotted many?"

"Four so far but I'm waiting for a full report. Right now they're all back in the ground except for one."

"Can we sabotage whatever's making them move?"

"We tried by laying down some explosives but so far nothing's worked. They're hermetically sealed."

"I've got some agents from the Green Dragon Force with me. They're upset and think we should have stayed in contact with Beffort."

"Well, that's not my job. They can come out here if they want to."

"Don't worry. They have every intention of jumping in and finding Beffort and his nephew."

Around noon the soldiers started to lose patience. Not far from their camp were several communes. Young people like them who did not look mean and had simply chosen a different life. Among the soldiers were both draftees and volunteers who understood this state of affairs. There was more and more talk about the Japanese woman, about not fighting the wrong enemy. At 12:30 some of the soldiers pulled out packs of cards. Only a few men were needed to watch the perimeter; the others could relax. At 12:45 someone asked to set up a television. After all, it was the fourth of July, a national holiday. The general refused but authorized the men to watch the President's commemoration speech at 8 pm as long as no adverse event occurred beforehand.

As if to ward off bad luck the general himself plugged in a television and set up two more in other tents for the men to enjoy the evening. Then everything went back to normal in the camp.

Beffort sat motionless on the metal platform under the huge satellite dish. Next to him, Lori Adams did not move either, staring straight ahead out of her blood-caked face. Strangely the temperature was falling sharply and neither of them was very hot.

"What do we do now?" the girl asked. "You untied me. You're taking a risk."

Beffort stared long and hard at her. "I'd like this all to end. I don't even know where I'm at anymore."

After a few seconds of silence the agent looked up at the enormous machine come out of the bowels of the earth, then back at Lori who did not answer. Her head had slumped slowly to the side.

"Wake up," he said, shaking her roughly by the shoulders. "Don't drift off now."

She opened her eyes and tried to smile. "It's too late, Beffort. You're way off on everything. Just leave me alone."

"We've got to get out of here. It might not be too late."

But his head was spinning. He knew they were in no condition to leave. The sun was beating down on his head. "Are you Madame Atomos?" he managed to ask.

He put his hand on his gun, the only solid thing left to him in this hostile territory where everything was going crazy. "I'm going to kill you, put a bullet in your head."

His trembling hand raised the bun but the girl had already passed out. Beffort was becoming more and more unstable and he knew it. He tried to point the weapon at the girl but gave up. What's the use? It would be better to try to survive rather than kill each other. His mind was in a whirl.

Beffort collapsed on top of his prisoner. The two bodies lay inert. Carried by the wind, the sand slowly buried them.

Chapter XIII

Phil Brang had bought his ranch five years earlier. At the time it was the best of best worlds. Madame Atomos was, of course, getting talked about, but all that seemed like another world to Phil and his family. For, Phil and his wife and two daughters lived in perfect harmony with the desert. He had rejected consumer society and was living happily with his decision. They could call him a hippie or any other name, he did not care. He had won his bet. He had found hope in the movement. The summer of love was gone from San Francisco: to reject his parents' values, to reject the access to a ridiculous social status that, summed up in buying a one ton fridge or a car bigger than your neighbor's.

Five years on, during the time of disillusionment for some of his friends who threw in the towel and dove back into the depths of the system, Phil resisted and was satisfied with the results. He knew the desert communes, his closest neighbors. There had been some problems since the arrival of certain gurus and Manson had not been the worst of them, but they were relatively rare, just minor incidents. Besides, Phil had a lot of friends, people like him who had held out. They helped each other out; all was not lost; it was possible to live differently.

Today Phil was watching the wall of military vehicles growing bigger around half a mile from his ranch. What were these guys doing here? The army in the desert was almost incomprehensible. His wife Sarah and their two daughters also gazed at the spectacle, dumbfounded. What enemy could these guys be fighting?

Phil saw Hess' motorcycle coming straight at him, kicking up dust behind it. Hess was his friend, a true maverick biker who belonged to no gang. They spent many long nights together discussing the new world.

"What's happening over there?" Phil asked. "You managed to get through the blockade…"

"There's a bunch of soldiers piled into the tents with all kinds of contraptions and vehicles. They didn't even pay attention to me."

"I don't have a radio. You know what's going on? What all this mobilization is about?"

"All of them, the army, police, the whole shebang is at the ready… They spotted some machines around here. That's the word in L.A. at least. They're all edgy about it."

"Machines?"

"Satellite dishes or something. There's one just over the hills."

"I haven't seen anything."

"You're too far. You can't see it from here. Anyway, it's gone back into the ground now. But it sounds pretty screwy."

"Satellite dishes that go under the ground? And they say we're the ones taking acid."

"It gets worse," the biker said. "There's a lot of tension in the city. The people are pretty pissed off."

"Pissed off at what?"

"Well, that's what's weird. It seems they're all pissed off at everyone under 25 years old with long hair. I'm wondering if their damned satellite dishes aren't just an excuse for them to start knocking us off."

"It's been a long time since there were problems with the youth."

"Yeah, but it's getting worse and worse. I know a few guys who got the crap beat out of them, almost a lynching. The people are becoming paranoid, I tell you. They're scared of us."

"That doesn't explain the army here…"

"They think something's going to come out the desert and massacre them. It's nonsense. They're all going crazy."

"Do you have an explanation?"

"No, but it might be a good time for you to leave your ranch for a while. I know enough people in the city who could put you and your family up…"

"I get it, Hess. You just said there were bad vibes in the city. I might as well just chill here with my wife and kids."

Sergeant Wood had made his investigation. It was quite a long time to listen to all the hippies and other groups of young people questioned all over the place. There was a lot of music, a lot of drugs and also a lot of utopia, but nothing that could put the world of adults in danger. For Sergeant Wood the only threat was Madame Atomos. There was no need to invoke Satan or the spirits of the desert! Wood had children himself and was pretty well in touch with how things were developing. He was far from a greenhorn and had a relatively open mind. Therefore, when he saw all the young people one by one assuring him that they knew nothing about any plot, he believed them.

The vehicle looked like it was floating over the desert. It was moving eight inches above the rocks and going fast. From a distance it could be mistaken for a zodiac but up close its body was smooth and metallic. On board two men, like fishermen, were observing the area.

Now they were hovering over the place where they thought they had seen two bodies buried in the sand and they got out to investigate. After verifying that the victims were still alive they gave them first aid and them placed them in the back of the vehicle.

The trip did not take long. When the vehicle stopped near a camp, the ground gaped open revealing a deep well to receive it. As it started descending the ground closed up behind it. If Manson had been there he would have noted that the desert dwellers' population had just increased by two new people.

Beffort woke up next to Lori in a pale blue room with a soft, dim light. He quickly tried to get his mind around the situation. The rising and falling of the girl's chest reassured him of her condition—she was still alive. It was his own condition that worried him or rather his condition in the Mojave at a time that now seemed like a distant memory.

Then he saw the cameras in the walls. He also recognized some details in the sophisticated layout and composition of the place. He had already seen it a number of times. He was definitely in a Madame Atomos hideout.

The diabolical Japanese was certainly watching him wake up. That was what the cameras were for. She saw everything. She controlled everything. Soon Beffort would hear her voice and she would come to see him. The thought of it was unbearable.

How could he have confused Lori with such a monster? He could have had suspicions but to be 100 % convinced?

Madame Atomos still had the power to get into people's brains, even Beffort's, though he had no idea how she pulled it off. Nevertheless, this was not the time to ponder but to find a way to warn the outside world.

What was happening outside? Had she already sown terror in the region?

The sudden crackling of a speaker made him jump, his whole body tensed up. He knew the sound. Madame Atomos was about to contact him.

"Good day, Mr. Beffort," the terrible Japanese woman said. "Here we are face to face once again."

More than half the soldiers were together in the tents. The card games had begun in order to kill time in what looked to be a endless afternoon. Some recruits plus the guards on duty were watching the desert and the few habitations under the crushing heat. They could see a truck stop in the distance over a mile away from the camp. Lance Corporal Molina knew the truck stop well having stopped there a few times when he was a civilian. The bar was where the freaks from the area and those just passing through would gather.

"What are you thinking about?" Molina asked his partner who was trying to get comfortable in the heat.

"I think things have really changed and I don't see my future in the same way I did when I signed up."

"What are you griping about? We're not in Vietnam."

"It's worse. I feel like we're going into battle against each other."

"Hey, c'mon pal, didn't you see that thing on top of the mountain? A grade A disintegrator! In less than three seconds we could all be wiped out! So, your lousy ideas…"

"Have you noticed anything?"

"Should I?"

"The silence."

"I hear the T.V. in the tent."

"No, I'm talking about the desert. It's more and more silent. The calm before the storm."

"Stop it. You're giving me the creeps."

"I hope we're not going to be fighting our brothers."

"What do you mean? It's your Mexican blood that's screwing you up."

"It's the people right in front of us. They're Americans like you and me."

"Sure, but they're not our target, numbskull. Come on, let's get into a poker game and get your mind off it."

At the Vargas camp the activity was intense. Material was being unloaded from trucks. Weapons were being stocked up on all sides. 100 sparkling motorcycles were parked next to the camp. Vargas had come up from the depths to supervise everything. Only the initiated could come to this place that was inaccessible to common man. The attack was scheduled to start soon. In less than four hours Vargas would contact Madame Atomos to tell her that everything was ready. In the meantime, he sketched out a number of plans in his head among which freeing Charles Manson seemed absolutely necessary.

"You're back on your feet," Beffort said. "I never believed in your disappearance. I guess whatever I did I was bound to run into you."

"I could say the same thing. However, this time I literally guided you to me, my dear Mr. Beffort, and it is not by chance that you are here. And this poor girl you thought was me, isn't that a laugh? Look at what a pitiful state you reduced her to. And I believe she's your nephew's fiancée."

"You've got Danny, too?"

"I have the pleasure of holding two members of the Beffort family. We're going to have quite a time."

The door slid open and two guards entered, two European men very different from the bikers outside. Dressed in dark blue uniforms they looked like on duty policemen. Beffort followed them down a few brightly lit corridors, then after passing a dozen doors the three of them entered a big circular room. Madame Atomos was waiting there, alone in the middle of the room. She signaled the guards to leave.

When he saw her Beffort wondered how he could have fooled himself and taken Lori for this creature he knew so well. Because Madame Atomos had not really changed in spite of the recent physical transformations that she performed on her.

Beffort felt uneasy. For several days he had rubbed shoulders with people who were weird, certainly, but thoroughly human. Here everything seemed sterilized. The sinister woman was dressed in a simple but elegant outfit, blue and black, which would have fulfilled more than a few Westerners' fantasies.

He himself felt dirty with his 3-day beard and the clothes that he had worn all through his desert trek. He was in dire need of a shower to wash off the sand that incrusted on his clothes and skin.

"You'll be able to wash yourself," the Japanese woman seemed to read his mind. "And you'll also eat so you can be in good shape to watch my little operation. You'll see everything from the inside. You'll be able to watch the destruction of the United States from inside Madame Atomos' very own quarters."

Carole was waiting for the right time. They had just sat down to eat but her father was in a bad mood. The problem was to find the right time to give him his present. Then she would have to talk and not let him interrupt her, to tell him the tickets were bought and the concert could not take place without her.

"You can tell me later," Alan said. "The President's on the T.V. I'll listen to his speech and then I'm all yours. I had a bad day today, you know, so I'm sorry if I'm a little out of it."

She knew her father. Frankly, he was often grumpy since his divorce, so his behavior did not mean that he was angry with his daughter. There was also his work weighing on him and worries that he never talked about.

The appetizers were gobbled up. Apparently it would not be a big dinner tonight. Carole had bought a strawberry shortcake that she had put in the fridge and was supposed to come with the present. Of course Alan never remembered his birthday and the word celebration was not part of his vocabulary.

She slipped away to get the present. It was the moment.

Alan was absorbed by the President's speech, so he did not see her leave or come back. When the speech was over he automatically turned off the T.V. as no one else was but him was interested in watching.

Then he saw the package on the table and Carole believed that it would click in his mind.

"What's that?" he asked.

"It's the fourth of July. Happy birthday, dad!"

Carole started to lose hope. Not only was her plan backfiring, but she was infuriated by her father's total indifference to her present. "Well, aren't you going to open it?"

Without saying a word Alan got up and disappeared into the living room. The girl's disappointment turned into a secret hope. Maybe her father would have something for her when he came back.

Alan did indeed have something to show his daughter. A 10-gauge shotgun that he had bought from a pachuco at the Mexican border.

Carole did not have time get scared or to ask about the Osmond Brothers concert. The shots rang out. Part of Carole's brain splattered against the wall next to the T.V. The shooter looked proud that her skull exploded so easily because Alan Beffort was standing there grinning from ear to ear.

Chapter XIV

He was not being impolite but Hess no longer bothered to ask for permission to open the refrigerator. He was part of the family. While he was fetching a cold beer, Phil rolled a joint. Hess was coming to sit on the sofa when he froze in front of the window.

"What's up," Phil asked. "Something going on outside?"

The biker took a minute to answer as he scrutinized the busy military maneuvers. "I can't see too well but things are moving out there."

Phil got up and joined him at the window. He, too, did not understand the reason for all the activity because both of them were looking in the wrong direction. When the huge ball of fire hit the farm, none of the five people present in the house saw death coming. Hess, Phil, Sarah and the two little girls were instantly turned to burning embers and died without pain and without asking any questions.

After 8 pm an attentive observer walking down a quiet street in Los Angeles could have thought of Christmas Eve when the good people have finally gone home to finish their preparations. One might also think of the start of a celebration hearing firecrackers go off in the streets. But what one took for firecrackers would quickly be understood as gunfire. Then the picture would come after the sound and our man in the street would realize the unthinkable because what was happening in the streets and homes of the city was truly a nightmare. All a man could do was pray. Or thank heaven or whatever that he was older than 25 and considered an adult, a responsible people. For, on this night took place the largest massacre of kids that America had ever known.

There were hundreds of bodies thrown out of windows and hundreds of others running around like puppets turned into human torches. There were babies smashed against walls and countless adolescents mutilated.

Our man in the street was lucky to be over 25 with short hair. He told himself that he should be taking part in the festivities and go home right away to discipline his daughter who has had it coming for a long time. Unfortunately his wife got to her first and had already finished the job. Little Julie, five years old, was lying on the floor of her room, drowning in her blood that was still flowing from her throat and filling up her mouth. The man looked at his wife holding the bloody knife and the two of them shared a sly glance followed by a smile as they stood over their child's corpse. Then they broke out laughing, which mingled with tons of other laughter bursting out at the same time all over the city.

Beffort, even though he was only 15 feet from Madame Atomos, was unable to move, to get closer to her. She had, however, never been closer. He listened to her speak all the while wondering if her voice did not have some kind of hypnotic force that he was powerless against. When he should have jumped at this woman, he just stood there and listened, as if it were any other perverse, egotistical speech.

"Right now as I'm speaking to you," Madame Atomos said, "your friends and fellow citizens have already gone into action and the apocalypse has begun."

"Yes, I know that you're preparing an attack against Los Angeles," Beffort responded. "What exactly are trying to do? Unite all the communes in the desert and march them into the city? That's not like you and it has no chance of success. We have an accurate census of the nomads here and the numbers…"

"Forget about your numbers, Beffort! As usual you understand nothing at all. As usual you talk only about yourself and your exploits. You know nothing about what's happening right now. I feel like you've regressed, which amuses me. When you've stopped amusing me, I'll kill you. Do you realize, at least, that if you are alive it's only because I allow it? Don't drop the ball, Mr. Beffort, and you have a chance to survive."

"So tell me what I should know."

"What you should know is that you will not die today or maybe even tomorrow because such is my will. Today I need you to bear witness to my power and to what your fellow Americans are capable of doing to their own children. Then maybe you'll admit that the people of the United States are not worthy of living."

Her words were far from reassuring to Beffort and the promise of being freed ran shivers down his back. He had always known that Madame Atomos was very intelligent and very dangerous. Moreover, considering the luxury and sophistication of this installation in the middle of the desert with all the guards, it was obvious that the Japanese woman was not only back on her feet but that she was stronger than ever. Her power to harm was in full swing. Her organization was about to make America tremble again.

"I won't leave without my nephew and friend," Beffort wanted to sound firm but he felt unsteady.

She was about to answer when the door slid open noisily to reveal a gigantic shadow. The man had opened the electric door with his bare hands, demonstrating his tremendous strength. He was a black man with shaggy hair who looked out of place in the aseptic environment. Such a surprising interruption could have been funny but Beffort was in no mood to laugh. The man's face was calm, even soothing, like he knew exactly what he was doing, like he was in control of the situation.

"We have to leave immediately," he told Beffort without looking at the Japanese. "You're not safe."

The black stepped boldly into the room. Beffort snapped out of his hypnotic state. He shot a glance at Madame Atomos who, strangely, did not react to the intrusion, then he turned to the black to warn him of the danger. The latter finally looked at the woman as if he had just noticed she was there and he burst out laughing.

"Don't get too rattled by the Japanese, especially the women!"

Beffort realized then that he was still in a frenzy and not yet completely himself.

Where the road left civilization for good and headed into the desert there was a 24-hour truck stop, an ambitious name for such a dive even if the drinks were guaranteed to be cold. The establishment, whose usual customers were mostly biker gangs, like Satan's Sadists to name only one, had been bombed out. The two tanks parked in front of what remained of the west wall made the place look like a battlefield in less time than it took a Hell's Angel to down his first beer. In the parking lot the bikes were scattered over the ground in puddles of gas and oil.

The inside of the building stank of blood and dust. The owners of the Harleys, who had been drinking when the place was hit, saw nothing coming. However, some of them were over thirty and had seen action in Korea. But there are times when a bomb cannot tell the difference between young and old, especially when it is sent by a soldier. It was with these deeply philosophical considerations that the men of the 11th division looked upon the wreckage caused by the attack.

"They got them good," the sergeant said to his men climbing out of the tank. "I think all the suspicious communes have been wiped off the map, which doesn't leave many left. The same goes for all the dives like this den of thieves. You made the good choice, boys. You're young, too, but you're on the good side, the side of order and American values. All the better for you!"

The sergeant was proud of his speech and looked at his men. They were young soldiers fascinated by the devastation of the old bar reduced to rubble. The sergeant figured that since he was not lucky enough to be in Vietnam, the present situation would make up for it. After a rapid inspection, noting that there was nothing to see and no one to help, he gave the signal for everyone to return to their vehicles.

"Someone's missing," he said. "I don't see Lance Corporal Ryan or my driver."

"They're coming," a soldier said. "They just had to throw up."

Half an hour later in Los Angeles the streets were full of lifeless bodies. The madness seemed to have stopped but it was far from calm. At the wheel of his

patrol car Sergeant Collins was slowly coming to, coming out of a bad dream, something vague and blurry like
he had suddenly passed out. He remembered watching
the President's speech on the small, portable T.V. that he
had brought in the car, and then... nothing.

He had to get back to base to make his report and
get some explanations from his superiors. Images were
coming back to him one by one. He realized with horror
what had actually happened. That pedestrian running
before him, the stunned face glimpsed for a second, then
his slamming down the accelerator, the young body
tossed in the air, the blood, the other pedestrians and his
own laughter filling the car, more and more hysterical.

Sergeant Collins was waking from a bad dream and
into a nightmare. He had killed people; he had knowing-
ly run over teenagers. Then he thought of his 15-year old
son who could have been one of his victims, whom he
could have killed if he had seen him. He stopped the car,
wiped his forehead and tried to calm his shaking nerves.
After a few minutes he started the car and headed back
to headquarters.

Less than two hours later, after the general panic in
the police stations all over the city, Collins learned that
his son would have been luckier to be on the streets because he was calmly murdered in his sleep by his mother
with three bullets to the head at point blank range. Less
than 15 minutes later the poor woman used the same gun
to kill to kill herself. Collins could have taken some
comfort in the fact that many of his colleagues were in
the same situation but he preferred, in good conscience,
to take refuge in madness.

At headquarters a semblance of organization was
back and the telephone lines were already less overload-

ed. As midnight approached darkness fell over California, which did not help the situation. All the municipal offices were in turmoil, reports were arriving constantly, each more frightening than the last. From the army's high command were coming in an overall estimate of the extent of damage caused by the troops stationed on the borders of the Mojave. There had been constant artillery fire for almost 30 minutes along with commando teams set out to destroy all life in the sector, giving no quarter and no warning.

Chief of Police Cunha had summoned his closest collaborators. He had stopped answering the phone so he could talk with his men without being interrupted every five seconds by a call for help.

"Can we make some kind of concrete report at the moment?" he asked.

"What we can say, though it's not confirmed yet, is that the crazed killing spree lasted a limited time, I'd say half an hour, and it started Tuesday evening around 8 pm in every house in Los Angeles."

"Is there an explanation for the phenomenon?"

"Not yet, chief. It would seem that most of the youth were targeted by the adults. But this isn't exactly true of the infantry recruits stationed in the Mojave, whose average age is 20. They're the ones who bombarded the mountains and killed a lot of people."

"Are those satellite dishes destroyed?"

"Partly, chief. But I think that's not the real problem. We have to wait for the report from the ground troops but these sudden riots took us by surprise."

"You're right. We have young recruits here, too, and no one tried to kill them. I don't understand. I've got shocking reports about abominable murders, scalped teenagers, others burned alive, sometimes with the help of law enforcement. And now the suicides. The hospitals are overflowing, not to mention the fires lighting up all over the city."

"I might have a theory," Sergeant Wood said, "even if it seems kind of premature."

"Out with it."

"We've lived through some pretty troubled times these last few years. Youth and protest go hand in hand and the Vietnam War didn't help. There's no movement on any campus in the U.S. that isn't against the politics of our President. I think tonight was a movement that sped things up."

"I don't get it. A movement against the youth?"

"Not against the youth but against what they represent. Our children disagree with us more and more. When we don't use them for cannon fodder in a conflict that's not theirs, we send law enforcement to kill them…"

"We're not here to talk politics, sergeant!"

"I'm just trying to explain to you that anyone, say Madame Atomos since we have to blame this plague on someone and I'm sure she's behind it, so Madame Atomos only boosted our fears. Our children needed change, they wanted the world to move and not live like us. There's a conflict about this and I think that's the rift exploited by the Japanese woman."

"By sending adults to massacre the kids?"

"Madame Atomos sent us to massacre our children thanks to our fears, thanks to our fixed ideas that are used as weapons by her. She just had to give us a push and we fell. I don't know how she did it, but tonight I'm sure of one thing."

"What's that?"

"I'm quitting the police."

The black man headed for Madame Atomos but she did not budge. When he got close to her his huge body melted into the Japanese. Beffort knew that he had been trapped.

"A hologram," he murmured. "I never would've thought it. But it looked so real."

The image of Madame Atomos had disappeared as if an invisible hand had turned off the program. The black turned and faced Beffort, smiling.

"This lady can do really incredible things. Even a simple hologram is like a work of art with her."

He had barely finished speaking when the room shook violently and a droning sound rang out.

"You shouldn't be here," Hawkins said. "Soon it'll be too late. You won't be able to get out and find the girl. Go on, you know the way, you still have a chance to escape."

"I came here for Madame Atomos and I won't leave without my nephew."

"He might be dead. And you might be too if you don't beat it. Don't play the hero, it'd be a pity. Someone's got to be saved."

"And Madame Atomos?"

"She's here and I'm going to find here. I've left her alone so far but she can't go on and destroy everything."

Beffort was fascinated by the determination and charisma of this man.

"Probably won't see each other again, Beffort. I'm going to hunt down this monster and make her disappear forever and I'll try to find your nephew too. But you take care of the girl. There's a reason she's here. Madame Atomos has been sending her damn waves over Los Angeles for months in order to manipulate everyone's brains. You were manipulated too, Beffort. You thought that girl was Madame Atomos because Madame Atomos is your greatest fear. But believe me, Lori deserves to get out of here. Quit stalling, get out!"

Hawkins was forced to scream to make himself heard. His voice was drowned out by the drone getting louder every second.

"Who are you?" Beffort bellowed.

"I'm from the force, don't worry about it. Run and find Lori, there's not much time."

"Is this hideout going to cave in?"

"You don't get it. This place is rising up. We're in a spaceship that's getting ready to take off."

Chapter XV

Vargas had always been the master. He knew that his formidable power over all the desert rats was good for two things: First for his ego, which could move mountains; then for his unshakeable faith in himself, while being aware that everything he said was a lie. It was exhilarating to lead crowds, even if they were scum. It was exciting to be taken for a new messiah and to tell his subjects to plant new crosses all over the desert to scare the good people through religion. Yes, Satan had returned. And he, Vargas, was Satan. He was unbelievably lucky to have met the Japanese woman who had got him arms and money for the revolution.

Vargas did not give a damn about religion or revolution. The important thing was to be the master. All was going well for him in the best of worlds as he serenely contemplated his camp as well organized as a military unit.

When the ground started trembling he remembered his own predictions of the apocalypse. The end of the world was about to come to the desert. The underground people would wake up and take over the world. Yes, fine, it was all nonsense that made him laugh for five minutes, especially when the others drank up his banter. The earth had no need to shake like this. He was going to end up falling on his face.

Everything happened very quickly in the camp. Vargas saw the first bikes topple over and he himself had to squat down to keep his balance. Then the tents collapsed while the men were running helter-skelter. In fact, Vargas could not see everything; he was not high enough to survey the disaster. He would have to be a vulture to have a good view. Several square miles of desert were sinking, revealing a bottomless pit that for many disciples must have been the entrance to hell.

Vargas' last thought before being swallowed up by the void was about that bitch who had used him.

Beffort and Lori heard the sound of the apocalypse behind them. The Harley 74 on which they were escaping had its throttle fully open on the road. They could not see the spectacle through the dark night. Their priority, firstly, was to get as far as possible from the place that was still shaking despite the distance now separating them from ground zero.

They rode for a long time, all the way to the suburbs of Los Angeles where they understood right away what was happening even though it was still too dark to gauge the magnitude of the wreckage. But they smelled fire. They headed for the nearest police station and were immediately transferred to headquarters where they met the officials.

When the day dawned on July 5, Beffort learned of the events of the night before. He told his own story several times, trying to keep his thoughts in order and in the right sequence.

"There are a few holes," he told the chief of police. "I, too, suffered the effects of the ray during my entire stay here."

The chief had no time to answer because he was receiving news of the utmost importance. A huge, oblong, saucer-like craft was hovering over Los Angeles. According to witnesses it was more than half a mile in diameter. As the sun rose, the shadow of the machine stretched over a good part of the city.

"I've seen flying saucers before," the chief said, "but never so big."

"A few hours ago the thing was buried in the desert. It's Madame Atomos' ride. I hope it's the only one."

"What do you think we should do, Beffort? Send the planes?"

"We can't do anything as long as it's over the city. One of your men, Hawkins, is on board, as well as Danny and Madame Atomos. We just have to hope it's not a combat vehicle."

After long minutes of silence the flying saucer moved slowly away from downtown and turned toward the sea.

"Follow it on radar," the chief ordered. "And this time ask the air force to send some planes but without orders to fire."

"We just have to wait," Beffort said. "There are people on board who I'd really like to see again."

The saucer did not seem to be flying in a straight line, which gave Beffort hope that something was happening inside.

"What was the name of the officer on board the saucer?" the chief asked.

"Hawkins."

"Hawkins? Okay, find out what unit he belongs to."

The saucer flying over Los Angeles would have scared the entire population of the city under other circumstances, but now, after the carnage that took place the night before, it was just another incident. Nevertheless, Beffort was relieved that it was leaving land and heading for the ocean. The combat planes were flying around it but observed nothing strange, except that the saucer flew as if the crew had a hard time controlling it.

"I'm sure Hawkins is going to succeed," Beffort said.

Lori was brought back to her parents with no unpleasant consequences.

Beffort, however, learned of his brother's suicide with the same weapon he used to kill his daughter. The news was too shocking to have a real, immediate impact. Beffort, like everyone else, was dazed and only became fully conscious of the deeds a little later. For the moment he was wandering through headquarters with a cup of coffee in his hand.

He got an open telephone line to contact his wife. The call was the only bright spot in Beffort's day: Mie was fine and soon he would be back with her.

Then things unraveled quickly. The saucer suddenly sped like lightning toward the west. The radars followed it for 15 minutes, then nothing. After some time it was surmised that the machine had crashed into the Pacific Ocean. A search was undertaken but in vain. The location was identified but the water was so deep it would take a miracle.

"The saucer will never be found," Beffort said. "We should expect anything from Madame Atomos. Maybe this is all a decoy and she's flying around unharmed on the bottom of the ocean. Maybe she'll leave us alone now that she has so much to rebuild.

Beffort stayed in Los Angeles for two more days. Although he was eager to see Mie, he went to the huge crater where Madame Atomos' flying saucer had been buried. Nothing remained of Vargas and his troops but a few burned bodies; the others were lost in the bowels of the earth.

The crosses were destroyed. The trailers and buildings, or what remained of them, were knocked down. All this in an attempt to erase the memory of the disaster. There were no more hippies in Los Angeles or rebel teenagers. Los Angeles had lost almost all its children and was praying that Satan had left the desert.

Some of the dishes that had been used to broadcast the rays were destroyed and others studied but their system was incomplete because they were all connected to Madame Atomos' saucer which served as network central and command post.

After counting the dead the citizens of Los Angeles went back to their routines. The city was now a city of old people.

Ex-Sergeant Wood stared wide-eyed at Beffort. "We haven't found anything on this Hawkins guy. Are you sure that was his name?"

"He said he was from the force, that's all I remember."

"He didn't give his rank?"

Beffort smiled. "Can you imagine the importance of a rank at that time, Wood? You think we were making formal introductions?"

"No, of course not. Sorry."

"It's nothing, Wood. Your question put a little humor in otherwise tragic events, it's okay."

"You'll be leaving us soon, I guess?"

"I'm taking a plane tonight but I have to see someone first."

They met in a quiet café. Beffort noticed how beautiful the young lady was. A true beauty, the kind that is not made with exterior trappings. He saw the girl as she really was and hoped with all his heart that Danny would find her again some day. Danny was a brave young man who was just starting his life and deserved better than he got. Lori was a worthy companion for him, a good woman. Madame Atomos had no right to separate them.

"Do you think I'll find him?"

The FBI agent was careful not to speak too hastily. He had already been wrong about so much. Today, with his brain free of outside influence, Beffort thought a lot about his nephew and he was convinced that he was still alive.

"I'm not just trying to make you feel better, Lori, but I'm sure he's not dead."

"Madame Atomos either?"

"I don't know. I don't want to talk about her. I'm leaving soon and I came to say goodbye."

"You're going back to your family?"

"I'm going back to my wife," he corrected her.

"And your colleague, the one in the flying saucer, you think he's still alive?"

"Hawkins? He hasn't surfaced either. The weirdest thing is that no policeman in L.A. seems to know him... But it's thanks to him that we got out alive."

"He wasn't a cop?"

"I really believed he was but everything happened so fast."

"What'd he look like?"

"Tall, black, with amazing light eyes..."

"Did he have a coffin by any chance?" the girl joked.

"When I saw him, apparently not. Why do you ask that?"

"There's a legend that's been going round the Mojave. A guy named Hawkins walking around the desert dragging a coffin. He's searching for the body of his lost wife and trying in vain to get a decent burial for her so her soul will stop wandering among the dead."

"You're talking about a ghost."

"No, no. This guy really existed. I never saw him but I know people who did. The guy became a myth. Some thought he protected the nomads by keeping evil spirits away. That's how a mortal can become a legend or a ghost if you prefer."

"And did he find his wife's body?"

"Not that I know. This was at the beginning of the '60s. The poor guy disappeared when a dam was blown up by Madame Atomos."

Beffort lowered his eyes.

A moment of silence followed. It was not that they had nothing to say but Beffort and Lori could not help staring at and listening to the city around them. There was a lot of emotion in the air and it was hard to sit calmly on a terrace pretending that nothing happened. Madame Atomos had left her mark. They could still hear the distant wail of sirens.

"It's going to take time to rebuild," Lori said.

Beffort stood up. He did not want to discuss it. Things were always the same. The evil Japanese woman left nothing but ruins and desolation behind her.

"I'm sorry, Lori, I have a plane to catch."

He picked up the file from ex-Sergeant Wood off the table. It was a file of recent events, pages of numbers, photos and reports that Beffort had to bring back to FBI headquarters. It all seemed so ridiculous to him.

He turned to the girl one last time. "Don't worry, Lori, you have the strength and the courage."

Then he disappeared into the crowd.

Tony was not blind or deaf. His five senses were simply absent but that did not mean that they were gone for good. The old Indian was sitting like always in his usual position, which meant that he was on a trip. His spirit was elsewhere and rarely came back to reality. Tony preferred his dreams that brought him to places that only he knew about but that many humans would have desired.

It was always the same comments: Tony is on a trip; Tony is nuts again; Tony is totally out of it... But the old Indian paid no attention. He had never been the victim of the slightest violence in the desert. The youth who came to see him just thought he was strange and had a lot of respect for him.

There was only one person who could interrupt his trips. And today the old Indian knew that his friend was coming to see him. The Jeep stopped next to the cabin and the Japanese woman stepped out, supple and agile like a sand cat. For the first time in months Tony's eyes came alive.

The woman sat across from him. She was beautiful and did not look her age. She leaned forward, her face only a few inches from the old Indian's.

"I feel like my sense are coming back for you," Tony said. "Or maybe you forced them to come back."

"It's only with you that I feel good," the woman said. "The United States is nothing but a huge dump but I feel calm here. You're like me, Tony, a victim of these white people who don't hesitate to massacre their enemies. Today they're even killing their children."

"Be careful, Kanoto, you're not in the United States here. You're in the Mojave Desert, in a world that still has unexpected forces, a world of magic and of death."

"Don't worry about me. I always knew how to get by with magic. And I made a pact with death. Today we won a battle against our enemies."

"I know, Kanoto. I saw everything on my voyages. What are you going to do now?"

"I'm going to let them be scared while I keep dancing with the devil. The pigs haven't finished paying their debt."

The old Indian looked outside the shack. "Is there someone with you in the car, Kanoto?"

"It's my driver. His name is Danny Beffort. But I'm going to let him go back home. I believe he has a fiancée in Los Angeles and I don't need him anymore. He can find his way back without a problem. I grafted a new motor brain in him and he's completely under my control."

Sitting at the wheel of the Jeep Danny was like a zombie, staring straight ahead. Every spark of life had disappeared from his eyes. There was not slightest emotion in him when he turned the ignition and headed back to the city.

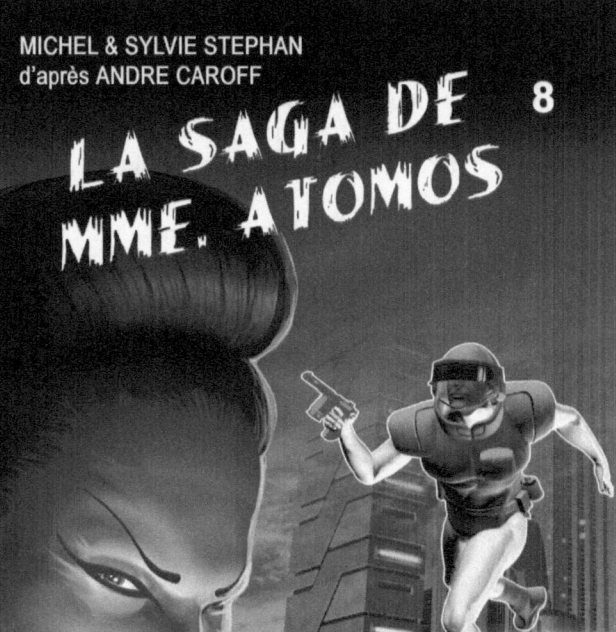

MICHEL & SYLVIE STEPHAN
d'après ANDRE CAROFF

8

LA SAGA DE MME. ATOMOS

RIVIERE BLANCHE

ANTICIPATION BCP FICTION

Madame Atomos parie sur la Mort

MADAME ATOMOS BETS ON DEATH

Chapter I

Tokyo, September 1947

Alone in his hotel room Ralph Bender was ready for action. He did not feel particularly worried. His mind and body were more disturbed by the heat than by the unavoidably stressful hours he was going to live through. See, Ralph had strengths: he was incredibly self-controlled and he was in almost perfect physical health thanks to long months of intensive military training.

Ralph had been in the US Navy for four years. He was three quarters American Indian, well-built and had astonishing, cat-like agility. His colleagues knew only one fault: he was totally deprived of a sense of humor and he saw no need to have one. However, it was recently discovered that he had another weakness: Ralph Bender had fallen in love.

The incredible history had begun three days earlier. Like hundreds of other American soldiers Ralph had disembarked in the port of Mikawa after the war in order to keep Japan safe and secure. The country was in turmoil. Hiroshima and Nagasaki had devastated the future of the Japanese and chaos was rampant in most of the country.

Ralph Bender had not participated in the war. Because of his age he had signed up late and during the conflict he had been assigned to administrative duties. The trip to the Land of the Rising Sun was to be a real maiden voyage for him. It was the first time he had left his native Nevada, not to mention the United States, to find himself in a country he knew absolutely nothing about until a few months ago.

Everything was different here: the smells, the colors and the sensation of an unknown world peopled with little men who were surprisingly kind in Ralph's eyes. Being almost 6 foot 5, Ralph stood head and shoulders above the hustle and bustle of the port. Like other American soldiers he did not have much to do except patrol the wharf and show his presence to keep things relatively calm. Scuffles sometimes broke out on the docks but acts of real violence were rare and only involved the natives who fought each other, especially over the thefts that happened everywhere because of the great poverty afflicting the country.

All this was only superficial, on the surface of things. Everyone knew who really controlled the territory, particularly the Americans who were fully aware of playing a secondary role in the situation. The real power was in the hands of the local mafia, the clan of Gurentai who owned all the bars and nightclubs and gambling joints in the city. Almost all the girls belonged to them, from the prostitutes to the dancers who often enough were one and the same. The money circulated in the dives and slums much more easily than in the open air. And the Americans knew about it because they were the prime customers of these more or less clandestine establishments.

One night Ralph Bender entered one of these bars. The young soldier not only lacked a sense of humor, he seemed totally immune to any emotion whatsoever. At the death of his father he had shown a semblance of grief but that was a natural reflex and had to be taken as such. His emotional range was as narrow as his shoulders were wide.

His vision of things was also rather simplistic. Bender was sure he represented the forces of Good because his life and actions had always been on behalf of justice and the values of his country. He had never cheated anyone. Even if he did not act friendly, he could boast that he was always honest with his fellow man. As for Evil, well, you had to fight against it. There were no half-measures. His father had been on the side of the law and he was following in his footsteps. When his tour in the world's most powerful army was over, he would return to Nevada and become a representative of order, a worthy successor to his father.

Ralph, in fact, was a big kid who liked to keep things organized in his head, for fear of getting completely lost in the complicated world of adults. He was, however, far from stupid—he just needed a little more time to grow up.

It was in this bar, the Golden Lotus, in the heart of the old port, that Ralph saw his destiny keel over. It was a bar for prostitutes that he and his friends visited regularly. Ralph usually just drank while the others went upstairs with the girls, but he did not seem to care and nobody said anything, being afraid of his wrath.

Ralph, who put everything in a specific compartment in his head, suddenly felt his internal file cabinet explode the second she sat down next to him.

Nor did Yomi Nomuna understand what was happening. She had been dancing and selling her body for two years to all the Americans, each one more despicable than the last in her eyes.

When they dropped the bomb, which cost Yomi Nomuna her whole family, she was five miles away from Hiroshima. She preferred to forget the nightmarish days that followed the explosion, the panic of the survivors, the burned faces, the tattered skin falling off and the grisly vision of charred corpses that littered the streets and sidewalks of her native city. In dazed horror Yomi had fled Hiroshima. By pure luck she was alive, but for a young woman alone in a devastated country, there were really not very many options if she did not want to die of hunger.

Well, one night she approached this American soldier without even looking at him, simply to get him into her sordid room and get as many yen as possible out of him. In truth, Yomi Nomuna tried not to look at anybody and was even starting not to look at herself. Everything was so foul and pathetic! But you have to live if you don't have the courage to kill yourself.

The two of the them, the GI and the stripper, found out that night that love at first sight was not a myth. Each of them experienced, like a gift from heaven and at the same moment, a rush of differing emotions.

Ralph felt thousands of neurons shoot off in his brain to keep the furniture around him from getting smashed up. As for Yomi, she felt a new palette of hitherto unknown colors rush into her mind, allowing her at last to paint new lines on the horizon. Of course, this was not very clear for either of them but they were sure of one thing—from that moment on life without each other would be impossible.

Then everything happened very fast.

From then on there was no doubt in Ralph's mind: Yomi had to go with him to the United States and become his wife. That was what he explained to the captain on board the plane he planned to take and the officer found the idea completely suicidal.

"Maybe this woman is just playing with you," he said. "You know perfectly well that she and her kind are under Yakuza control. The Japanese hate us, which is the least you can say. Try to take away one of their women and things could explode at any moment. We keep the population in order through fear but the Yakuza are as powerful as we are, maybe more because they're among their own. No, it's absolutely out of the question that this woman will board a military plane."

"I've thought of everything," Ralph explained. "She finishes work at 5 am. I'll pick her up like I was just another customer. I'll drive her to the airport and the plane will take off at 9 am. It's a one-way trip to freedom. My mother will be waiting for her at the airport and I'll join her when I get back in six months. Then she'll become an American citizen. The only problem is getting on the plane, the papers and all that. You can authorize it through the army."

"The problem is more the mafia who's controlling her. The Yakuza have no pity and will never let her leave, you know that!"

"We'll have four hours to get on the plane. If the papers are in order and if you help me, there won't be a problem. They'll just think she left to spend time with a customer. They won't see anything out of the ordinary."

"If the Yakuza found out that one of their girls was taken away by the Americans, it'll be a bloodbath and we'll have a very hard time stopping it."

Silence fell over the room. Ralph had voiced his argument and saw no need to say more. Captain Carlson, even though he thought the idea absurd and dangerous, had a real soft spot for Ralph. He did not always understand this young man who one had to admire for his somewhat clumsy and childish dignity but who was surprisingly sincere. And he surprised himself when he so readily agreed.

"Well, okay, I'll cover for you. The airport will be informed to facilitate the check-in tomorrow morning. But I warn you, Ralph, you're risking your own hide along with your girlfriend's. You'd better take all necessary precautions."

Since he had met Yomi, Ralph's face had become more and more expressive. One felt that he would have trouble hiding the new feelings that intensified his craggy face. Captain Carlson had noticed this but he did not crack a smile. He had been friendly enough during their meeting.

"It's my day of leave," Ralph replied. "With your permission I think I'll get a room in the old port district. Like that I'll be all ready to pick up Miss Nomuna. I'll be back around noon."

The captain made a slight motion with his hand, which was more like a benediction than a military salute, and Ralph left the room wiping the sweat off his forehead. He borrowed a Jeep from the army and found a hotel room in the old port.

Tension was mounting in him even though he had no reason to worry. He would just show up like a customer, which he had already done more than once. He could very easily pick up a girl and bring her back to his place; men did it all the time. Ralph decided to go to the bar at 3:30 am to get a feel for the place and see if he could spot anything suspicious.

In fact, the bar looked normal. It was surprisingly big with respect to its narrow entrance. All the action was downstairs in a huge room permanently filled with the smoke from the American cigarettes. The GIs were practically the only clientele of the place. Ralph recognized some of his comrades-in-arms but they paid no attention to him. The girls were twirling sensually around the tables. Sometimes one of them would fall limply at the knees of some solitary sailor. When the striptease was over Ralph was supposed meet Yomi outside at 5 am sharp. They would get in the Jeep and go back to the hotel before heading for the airport.

Yomi was not in the room but he had no reason to be alarmed. She was probably changing in the back. However, Ralph noticed some Japanese men dressed in black near the bar. They obviously belonged to the Yakuza who controlled the amphetamines, pornography and prostitution. These were juicy markets since the Americans had landed in the devastated islands and the Japanese mafia was rolling in it. All of this made Ralph sick.

He lit a cigarette and left to wait outside. In five minutes Yomi would be with him in the Jeep and in less than 12 hours she would be meeting his mother. He still could not believe it. He decided that right now he should concentrate on his role: a customer waiting for a girl to take to his hotel.

At 5 am a whole group of GIs, some of them seriously inebriated, left the club. In the midst of them Yomi was laughing and joking, chatting with the sailors as if they were all leaving the theater after seeing a great film.

When she sat in the Jeep next to him Ralph detected no anxiety on her face. He turned the ignition with a steady hand and felt Yomi's body nestled against his. So far everything was going smoothly.

They spoke not a word during the short trip to the hotel, saving themselves for later when they would be married, when they would be Nevada, in the family home... At the moment they were risking their lives and they both knew it.

At the hotel, however, Ralph asked, "Did anyone suspect anything?" His mouth was dry. For the first time in his life Ralph was scared. Love had also freed this emotion, a new one for him.

Yomi did not answer right away. He felt like she wanted to say something but the words would not come out. A strange spark glimmered in her eyes.

Ralph was disturbed. He was not aware of what was happening until the young lady collapsed in the armchair with her head dangling. Then he knew. He realized by the smell that Yomi was drunk. She had drunk, no doubt to deal with the stress and give herself courage.

Yomi raised her head and smiled as the revolting stench of whiskey filled the room. "Everything... is... perfect," she stammered.

Ralph realized that he was going to have to take her to the plane in this condition. Impossible to do otherwise. It would make her hard to transport; she might even fall asleep in the Jeep. Apparently the amount of alcohol she had ingested had knocked her out, but would not be a disaster as long as she was not caught. They had a chance.

At 7 am, when he put her in the passenger seat of the Jeep, Yomi was snoring and the streets were still deserted. The dawning light of day was slowly chasing away the darkness but the heat was still intense, which Ralph had a hard time with. It was nothing like Nevada. It was a wet, sticky heat that mixed with his sweat and glued the clothes to his skin in a disgusting way. But was it really only the heat? The young GI told himself that he still had a lot to learn about fear.

The Jeep was now crossing the suburbs of Mikawa. Two years after the war, the sight of these ruined districts was still frightful—nothing had been rebuilt as ordered. Poverty and corruption were rampant. The Americans were getting used to the Japanese mafia and leaving them alone to the detriment of the local population, in the same way the soldiers (with pleasure however) were getting used to the Japanese whores.

And Ralph Bender was now driving in an army Jeep next to a young, drunken Japanese woman with whom he had fallen in love. He started thinking about Pearl Harbor and almost ran over a kid squatting on the road, a kid missing an arm and with a bloody face. The Jeep swerved but stayed on the road and continued on its way.

When they were outside the city, Ralph started screaming. He screamed to get rid of all the rage that he felt for the madness of the world but his cries did not wake up his passenger.

During the whole trip he kept a constant watch on the rearview mirror. Traffic was flowing and he saw no one following them. They got to the airport around 8:30. The twin-engine plane leaving for the United States was already on the runway. All Ralph had to do was hurry up and put Yomi in her seat as quickly as possible and watch the plane take off for America.

He stopped at the parking lot and waved to the guard who let them through no questions asked. After parking the Jeep Ralph shook Yomi, who woke up without too much difficulty. When he saw a black sedan stop right behind them in the parking lot, Ralph's muscles tightened but the Japanese family that got out looked innocent enough.

As they headed for the entrance to the terminal Ralph had to hold onto Yomi, squeezing her body tightly against his. He thought they had finally made it since he saw nothing unusual around them.

Ralph knew that the check-in had been informed about the young lady's arrival. He also knew what was happening when the officer asked them to wait a minute. The two employees and the policeman were speaking in Japanese but Yomi was in no condition to translate. They made them wait! But everything had been pre-pared! Carlson had taken care of the papers; there should be no hitches. And yet the minutes ticked off.

Through the window of the terminal Ralph saw the first passengers boarding the plane. He felt a knot form-ing in his throat. It was obvious that something was wrong; the wait was too long. Or maybe it just seemed long to him because he was getting more and more nerv-ous.

The officer ended his conversation and gave them a smile, telling them that all was in order. If the young lady wanted a blanket the stewardess would be glad to get one for her.

Less than ten minutes later Yomi Nomuna was fly-ing off to America.

Ralph would join her soon and the two would spend a number of happy years in the land of liberty where an-ything was possible for whoever was willing to work at it.

Chapter II

Nevada, November 1970

Ernst Hartmann felt sick to his stomach. Since yesterday events were unfolding much too rapidly to his liking and had dragged him into a whole series of premature actions. Years of experience had taught him that haste never made anything but waste. But the Atomos Organization had decided otherwise and he would have had to be pretty shrewd to change their decision. Maybe the younger ones like to fulfill themselves in action and in this sudden commotion they saw an opportunity to do so.

When Ernst Hartmann looked at the driver of the Mercury Cougar sitting next to him, he realized that he did not like this kid. He would even say he hated him. At 25 years old (Hartmann figured he could not be older) the young man wanted to defy the elements by driving as if he and the car were one. Hartmann wanted to smash the yokel's head against the windshield to give him just a little sense of values. But Hartmann was not a killer. He was not violent either. Except in his head, of course, where he imagined inflicting the worst tortures on others, though he could never actually do it. Because he lacked real perversity Hartmann was bitter and aware of being nothing but a timid old man. His brain, on the other hand, had many abilities that could make him money in the richest country in the world. For, Ernst Hartmann was a genius physicist. It was for his scientific knowledge that the Atomos Organization hired him.

The driver was called Speedy, a pathetic nickname. This type of guy, full of himself, always had to call himself by the quality he thought he possessed best. If recent events had not caused such a ruckus, this guy would not even be driving the car. Moreover, this so-called Speedy did not even know who he was working for.

The Organization sometimes employed little Hispanic hoodlums to perform less important tasks. Generally it was for manual labor or, as the case here, as a chauffeur to drive from Santa Ana to Las Vegas. If one of the young greenhorns was unlucky enough to learn a little too much about the mission, he always ended up with a bullet in the head and his body dumped in cement to be used as road filler across the Mexican border.

But there were too many things to be settled now for Speedy's life to be in danger anytime soon. Ernst Hartmann had not received any particular instructions about the kid simply because no one had time to give him any. In Las Vegas he would contact members of the Organization who would decide what course to follow.

Since Hartmann started working for Atomos he had never seen such feverish activity. He had to act fast, very fast, and the scientist knew the reason for the hurry. The crash of the flying saucer!

The wreckage was still hundreds of miles off the Californian coast but the authorities would end up finding it sooner or later. Madame Atomos had no desire for her saucer to fall into the hands of the FBI and their aeronautic experts. It was out of the question. First of all because the structure of the engine had to remain a secret but especially, and this was the main reason for their racing, no one could know what these flying saucers were really meant for. So, everyone was in a rush, on the border of incompetence and improvisation according to

Hartmann, who agreed, however, that time was playing against them and they could not afford to delay.

During the final months of WWII, while the superpowers were competing with each other to develop an atomic weapon, the physicist Ernst Hartmann was part of a very small team of German scientists studying the issue. He had been the first to demonstrate that it was possible to trigger and control a chain reaction in a mixture of uranium oxide and heavy water. It was not the excessive and unpredictable destructive potential of a nuclear weapon that stopped the Nazis but the lack of finances. Toward the end of the war the destruction of the main underground bases kept Hitler from completing his projects.

After Hiroshima and Nagasaki, the Americans continued their research. The nuclear arsenal was still in its infancy and they faced the same problem: how to control the chain reaction? The Manhattan Project was launched and a laboratory town built 35 miles outside of Santa Fe in Los Alamos, which saw the final assembly of a device that would raise many questions among the Americans. It was, in fact, a bomb based on the method of electromagnetic separation. This method, in which uranium in gas form passed through a magnetic field of constant force, would prove to be unbelievably effective and caught up with Ernst Hartmann's work ten years earlier. At this stage the bomb was not operational because it was missing a crucial piece: the detonator/mitigator, which the physicists refused to build because even if the mitigator, as its name implied, could slow down the rapid progression of neutrons and consequently the destructive power of the bomb, its manipulation was still uncontrollable.

The project, therefore, remained at this stage. The fabrication of a prototype quickly yielded to the manufacturing of more reliable and more accurate bombs based on other methods and the Americans closeted the first model, the result of the abandoned project, in the subterranean storage of the Los Alamos lab town, figuring to destroy it later. They were in no hurry because without a detonator/mitigator the device was completely harmless and the Americans were convinced that no scientist in the world could build one.

But the Americans did not know Ernst Hartmann. They had only heard about him working in the field. At the end of the war the German physicist joined neither the East nor the West but flew off to South America with the help of the Vatican.

A few years later the Organization went looking for him in Buenos Aires and offered him a significant amount of money to put his skills to work for Madame Atomos. The same Organization had just managed to steal the first model of the bomb, which had not been a particularly difficult operation since the US Army had always figured that without a detonator/mitigator there was no need to be overly cautious about its storage. For the military it was just an unfinished weapon waiting to be destroyed.

The German physicist devoted more than five years to unravel the mystery. More than five years and untold sleepless nights. But he always knew that he would succeed.

In truth, if the war in Europe had not ended soon, he would have realized great things for his country because there too they knew how to be generous. Great powers are always on the side of genius.

Thanks to Ernst Hartmann, therefore, the bomb became operational.

Madame Atomos' objective was to wipe Las Vegas off the map, along with Area 51 where the wreckage of her flying sauce was being transferred.

So, today, driven by young Speedy, Hartmann was bringing the detonator/mitigator. The operation presented no risks expect that everything was happening too fast for the scientist and he was starting to feel really sick. Maybe it was due to age. Ernst Hartmann was almost 60 and he did not feel cut out for a race through the desert, even if the detonator was safe in the back of the Mercury, protected in a lead case.

Hartmann was about to ask the driver to slow down when the car pulled into a restaurant, skidding to a stop in a big cloud of dust. The German was thankful that he had fastened his seatbelt.

"I'm gonna buy some smokes," Speedy said. "I won't be long, Hartmann."

The scientist cursed the young man to himself. This little Mexican was obviously mocking him. After all, he was the pro, the boss who should be giving the orders. A few years before in Hartmann's native country where he served with unflinching loyalty, a young moron like this would certainly have been in trouble with the authorities and never would have spoken to him like that. But he cursed himself too for being a coward and for being troubled by the driver's physical beauty. Hartmann got out of the car to chase these thoughts out of his mind.

It was the dead of night now and the sky was full of stars. The fresh air blowing down from Mount Wilson felt good and helped wash away his nausea. He did not keep track of the distance they had traveled but he told himself that soon they would be in Las Vegas, sooner than expected. But the little man was still driving like he was in charge.

Ernst Hartmann walked around the Mercury. He opened the trunk and felt the lead case. The object was small but the damage it would cause would be unimaginable. An explosion more powerful than had ever been seen before.

The scientist coughed nervously and a dim smile crossed his face. He felt more excited than a child on Christmas morning. He wanted to let his joy explode, like a volcano, ridiculously, like you see in the movies or cartoons. Hartmann was no longer nauseated and he almost felt a liking for Speedy, probably because he was not behind the wheel. So, nothing was keeping him from letting go a little.

He burst out with a demented laugh that echoed in the night. Who cared? Whoever would mock him would soon be turned to ashes.

Ernst Hartmann closed the trunk but had to hold himself back from screaming out in joy. Only his body expressed it with short, uncontrollable, almost obscene jolts. And that was when he saw them and felt his whole nervous system short circuit.

Two police motorcycles parked right next to the entrance to the restaurant. He should have seen them earlier and that jerk of a driver too—he had to stop here of all places to buy his cigarettes!

Mexicans are really a degenerate race, Hartmann thought as his hands started trembling. This was one too many emotions to feel in the same evening when he should be arriving in Las Vegas.

Speedy was taking his time to buy his damn cigarettes. The rules, however, were clear: even if a mission faced no danger, it was absolutely out of the question to take unnecessary risks. Madame Atomos was never lenient on the punishment for such transgressions. Moreover, this idiot had entered a place where there were already policemen. Maybe these cops were the reason Speedy was taking so long.

When the driver finally appeared, Hartmann felt like an eternity had passed. The young Mexican was walking fast, springing like a deer. With a big smile on his face he sat behind the wheel and offered a cigarette to the scientist.

"What the hell were you doing, damn it? You were in there for an hour!"

Speedy looked at his watch in surprise and shot back, "Nah, it was less than 15 minutes, Hartmann. I just drank a beer. A quick one. I didn't want to make you wait. You're the boss."

Ernst Hartmann did all he could to look mean and threatening but all he managed to do was scowl sullenly. He ordered Speedy to drive more slowly and the Mercury got back on the road in the starry night.

"You didn't see the two cops at the diner?" Hartmann asked after a few minutes.

"I didn't see anything at all. It was crowded. I didn't have time to see much."

"I mean the two cop bikes parked at the truck stop. You really didn't notice them?"

Speedy shrugged his shoulders and shook his head. While the car was cruising down the highway Hartmann kept turning around to check if anyone was following them.

"There's no one. I'm checking my rear-view mirror. I'll know if someone's following us."

"Shut up!"

The scientist liked this answer. It was clear and proved to both of them that he was still the boss. He was not feeling sick again but the sight of the two motorcycles was disturbing him for no good reason. The cops could search the trunk as much as they wanted, they would not notice anything. The object they were transporting was beyond the scope of ordinary policemen. For them it would be some simple device bought in any electronics store.

Nevertheless, when he saw Speedy's eyes riveted on the rear-view mirror Ernst Hartmann knew that something was wrong. Perhaps the time had come, the time when they would have to go into action. And the German was scared because he was not ready. He was hired for his intellectual skills. He was not being paid to risk his life.

"Maybe it's not the cops, Hartmann. Maybe it's just two bikers…"

The scientist forced himself to turn around. He clearly saw the two lights behind the Mercury and they were obviously two motorcycles but in the night he could not tell if they were police.

"Why don't they just pass us?" Speedy barked, starting to regret having stopped for cigarettes.

At least they won't find anything, Hartmann repeated to himself, clinging to the thought.

The two men realized that it was the two cops. For a long while the motorcycles held a steady distance behind the Mercury, then they suddenly sped up, passed the car and disappeared into the night.

"Anyway, they wouldn't have found anything, right, Hartmann? Except the shiny toy you put in the trunk, right?"

Hartmann wondered whether his travel companion was having fun with him or the jerk knew nothing about the importance of their mission. It was only because things had happened so quickly that the kid was made his driver. Normally the Atomos Organization would never trust a job like this to such an idiot.

The cops seemed to be gone for good. The scientist tried to evaluate the risks they had run. The results he came up with were the same. Nothing and no one could make a connection between the Atomos Organization and this ordinary car driving toward Las Vegas.

The FBI knew about Ernst Hartmann's past activities, but since the beginning of the 50s the scientist was living in South America as an American citizen. His papers were in order though his identity had completely changed.

Hartmann started to relax now. At the speed they were going Las Vegas was at least an hour away. Once there he would get in contact with other members of the Organization who would tell him what to do next. Maybe they would have to take care of the driver, make him disappear. He would get what he deserved, the little jerk. With his big mouth he might ask a lot of questions or brag and talk too much, which would be worse.

The Organization had strong-walled compounds and that was a great advantage. Thanks to the members on the base it was getting more and more powerful. When the detonator arrived at its destination things would go quickly. One could always count on Kanoto Yoshimuta!

Kanoto Yoshimuta, Madame Atomos in person! What would this little bastard do if he knew the real name of his employer!

Ernst Hartmann watched his driver staring at the road. In spite of everything, he could not help being seduced by his youth and his admirable body. He himself had never been so lucky. Hartmann was born with an unattractive physique that he camouflaged under expensive clothes. That was why he admired this young man's beauty.

The scientist wondered if by chance Speedy might be homosexual. To have relations with him right there in the car or on the side of the road—they had a mission to accomplish right now—but later, maybe the two of them could get together, right before the attractive young man was executed. He would love to use that body. Ernst Hartmann felt his old demons resurface. His upbringing tried to convince him otherwise, but the fact is that he was never attracted to women. He had experiences with the strange creatures of the other sex but they were always doomed to failure.

As for religion, it had been a long time since Hartmann believed in anything. Right now it was Speedy who was the object of his desires. His eyes were fixed on the young Mexican's face, which looked concentrated only on driving the car. Apparently the two police bikes cooled his jets and he kept the Mercury at a reasonable speed.

Ernst Hartmann risked putting his hand on the young man's thigh and started gently caressing his leg. Surprised, Speedy stopped watching the road for a moment. With a quick, firm movement, he pushed the hand away. A heavy silence followed as the two of them watched the road. But Hartmann's passion was far from extinguished and his desire was so strong that he touched the driver again. But this time he was repulsed right away.

While keeping a firm hold of the wheel, Speedy started yelling at his passenger, "Leave me alone, you fat pig!" He repeated the phrase two or three times, screaming at the top of his lungs. Then the boy slammed on the accelerator. The Mercury shot into a 180 degrees turn and took a dirt road leading into the highlands.

Hartmann was thrown back in his seat. The Mercury, although driving far over the speed limit, stayed straight and steady on the gravelly road leading away from the highway. Speedy was still yelling, crying out in disgust and revulsion. All of a sudden he calmed down, seeing himself driving way too fast and too wildly.

But the speed of the car, which was not built for this terrain, made it drift off to the left. Speedy tried to compensate. Too late. He slammed on the brakes but the vehicle flew off the road and crashed into a dry riverbed ten feet below.

Hartmann was just an innocent bystander of the fall. There was a momentary pause in time and space when the car soared off the road, then the crash. A loud thump that filled up space. Flesh mingled with metal. Everything happened so fast that Hartmann did not have time to be scared. He lost consciousness.

Chapter III

When the physicist woke up, he was straightaway seized by fear. He did not think about wounds but about his mission that might be irremediably compromised because of his flirting. Madame Atomos would never forgive him if he failed in his task but got out alive. It would be better for him to die in the accident than suffer the wrath of the terrible Japanese woman.

How much time passed since the crash? A few minutes, give or take. Ernst Hartmann did not feel like he had blacked out for long. He looked at Speedy and took a long time to understand that the young man was dead. The little Mexican was twisted into a position that life would not allow. His body looked intact but his eyes were popping out and his head formed a weird angle with his neck. There was no doubt about it: he was dead. The scientist thought, not without some regret, of the vertebrae collapsing under the shock and crushing the spine.

Since he did not feel any pain, he started to wriggle out of the car. The crash had opened the door and the vehicle was leaning toward the passenger side. It had fallen right in the middle of the small river, which had been dry for years. Hartmann carefully extracted himself from the wreck.

After a few minutes, after checking that he was un-injured and telling himself that some old men are lucky, Ernst Hartmann came back to reality, listening to the noises around him. Besides the sounds of nature there was the hum of Highway 93 passing nearby. Apparently no one had seen the accident. Therefore, he was alone with the corpse of a driver.

For a second several thoughts crossed his mind and he realized that his body and mind had gone through the wringer. He also told himself that this was no time to get wild and whimsical when his mission, if it were not completely ruined, was off to a really bad start.

Hell, all he had to do was transport an object from point A to point B! What difference did it make if it was a TV set or the crucial element for a goddamn bomb destined to blow up half the state? It was imperative that he complete the mission.

Ernst Hartmann tried to take a few steps and was relieved to feel his motor skills intact. He opened the trunk and picked up the lead box, which did not look damaged from the crash. After slowly opening the cover he saw the detonator/mitigator in perfect condition, looking like one of the new gadgets that you buy for children at Christmas.

The physicist affectionately rubbed the curves of his invention, brushing it with his long, slender fingers. This technological marvel had come directly out of his brain, so he was the only one who could make a serious examination of its condition. A quick check told him that everything was okay. The most important thing was that the structure was unharmed.

He had no time to lose. He had to get the detonator to a safe place and act quickly. Even though it was late, anyone could come by at any moment. First of all he had to find a bag strong enough to hold the object. Right away he thought of the backpack that poor Speedy had tossed onto the backseat. He quickly dumped out all the clothes and slipped the detonator delicately inside. It was perfect and did not weigh too much. After adjusting the straps he walked down the dried up river. He had escaped the worst disaster but the hardest part was yet to come: now he had to find a way to tell the Organization.

He waited until he was far from the car before climbing out of the riverbed to look for some kind of marker to give the Organization so they could send help as soon as possible. The night was clear and after walking for half an hour Hartmann saw a simple, wooden sign standing at an intersection, which read: Salvation, 4 miles.

With a trembling hand he grabbed his transmitter. A man's voice came through and asked him to identify himself.

"Hartmann here. This is Hartmann. There's a problem. We had an accident."

After a few seconds of silence the voice came back, "Be more precise, Mr. Hartmann. Are there casualties or material damage?"

"The driver's dead. The accident was his fault. The guy was a real public menace. I'm not hurt, not a scratch. I've got the package and it's fine. But the cops could show up anytime, if they haven't already."

"Don't panic, Hartmann. Are you far from the vehicle?"

"I don't know. I can't see it anymore. I... in fact, I can't see the road. I must be at least a mile from the accident."

"Well done. You showed initiative. Can you tell us where you are so we can help?"

Well done. Hartmann wondered if he should take this as ironical or if the guy really did not care about him. He felt like he was talking to an ambulance driver. And he was always suspicious when people talked to him in a calm, reassuring voice. Especially when it came from the Atomos Organization. He knew that despite their smooth talking these people were not going to do him any favors.

"I'm standing in front of a sign that says some town called Salvation is 4 miles away."

"Salvation? Okay. Leave your transmitter on, Mr. Hartmann. We'll try to come get you as soon as possible. I advise you to stay away from the highway and head for the town. And keep a low profile, of course. We'll find you."

Hartmann's hand dropped to his side. He had never felt more alone.

When Madame Atomos' flying saucer crashed off the coast of California[1], the work of raising the wreck started immediately in spite of the difficulties of the undertaking. Dr. Creighton, who had replaced Alan Soblen, was an old friend of Smith Beffort. He was in charge of the operation and of studying the remains of the saucer. Being a scientist working for the FBI Creighton could not avoid certain restrictions. Obviously his presence was tolerated in this area that been reserved specifically for military and scientific personnel belonging to the army and even though he was known and respected up and down the ranks, he realized that Area 51 was most assuredly the only place in the US where one is not allowed freedom of movement. Of course he knew the physicist White as well as a few other scientists here, but sometimes he wondered bitterly whether he might have more freedom in Red Square.

Area 51 was located in the middle of the desert. It was huge and could hold all kinds of machines, which

---

[1] See *Madame Atomos Sows the Whirlwind.*

was, as far as could be seen, why a large number of engineers and physicists worked here. The flying saucer had not yet been completely recovered because it was an impossible task for the moment, but some essential pieces had been brought to the base and their nature puzzled all the experts, Dr. Creighton included.

Like all passionate people Dr. Creighton was only interested in his work. He had been an engineer for many years and his peers always found him fascinating. He seemed to be a real genius. He gave but passing attention to his clothes, only his clean, white shirt keeping him from looking too scruffy. He was still a young man, around 40, who had acquired a considerable amount of knowledge. And he shared with Smith Beffort one point in common that brought them together: they had both dedicated their lives to fighting the sinister Japanese woman. After the death of Dr. Soblen[2] the battle became more and more of an obsession. Almost a Holy Grail.

Since Madame Atomos' saucer crash, the activity in Area 51 had doubled. Creighton ran into people he had never seen before, convoys came regularly onto the base and air traffic was constant. He felt more and more alone until he had the nice surprise of seeing John Pierce, one of his old colleagues from the University of Pittsburg.

"How's your morale since you got to this wonderful place?" Creighton asked Pierce, who was watching a truck enter the base.

The engineer did not recognize him right away. He ignored the question and replied, "Are you bringing the saucer here in separate pieces?"

"No, it can't be transported. For the moment we're just bringing in a few pieces we recovered."

---

[2] See *The Revenge of Madame Atomos.*

Then the engineer adjusted his glasses and stepped closer. "Creighton! I should've figured I'd see you here."

"It's not such a small world but Area 51 is real magnet for people like us," Creighton remarked while shaking his colleague's hand.

"It's a beehive of activity here. I guess this machine will keep us busy for a while."

"Can you believe it, a flying saucer in Area 51! It's the first time I've seen such a thing!'

The engineer smiled and asked, "Have you made much progress?"

"It's still too early. The more I see, the more questions I have."

The rumbling engines almost drown out their voices and Pierce shouted that they should continue their conversation in a quieter place.

"You're right. Let's go to the locker room. We can talk there."

When they got to the small, rectangular room with 10 lockers, a small cot and a brand new coffee maker, the two men appreciated the sudden silence.

"So, as I was saying, this flying saucer we're just starting to study is going to present a lot of problems."

"What kind of problems? Unknown materials?"

"It's not exactly that. In truth, it's a lot more complex. There are unknown materials, for sure, more like fusions, weird combinations of things. But as surprising as that is, there's nothing really exceptional there, even if the saucer was made with cutting edge technology, I'll admit."

"What do you mean, Creighton?"

"Well, the question I keep asking, and I'm not the only one, is what's the real purpose of it?"

"The purpose?"

"Yes, yes, I know what you'll say. You'll say it's a weapon and with ten more just like it there won't be a living soul left in the United States. No doubt you won't be entirely wrong. You'll also say that the dreadful woman's technology has reached extraordinary heights."

"That goes without saying."

"So why did the flying saucer, which must have cost as much as our space program, crash into the sea on its first flight?"

The engineer did not answer.

"Did you know that it was also buried underground?"

"Yes, I know. I was in L.A. when it took off. But what are you getting at, Creighton?"

"I don't know, but I'm looking. That's why I'm here."

"I feel," the engineer observed, "like you've got some idea."

"Of course I do. But it's too early to talk about it."

"Come on, there's no harm in it."

"Sure there is. I could be called a nitwit. By you and all my distinguished colleagues."

"You know very well I'd never say that."

"Well, let's wait all the same because I'm not really sure about my theory. I don't have enough to go on yet. But one thing is certain: this machine was built for something completely different than what it appears and when I explain to you what I think, it'll knock your socks off."

Ernst Hartmann progressed slowly along the gently sloping path leading to the desert plateaus. All vegetation had almost completely disappeared so the man was out in the open. From the start, he had seen no vehicles but he was waiting anxiously for his transmitter to send a message.

He was getting tired but his legs did not hurt. Sometimes he felt like he was turning into a ghost, insensible to pain, but he could feel the desert air becoming colder and colder. The bare rocks looked like they were melting in the darkness. Hartmann felt like he was in the middle of nowhere.

Then his transmitter started vibrating and he almost dropped it. He swore as his trembling hand grabbed it. "Hartmann here. Have you located me?"

"We've located you, Mr. Hartmann. You're on Temple Bar Road and if you continue on it you'll arrive in a town. How far have you gotten?"

"I must have walked for two hours. I don't know what else to tell you. I've still got the backpack and everything's okay. When can you pick me up?"

"Don't worry, Mr. Hartmann. Keep on the road and you'll come to Salvation. It's deserted, a perfect place for you to rest. You'll be safe there while waiting for us."

"Hurry up. I don't feel so good."

"Relax, Mr. Hartmann. Whatever you do, take care of the bag. A team is already on the way. Try to get to the town."

The scientist was about to respond but the transmission cut off. The conversation was over.

He should not have stopped because when he started walking again his body was completely numb. He continued on the road, strictly following the instructions given to him. The sky was slowly lighting up from the pale moon that cast eerie shadows over the desert landscape. Ernst Hartmann had the unpleasant feeling of being on the planet Mars.

Salvation finally appeared. From a distance he saw only the outlines of buildings. A ghost town lost in the desert vastness. As he got closer the buildings became clearer but he was too tired to make out any details. His whole body was cold. When he got to the first structure, a crude wall almost fallen down, he wrestled off his backpack. Nothing else really mattered except that he had to hide it somewhere.

As he was dead tired he decided to sit for a minute to gather his strength but his body felt the irrepressible urge to lie down. He fell over onto the ground and almost felt good. In a matter of seconds he fell into a deep sleep. His first dream was of Benzenstein during his childhood.

Chapter IV

A big sign at the entrance to the town summed up the situation well: Don't play around with marijuana. In Nevada Possession is 20 years. Selling is a life sentence.

Jack Dickerson no longer worried about that problem. Since he started doing cocaine life had become rather generous to him. For almost eight years he was the manager of the Imperial Saloon, one of the most popular casinos in Las Vegas. Being at the end of the Strip near the Mandalay Bay gave his establishment a great location. He could proudly say that his casino, despite its modest size, could hold its own against any other establishment on the Strip.

He was lucky but he was not stupid.

Ten years earlier he had arrived in Las Vegas and set up a garage in the western suburbs. His rent-a-car business went bust. He had invested all his savings in the broken down garage but in the end he saw that the clientele was... let's say, a lot more chic than he thought at the start. The cheaply repainted Chevys and Cadillacs had no takers and after six months Dickerson had to declare bankruptcy.

When some men came to see him to offer the management of a casino, he saw right away that the guys were not on the up and up. First of all they were a lot better dressed than him. Then in spite of the temperature bordering 110 degrees, they kept their shirts buttoned up and their ties neat and straight.

But even if he came from a state that was full of hillbillies Dickerson was smart enough to know that the Mafia held sway in this city. It was public knowledge that the Las Vegas casinos were ideal fronts to launder money.

The two guys—the third had stayed in the car, ready for any eventuality—had met him in an expensive bar outside of Discovery Park. The deal was simple: they offered him the management of the Imperial Saloon, a well-established casino that brought in more than enough money every week. Dickerson would take care of the casino and these three guys would take care of the transfer of funds. All Dickerson had to do was sell his old garage and let himself slip sluggishly into luxury and idleness. He told himself that he could be diving head-long into serious trouble but the idea of running back to his hovel with his tail between his legs was unbearable.

Therefore, he accepted, fully conscious that he was working for the local mafia. But he convinced himself that after all Las Vegas was a city built on money laundering and the city council itself was thoroughly rotten with corruption.

Very quickly, Dickerson also realized that he was not the kind to be bothered by scruples. That was when he was younger and the money he earned brought him women despite his big belly and ugly face. Then there were the drugs, which soon dominated his life. Thus, his fate was sealed.

The first year, while Dickerson was still trying to find out where the scam was, he figured he would end up buried in an underground parking lot or see a swarm of cops arrest him and lock him up for 20 years. But nothing like that happened and the years rolled by.

From time to time he got visits from the Organization, always polite and courteous. And his bank account grew daily. After a few years, except for the round trips to Hollywood in his Cadillac convertible, the guzzling of mescal and getting high on ether and other substances that had yet to be classified as narcotics, Dickerson found himself without much to do.

One day, the sheriff's department found him in the middle of the Mojave Desert on Highway 95, his Cadillac wiped out, halfway off the road. Luckily for Jack Dickerson the girl sitting in the passenger seat had just turned 18 but their semi-conscious state landed them in jail. Dickerson managed to take care of it but his reputation as an alcoholic and inveterate drug addict had sullied his image and credibility.

The Organization got wind of his behavior, so Dickerson was expecting a reprimand or, what would be worse and insupportable for him, to get fired from his job. He had everything ready, excuses, regret; he would admit his misconduct, his pathetic behavior, and promise to change...

When the two men arrived for their usual visit, it was barely past dawn and Dickerson was still in a bathrobe. A girl, even more beautiful than the night before, was lying in his bed. When he held out his hand to shake, one of the men, who looked hostile today, in a split second had the right arm pinned to the table. Dickerson was expecting him to break his wrist but instead he saw the second man take out a handgun and place the barrel on his palm. The bullet went through his hand with a dull explosion. The girl started screaming in terror but he barely heard her. One of the thugs went to calm her down and Dickerson never saw her again.

After that day, he behaved himself. He never again took a high-class whore through the desert, high as a kite and yelling behind the wheel of his car. Besides, with his mutilated hand he could not drive anymore. A bullet that size did plenty of damage.

He continued to take drugs, a little acid here, a little cocaine there, everything that was easy to get. But he was a sad drug addict. Alcoholic as well. He sat around and listened to jazz records while drinking huge amounts of mescal but he never left the casino.

The men from the Organization came for their regular visits, charming and smiling as if nothing had happened. A good lesson is what he got. Don't go howling with the coyotes in the desert at night.

Now this morning started like any other. The casino manager felt no better or worse than usual. He was in his bathrobe like every morning. The thermometer was already over 100 degrees. From his apartment on the third floor of the casino he saw the car pull up to the curb. It was always the same black limousine giving the impression that these people never changed cars. But when the two men entered his apartment he saw right away that something had changed. He felt it in his bones and like an old memory coming back he suddenly felt his lame hand hurting.

"We have a little bad news for you, Mr. Dickerson," one of the thugs said, putting his hat on the small, blue marble table in the entrance.

Jack Dickerson had a knot in his throat. They were going to fire him even though he had done nothing wrong in four years. He had managed the casino as best he could, meaning he kept his mouth shut and never traveled more than two miles from the city.

"Is there something I did you didn't like, gentlemen?"

Now that he knew better he was waiting for one of the psychopaths to cut off his hand or shoot him in the foot. But from the expression on their faces he knew that it was nothing like that.

"Mr. Dickerson, except for your minor misconduct a few years ago, which was rather embarrassing and disagreeable in the end, we have absolutely nothing to complain about you. But you have to understand that you can't manage this casino forever."

"But you... you'll ruin me!" Dickerson spluttered.

"No, we're letting you go with a tidy little sum. With all the money you've saved over the years I think you'll be more than comfortable. Anyway, the Atomos Organization needs to take over the business. I advise you to pack your bags as quickly as possible."

Jack Dickerson started to get angry. He felt like a complete idiot: he had accepted this deal and got a hole in his hand only to find himself fired like a common employee. Even with the millions of dollars he might get, he was going to turn back into a loser. Mediocrity and stupidity was written in his genes. Packing his bags and obeying these guys instead of socking them in the face like they deserved would only reinforce the idea that he was totally worthless. However, unable to protest, he flopped down on the bed started searching for his underwear with his good hand.

When the guy mentioned the Atomos Organization he did not react and he felt even stupider!

He had only a few seconds to think about it. Still lying on the bed, his eyes closed, suddenly he could not move. He opened his eyes when he felt the pillow drop on his face, smothering him. The P38 fired two inches away, blowing his skull to bits.

This time the weapon had a silencer and besides, there was no woman in bed to scream in fear.

Ernst Hartmann was startled awake, shaken out of a pleasant dream to find himself in a nightmare. A few seconds earlier he was with his parents at a birthday party before snapping out of it, back into reality, with all his aching bruises and the heat getting hotter every second.

He looked up. No cloud in the deep blue sky. The Mexican's backpack was still at his feet and what he thought was a wall a few hours ago was in fact the ruins of a chapel. Good God, what an eerie place! With all these ruins there was no doubt about it: Salvation was completely deserted.

Hartmann struggled to his feet and started inspecting the town. Maybe he could find a source of water to quench his thirst. If not he would have to wait for the Organization, which should arrive soon. He had clearly indicated his location and the man had clearly understood. Therefore, there should be no problem.

As the physicist shuffled down what must have been Main Street, he was surprised by the height of the weeds. He was in the middle of the desert here but the vegetation seemed adapted to the dry ground and atmosphere.

At a rough guess Salvation must have had 100 houses. Hartmann could not say exactly what was wrong but something was troubling his mind. When he went back and entered the chapel the problem was obvious. The building, although partly demolished, was also partly taken care of. It was not noticeable at first glance but on closer inspection the small, central altar, the cross and the stained glass windows were still intact. And they looked clean.

Ernst Hartmann thought of a religious organization or a group of students, but on second thought, he did not care at all. Anyone could come in and mop the floor twice a day if they wanted; he had other things to worry about.

A vehicle finally arrived. Hartmann noticed the raised chassis: it was a pick-up truck customized for desert driving, able to go off-road in any terrain. The Atomos Organization was always equipped with the best material for all occasions.

Like a giant mutant insect the black truck stopped silently six feet away from the scientist. What a surprise when Madame Atomos in the flesh stepped out! It was really Kanoto Yoshimuta driving the truck through the desert. The Japanese woman always looked elegant. Her black suit was a perfect match with the truck.

Of course Hartmann was scared. First of all because he was not expecting to see Madame Atomos in such a place and secondly because he felt responsible for all the complications. Last but not least because the sinister Japanese woman was smiling at him.

"I hope you didn't have to wait long, Mr. Hartmann?"

He held out his hand and answered with a smile. Although scared out of his wits, he was about to open his mouth and try not to babble but she beat him to it.

"I know what you're thinking, Mr. Hartmann. You're surprised to see me walking around alone on American soil and you think it's not very wise of me. But believe me, in spite of all the police looking for me, I can still go to any crummy restaurant and eat without anybody paying attention to me. And do you know why, Mr. Hartmann?"

The scientist found nothing to say. All he could do was gulp.

"Simply because the publicity about Madame Atomos has made her the icon of evil, a practically unreal character for most people, so nobody would ever think of her when seeing a Japanese tourist. Am I right?"

"Certainly... You ought to know the risks."

The woman slowly removed her huge sunglasses. "Of course with this kind of accessory hiding part of my face and with my hair pulled back, it helps a little," she joked.

"Uh... yes, of course."

"Do you have the object?" she abruptly changed the subject to cut short the small talk.

Hartmann held out the backpack as a second pick-up, identical to the first, pulled up behind Madame Atomos.

The Japanese woman took the backpack and said, "We've lost a lot of time but the important thing is that the detonator is still in working order. You can get in with my men, Mr. Hartmann. They'll drive you to Las Vegas and give you complete instructions. I've got to go too. A more discreet vehicle is waiting to take me across the border. Although I don't have much to fear here in the desert, I can't tempt fate, especially since we're not far from the accident. But you see, with such inexperienced and young workers like that driver, I'm forced to check everything myself. In the present case we're pressed for time but I'll make sure that this kind of thing never happens again."

Ernst Hartmann felt even more uneasy. He did not like her ironic smile, her inquisitive eyes or her innuendos that seemed to see right through him. But he also knew that he was the only one who knew how to fit the detonator to the bomb. He was the brain, the indispensable element for a smooth operation.

When he said goodbye to Madame Atomos, his thirst disappeared, replaced by a much more uncomfortable feeling. He stepped into the big, black truck and squeezed in between the two men in the back seat. Once settled in he risked a few words to relieve the tension.

"Your boss was smiling today…"

The driver looked in the rear-view mirror. The others turned to him and smiled as well. This time Hartmann knew that his fear would not go away.

Madame Atomos turned the ignition. She had one hour to cross Nevada before meeting the private plane that was waiting to take her safely over the Mexican border. The pilot was a true blue American who had switched sides. She knew him well because she had traveled many times with him between Mexico and the United States. His service record had never attracted the slightest attention.

The Japanese woman was in a good mood because she had recovered the piece that would allow her to blow up Las Vegas, that temple of money and corruption that ruled the United States. At the same time she would wipe out all traces of Area 51 where they had brought the wreckage of her flying saucer. She would blow it all up before the experts had time to find the secret of its design.

The pick-up had been driving for 15 minutes when Madame Atomos was tempted to pull off the highway at a bar. She had a strong desire to order a drink from a hick bartender without being recognized or maybe to flirt with one of the redneck freaks who could not see what was right in front of them. Yes, she wanted to make a stop. Just for the challenge, to dance with the devil. But it was really not the time. She had a tight schedule with the pilot and the operation was too far along to risk it by being reckless or just to satisfy her whims.

To dance with the devil! She liked the phrase. She liked repeating it, back and forth in her native language and English. In the two languages it sounded nice. For the Americans, she was the devil.

One never knows exactly where he is.

Right now she had to find the turnoff for her meeting. It was not far but in the vast, monotonous landscape everything looked the same and Madame Atomos had to concentrate so as not to miss it.

She stopped on the side of the road to look at a map. That was when she saw a police car pulling up behind her. Her first reaction was to reach for the glove compartment where she kept her paralyzing pistol, but she held herself back. The officer was already coming up to her window. Besides, there was no reason for trouble. She was just a common tourist and he was just a hick sheriff with, however, a nice body and an impressive bearing in his uniform.

The man saluted her as he walked casually around the car. Madame Atomos wished she had grabbed her weapon. She could have taken care of business more quickly. The country bumpkin (he really was one) took off his sunglasses and started making the usual show of things, his eyes wandering from the car to the driver. Madame Atomos was in no mood to play around. She was going to wait for him to ask for her papers and then grab her weapon and be done with it.

After taking his time to examine the license plates and the tires, the policeman approached the window and leaned in. "Hello, miss. Have you looked at your tires lately?"

Kanoto Yoshimuta saw the sheriff's face and his frozen expression that made him look like he was wearing a mask. Could be the result of plastic surgery gone wrong. She looked away, knowing that it was not very prudent to stare at a policeman on duty.

"My tires? No, why, is there a problem?"

What was this hick's problems with her tires? Her men always checked to make sure her car was in perfect condition.

"I'd say! It's not legal to drive with bald tires like you've got. I'm going to have to hold your car."

Madame Atomos decided to go into action. She had no time to waste with a country sheriff full of self-importance and delusions of grandeur.

"I'll show you my papers," she said, reaching for the glove box.

Then she caught a sudden movement out of the corner of her eye. She never would have thought it was possible to move so fast.

In a split second the sheriff had caught her hand. Madame Atomos could feel his breathe on her face and before she could make a move her two wrists were locked in handcuffs. He was incredibly strong and fast.

That was how the formidable Madame Atomos was taken by surprise and put out of action. One never knows what form the devil will take.

Chapter V

For the past few days Smith Beffort had not recognized the FBI offices. Huge cables covered the floor and the personnel were in constant motion. The only upside this morning was the reassuring presence of the coffee machine that was an oasis of calm amidst the perpetual commotion. As he was putting a coin in the machine Beffort saw the photocopy manager waving to him. He cracked a smile when the little man hustled over.

"It's a hell of a mess here, isn't it, Mr. Beffort?"

"I feel like it will never end. I didn't think an internal move would last so long."

The employee's face became more serious as he searched his pocket for a coin. "It's not just the offices that are moving. They decided to redo the toilets on the top three floors and now these down here are the only ones working. With all this junk there's a line a mile long."

"Besides that, what's new?" Beffort raised his voice to be heard over the drilling noise.

"Well, it's getting harder and harder to keep the copy machines running in this mayhem."

Smith Beffort looked at him sympathetically. Since the two men worked on the same floor, they knew each other well and their mutual understanding allowed them to communicate with body language as effectively as with words.

"In fact, Mr. Beffort, I didn't come over here by chance. The boss wants to see you."

"I hope it's not too urgent. My coffee's still hot."

"If I were you, I'd finish it first. Your seniority gives you some privileges."

Beffort smiled.

The new boss' name was Jonathan Forbes. He was the younger brother of Sam, who had lost his life in the fight against Madame Atomos.[3] Jonathan Forbes had been appointed by J. Edgar Hoover himself and he was a little younger than Smith Beffort.

His education as a lawyer at Harvard and his recent nomination to such an important post had made him pretty strict. In appearance only, though. His affected stiffness masked his fear of not living up to the expectations of more experienced collaborators, including Beffort who was in charge of the Atomos file from day one and had complete control in the matter.

You could always discuss your opinion with Smith Beffort but Jonathan Forbes knew that the federal agent always had the last word because the FBI knew about his battles, his history, his failures and his suffering. Nevertheless, to establish his own authority Jonathan Forbes had no choice but to not share Smith's ideas, to disagree with him and offer other solutions. No one, however, was fooled.

Smith Beffort crushed his cup and swore. Even the trashcan had disappeared. He kept it in his hand. When he entered Forbes' office, a man was already there. He was sitting in the back and it was hard to see his face in the shadows.

Beffort nodded at him and turned to Forbes. "You wanted to see me, sir?"

---

[3] See *The Terror of Madame Atomos.*

"Yes, I wanted to talk to you before you left. You have carte blanche in pretty much all sectors except Area 51, which remains, as you know, a strictly military territory. Even if colleagues like Dr. Creighton are actually leading the investigation."

"I know the military's reluctance to let anyone intrude in Area 51 whether it's the FBI or civil engineers and technicians. Don't worry, I won't stay there long. Dr. Creighton is studying the debris from Madame Atomos' saucer right now and my presence at the site isn't really necessary unless of course they turn something up for us. I just want to see how far Creighton and his team have advanced."

"And do you believe in this Atomos lead around Las Vegas?"

"The Green Dragon Force told me that a young Mexican, known to work for the Atomos Organization, died in a car accident outside of Las Vegas."

"He was part of the Organization?"

"In a way. The Green Dragon has been watching certain installations in Mexico for months. With the means at their disposal, of course. I have to say that the Mexican government is not very cooperative. This young man was suspected of being a low level worker who did occasional jobs for the Atomos Organization. He mostly worked as a driver."

"Which leads us directly to the theft of the bomb from the army a few years ago, even if the theory is a little far-fetched."

With a discreet nod Smith Beffort reminded Forbes that a stranger was there listening to their conversation.

"Excuse me," the FBI chief said. "I haven't introduced you to Hunter Robinson, a journalist and writer. He's going with you to Las Vegas. Mr. Robinson is working for *Rolling Stone* and swears that he won't bother you in your investigation."

"I guess he can tell me that himself," Beffort said as the journalist stood up to shake his hand.

Forbes said, "Can you wait outside, Mr. Robinson, while I talk with my agent? I promise it won't take long."

The man had barely shut the door when Forbes continued, "I had no choice but to let him in, Beffort. We're getting pressure from all sides. The people want to be informed."

"If I'm not mistaken, the people are informed. They're the first to know when the plagues unleashed by Madame Atomos are coming for them!"

"Don't pretend like you can't understand. The people want to know what measures are being taken to protect them. I gave my word, so you have to take this guy with you on your trip. Then, well, you can lose him in Las Vegas or Area 51 if you want."

Beffort was squeezing the cup in his hand tighter and tighter.

"So, Beffort, we were talking about that bomb…"

"Yes. As you know it was stolen from the army in 1963 at the White Sand base. A bomb in transit, in a way. You know the facts."

"I also know that it wasn't specially guarded because they thought it was harmless without a detonator."

"Yes, but for a long time Madame Atomos has had the technological means to build a working detonator."

"I know your arguments, Beffort, and there's nothing, absolutely nothing that holds water! It's not enough to have adequate technology to build the thing. You also have to know the whole series of initial calculations and be able to design a suitable detonator. That wasn't possible in the past and it's still impossible today. The data to build this kind of completely obsolete bomb disappeared a long time ago. It's like the mold was broken."

"You're very well informed, Mr. Forbes. With regard to the bomb, the initial calculations were not made in the U.S. in the 50s but in Germany during WWII. The bomb, with its unrivaled power, was planned to be operational in Europe before the end of the war. Fate decided otherwise. Then after Hiroshima the research went over to the other side."

"Even allowing that the Organization took the bomb, it's still harmless and the most cutting edge technology in the world can't change that."

"Absolutely. But you're missing the point. You're speaking about advanced technology when you should be looking for an advanced researcher."

"What do you mean?"

"The engineers, the designers of the bomb were all German. A lot of them are dead. Maybe two captured by the Russians. But for years now one of them has been living in Argentina under a false name and he can travel freely in the United States."

"That doesn't give us much to go on."

"His name's Ernst Hartmann. The Green Dragon found his fingerprints inside the crashed car. They were in our archives because of his scientific research for Nazi Germany and we've had an eye on him for a little while because we thought he might have links to the Atomos Organization, that he might have been 'recycled' so to speak. Moreover, in the trunk of the car we found a lead case. Empty!"

"But there's no proof that the lead case contained a nuclear detonator."

"That's right. Maybe Madame Atomos was waiting for delivery of a high-tech toaster. After all, even if she's the most wanted criminal on the planet, she's just a woman."

"Spare me your sarcasm, Beffort, it's not funny. So, you figure that Madame Atomos is getting ready to set off a bomb in Nevada?"

"And the Organization seems to want to act fast. If my hypothesis is right, the range of this super bomb is big enough to destroy all of Area 51 among other things, which would put an end to our investigation of the flying saucer. Maybe that's the ultimate goal of Madame Atomos."

Silence followed. Jonathan Forbes, staring blankly, was thinking of the files piling up on his desk. He replied, "Even if you're right, Beffort, you have nothing, not the slightest proof. Where are you going to start?"

The FBI agent shook his head.

Forbes continued, "A seat's been reserved for you on a flight at 1 pm. You'll travel with Mr. Robinson. But rest assured, he won't be staying in the same hotel as you."

"Thanks for the favor," Beffort joked.

The two men shook hands. Deep down inside Forbes had a great deal of admiration for his agent but he had never had such an empty feeling as he felt at this moment. He had no clue as to why. Secretly he hoped that Beffort was wrong.

Beffort called Mie to tell her of his departure and assure her that his trip would not be long. A few days, give or take. And if it lasted longer, she could always join him in Las Vegas.

"But that's impossible, Smith! In my condition, no airline would let me get on board. And personally I have no desire to have a baby on an airplane. No, do what you have to do and come back to me as quickly as possible. The baby and I will need you."

Mie's voice was full of joy and promise. Since she found out she was pregnant, happiness had finally returned.

At the airport Beffort got on the plane headed for Las Vegas, accompanied by the journalist from *Rolling Stone* who seemed delighted to be at his side and ready to stick to him like glue. Hunter Robinson was very "presentable" and looked healthy and athletic, which did not fit his reputation as a *gonzo* journalist. During the entire flight he explained to Beffort his theory of the "new journalism" that he practiced and how he tried to live to the fullest the events in the field.

"I lived for months with the Hell's Angels. That was a fantastic experience. I wrote a book about it. Today you have to give the readers a different idea about journalism. You have to give them something that'll disturb them, challenge them, put them in touch with reality. For my next book I'm going to infiltrate the Atomos Organization. Live for six months with that gang of degenerate chinks."

The FBI agent was listening to him. He was watching the deep blue sky and the high clouds that were hiding the sun. The plane would land in less than one hour in Las Vegas and Smith Beffort's thoughts were with Mie. In his crazy battle against the Atomos Organization the few moments of happiness he had known were those he shared with Mie. He realized how lucky he was to have her at his side. In these magical moments when his

206

tranquil mind thought only of her, nothing else mattered, especially not an overexcited journalist whom circumstances forced him to put up with.

"Well, when the Hell's Angels chief arrived," Hunter Robinson babbled as he opened his third can of beer, "I said, Hey Man, is your fucking bike…"

"It's time to fasten your seatbelt," Beffort cut him off. "We're landing."

After landing in McCarran airport where the Las Vegas chief of police was waiting for Beffort, Robinson shook the FBI agent's hand and promised to stay in town to follow his investigation. Beffort thanked him politely and had the officer drop him at his hotel.

When Beffort was finally alone in his room his first thought was to call Mie. After that he made some calls to various members of the Green Dragon Force. He also had to contact Dr. Creighton but he would do that later. One thing at a time.

He met the chief of police in the hotel lobby and they went with several other policemen to the garage where the Mercury was being meticulously searched before examining the lead case. Smith Beffort was more and more convinced that Madame Atomos was preparing an imminent attack. The bomb she would explode could cause unheard-of damage all over Nevada if that was really her goal. Las Vegas and its surroundings, including Area 51, would be reduced to ashes.

For the moment the best solution would be an immediate evacuation of the city but Beffort knew that it was impossible. However, he had to convince the Army Security Agency and the mayor of Las Vegas of the potential danger.

He made a quick review of the situation with the men. "The City has been warned of the risks, meaning that I never thought the evacuation of Las Vegas would be on the agenda since we don't have any concrete proof at the moment. Maybe we'll get lucky in the next few hours and we can clear things up. I hope so because the bomb is most likely already in place and ready to go off at any time.

Ernst Hartmann was driven to a hotel belonging to the Atomos Organization. The trip from Salvation to Las Vegas was quiet and now in his room Hartmann had a chance to relax a little and drink something. He put on some new clothes so that he once again looked like the respectable German citizen he had always been.

For years, in fact since it was stolen from the army, the bomb had been stored in the third level underground of the hotel. It was relatively big with the weight and shape of a good sized car. The third level had once been used for parking, up to five levels down, but now only the first level was reserved for customers along with an outside lot around the building.

Ernst Hartmann thought he had arrived in another world when the private elevator brought him underground. Another world that strangely made him think of Peenemünde and its Army Research Center. As if the architects of this subterranean world had wanted him to feel comfortable in a familiar setting. The farther the elevator descended, the farther back in time the physicist went in his memories.

When they got to the third level, they had to take more stairs to get to the bomb. It was from another age but still had terrifying power. Since it had never been used nobody could predict the extent of damage it would cause.

In less than an hour Hartmann knew that he could make it operational. His technical knowledge and the long awaited detonator would make short work of it. Then he would have to flee. As far away as possible. Into a another state or better yet into another country. The scientist would undoubtedly go back to Argentina.

The time of the explosion had been left to chance. That was where Madame Atomos' genius showed. She had calculated all the probabilities for the bomb to go off at some time between one minute and one week. Probability? Chance? Were they not in the gambling capital of the world?

Standing in front of the bomb that had been waiting all these years, Ernst Hartmann took out the detonator, which had not left his side since his arrival, and noticed that his hands were starting to tremble again.

Chapter VI

Kanoto Yoshimuta felt the sheriff's hand crushing her wrist and then everything happened in a flash. She was still in shock when the cop asked her to step out of the car. She could have run but under such circumstances what was the point? It would be better to wait for the right moment.

Being caught by surprise she could not get over how quickly this policeman had been able to get the better of her. She climbed into the back of the police car. Calmly, with the same attitude she had from the start. Calmly and without saying a word, still in handcuffs that restricted her movement.

The sheriff started the car. His face was like stone. He did not talk about tires anymore, but was it still necessary? Did the man know whom he was dealing with? While staring at him Madame Atomos thought fast, running through the possibilities that remained to her. Out of her car it was impossible to contact the Organization.

The squad car drove slowly through the desert town in the middle of the street. The sheriff was careful to avoid bumps and potholes.

There's absolutely no one in this town, she thought. *Where is this madman taking me?*

"Where are you taking me," she finally blurted out. "I think I have a right to an explanation."

"Your two front tires were bald and the license plate covered in dirt. I'm bringing you to the station according to procedure."

Kanoto Yoshimuto was about to complain about the handcuffs when she realized that the man might not know who she was and that it would be wiser to obey for the moment. So, she just looked thoughtfully out the window.

It was a setback, certainly unexpected, but just a minor setback.

The car stopped in the main square of the deserted town in front of what was supposed to be the police station. There was not a living soul in the ghost town. The sheriff jumped nimbly out of the car and opened the back door.

"The city's deserted but it needs a guardian," he explained with a smile that the Japanese woman thought looked more like a nasty grimace.

Then he grabbed her firmly by the arm and dragged her into the building. The cool air was a nice surprise after the heat outside. Madame Atomos was not expecting to be in such a clean and tidy house, which suggested a woman's touch. A couple obviously lived here and that was reassuring. But the really strange thing was the strong perfume that she could smell everywhere.

The sheriff brought her into a cell that, like the office, was part of the residential home. For the first time in her life Kanoto Yoshimuta found herself behind the bars of an American prison, which would have worried her to death if it were not a jail in a ghost town.

With only minimal furniture the room looked like a drunk tank or at least a holding cell where one did not stay for long, which would be the case with Madame Atomos if the policeman did not know her real identity. The car registration was in order and her driver's license was a perfect counterfeit, which should fool anyone, especially a cop in the boondocks.

The man was slow but self-assured. She could not help staring at his face.

"What do you plan on doing with me," she spoke firmly. "I can't waste too much time with all these formalities. There are people expecting me and they'll start to worry."

The sheriff carefully examined her papers, turning them over while glancing at Madame Atomos. Being a conscientious official he took his time.

"I won't keep you here for long," he answered in an eerily calm voice. "I know who you are. I recognized you right away, Madame Atomos. I was lucky to get you here without a problem. Now you are locked up and I feel better because I have a lot of things to do and I can't deal with you right now. You're very nice but I have a lot on my plate."

Kanoto Yoshimuta was taken aback by the absurdity of what he just said and by the surreal setting. Although it might be useless to deny his accusations, his speech was so senseless that for a moment she doubted the reality of the situation.

"Sometimes I have to go away," the sheriff continued. "I have to take care of my wife who is very sick. We live alone here because the Lord did not want to give us children. But we get by." This time he had a real smile. "Pretty good, too. You've got to admit that it's not always easy to live in a place like this."

Madame Atomos was puzzled. Was she dealing with a crazy man here?

"I'll bring you something to eat very soon. If you need anything at all, don't hesitate to tell me. I'll do all I can to make you comfortable. Within my means, of course. But please, for now, don't ask me any questions. I have a lot of work."

The situation was far too unreal for the Japanese woman to say anything. Faced with the absurdity of this place she had to think up a plea that would get through his twisted mind.

When the sheriff disappeared she was alone. From her cell she could see the pale green walls of the kitchen through an open door in front of her. Flowers were in vases placed pretty much everywhere she could see along with knickknacks trying to hide the walls. She felt desperately empty in her cell that had only a narrow window to let a few rays of light filter in. And then there was that smell, that heady perfume that was almost unbearable...

Madame Atomos squatted down on the floor of her cell and forced herself to analyze the situation. Her brain was working at full speed. Even if escape seemed impossible, she could not convince herself that she was in any real danger. She just had to ask the right questions.

"My name's Ralph Bender," the sheriff said when he came back with some bread and fruit. "I'm going to open the door but I'd like you to stay calm. Later, when you know me better, I'll take off your handcuffs. Maybe we'll even eat together."

"What exactly do you want from me, Mr. Bender?" she asked coldly.

"We have a lot of things talk about. We have a past in common. So, I'm going to have to keep you here for a little while."

"Is it pointless for me to ask you to let me out?"

"You obviously think I'm crazy and I owe you an explanation. You'll have it in good time. But you know I really can't let you go. I'm the sheriff and you're wanted by all the police in the United States. So, right now it's better for you to stay here. And don't worry, I have no intention of giving you to the FBI."

There was a moment of silence.

"I told you that I have my reasons. I'll explain everything later. For now I advise you to build up your strength because I won't be back for a while."

Kanoto Yoshimuta was worried. The sheriff walked away slowly. He did everything slowly, a little contrived perhaps, but still graceful for such a big man. And yet she did not have time to analyze all the bizarre and surrealistic information bouncing around in her head since she ran into this fiendish sheriff. The important thing now was to evaluate her chances of escape and plan on how to do it.

When Ralph Bender turned around to close the door behind him, he shot a weird look at Madame Atomos, a look totally devoid of hate or violence which for the first time threw her off balance. His sympathetic eyes might be hiding a terrible madness, she knew, but she had to find a rational explanation for it.

Was the sheriff just pretending? The idea, *a priori*, did not make sense. He did not look like he was pretending, so there must be something else behind it all.

After one last glance at his prisoner, Ralph Bender disappeared into the kitchen. She heard some muffled sounds behind the door and then total silence fell over the whole house. Madame Atomos examined every nook and cranny of her cell. It must originally have been just another room in the house but later converted to hold prisoners. It was no bigger than 10 by 15 feet. The steel bars from floor to ceiling were unbreakable. The modern door was also made of steel. The only window in the room was a small opening that gave the prisoner a narrow view of the arid landscape outside.

Madame Atomos understood rather quickly that it was impossible to escape but her brain continued running at full throttle. She had to forget, at least for the time being, the absurdity of the situation and concentrate on what she could do to get out.

She also knew what her prolonged absence would mean for the Organization. The orders were strict and the consequences of all this could be very dramatic. The operation had been planned in a hurry but everything had worked—pretty much everything. In any case, she could not let a two-bit sheriff screw it all up. It was not right! But it was foreseeable. It was the monkey wrench, the unexpected glitch at the last minute... Anyway, whatever the price she had to pay, the operation could not end in failure. It was all planned for the final success. Madame Atomos might not be there to witness the grand finale but she knew the rules from the start and accepted them like any soldier devoted to a cause.

Escape seemed impossible but so did any contact with the outside world. Therefore, all she could do was wait for the sheriff, this Ralph Bender, to come back. The fat redneck who was maybe going to change the course of history. But he was not really a fat redneck. First of all because he did not look like your average American. The guy obviously had some Indian blood in him. And his appearance was far too strange. In spite of being fat he seemed extremely agile and strong. His face, too, was weird with its frozen features except for the eyes, which looked gentle... It was pure kindness, not madness. She could see it in the eyes. Since the bombs exploded in Hiroshima and Nagasaki she had seen thousands like them and she was sure that the sheriff meant her no harm. It was small comfort but it was the only hope she had. She had to cling to it.

The thick walls of the house kept out the heat. When night fell, Madame Atomos was surprised by the sudden change in temperature. Shadows started slowly creeping through the room until it was completely dark outside. Only the light bulb on the other side of the bars gave off a feeble light. It softened the atmosphere in the cell, making it almost intimate. She sat down and calmed her mind. She was expecting nothing, knowing that it was useless to try anything at the moment.

Faint noises came from the next room. Someone was walking around slowly. No, slowly was not the right word; it was more like someone having trouble getting around, someone handicapped or old who could barely walk. More like an old person because the steps were unsteady and slow. Ralph Bender probably lived with his mother, which came as no surprise. Well, Mrs. Bender and her son the sheriff had just captured Madame Atomos, the most wanted criminal in the U.S.

The Japanese woman was staring at the door in front of her now. Bender's mother (if it really was her) was about to pay her a visit. Instinctively she approached the bars to hear what was happening in the other room. The footsteps were gradually coming closer and Madame Atomos imagined an old woman struggling across the kitchen, curious to finally see the face of the prisoner.

But a door slammed somewhere in the house and she recognized Ralph Bender's voice.

"Be careful, Yomi," he said. "You're still very weak. You shouldn't be up, it's not sensible."

The sounds became clearer. Ralph Bender must have been moving chairs or heavy objects in order to help his mother or his handicapped wife. A line of light appeared under the kitchen door and Madame Atomos realized that the whole scene had just taken place in the dark. She heard a chair scraping over the floor and guessed that the sheriff was helping his companion to sit down.

"There, you'll feel better like that, Yomi. Don't move around so much. If you need anything, ask me."

Madame Atomos heard a little plaintive groan in a soft, almost child-like voice. It was certainly not an old lady. Bender's wife, perhaps, or his daughter? But after all, what difference did it make to the prisoner? Kanoto Yoshimuta was about to sit back down when the sheriff's form appeared in the doorway. In the shadows his size was even more imposing. He was still in uniform and his Stetson looked permanently glued to his head. Behind him a woman was sitting on a chair, a small and frail woman whose face Madame Atomos could not see behind the mass of dark hair.

The policeman closed the door, almost apologizing. "That's my wife. I'm a little upset because I didn't want you to see her yet. She's not presentable. An accident. A serious accident. But she's recovering little by little…"

His face suddenly lit up.

"Don't think it's a tragedy. I mean the accident… it happened a long time ago. You know how it is, it takes time to… how do you say it… rehabilitate."

Madame Atomos thought that Ralph Bender was playing with her. He knew very well that she did not give a damn about his wife! He wanted to pass himself off as an imbecile but he was far from it. But what was the point of all this? She did not know what to say. Besides, she had no desire to say anything and decided not to open her mouth, just stand there and listen to what he had to say.

"She wanted to see you," the sheriff continued. "I told her that it wasn't time yet. Patience, the time will come. I think the three of us might even be able to eat together one of these days… If you act reasonably, of course."

While talking, Bender slid his hands down the bars. At one point he started fidgeting with the electronic lock as if to make sure that nothing was wrong.

"I know you have a lot of questions. That's normal. It's because you don't know the whole story. But don't worry, very soon you'll have the missing piece of the puzzle. Whatever you do, don't think that this doesn't concern you. You'll be making a big mistake!"

The sheriff leaned slightly forward, bringing his face down closer to Madame Atomos.

"I'll tell you a secret," he almost whispered. "My wife is Japanese, too."

Kanoto Yoshimuta did not react. She was more and more convinced that remaining unemotional was vital for her. The sheriff straightened up and rubbed his chin, clearly lost in thought.

After a minute he went on, "Tomorrow night we'll eat together. Then you'll finally understand us, my wife and I. Yomi is really anxious to meet you. But anyway I can tell you one thing and believe me, I'm being sincere…"

He paused a moment then spoke in a monotone.

"It's that you have absolutely nothing to be afraid of."

Chapter VII

Smith Beffort understood the situation perfectly and he had a strong feeling of "déjà vu". True, the evidence was scanty, not to say non-existent, certainly not enough to justify evacuating a city the size of Las Vegas.

It was almost 10 pm when he was sitting in a fancy restaurant with Dr. Creighton. The last few hours had flown by: he had to go from his hotel to the morgue, then from the morgue to the garage while passing through different hotspots of Las Vegas. Therefore, he was more than happy to take a breather with someone he considered a good friend.

"Your job isn't going to be easy," Creighton stated after listening to Beffort explain his theory.

"I'm not sure I believe it'll work, you know. Too many gray areas, not enough proof. If you want to know what I really think, I don't believe 100 % in this story."

"And you'd like me to say something to motivate you?" the doctor joked.

"You have your own work, Creighton, and it's no walk in the park."

"Maybe I could, in fact, find a link between the flying saucer and your theory. I'm going to tell you something, Beffort: we're on the brink of discovering something about this saucer. I don't know what exactly yet but I think that whatever it is will be important enough for Mama Atomos to want to destroy the machine before we find it."

"I don't quite understand what you mean by 'on the brink of discovering something.' It seems to me that we have sufficient means to understand this technology, no matter how advanced."

"Yes, Beffort, I've already talked about that with my colleagues on the base and with the military. The technology itself, even though it's very sophisticated, poses no problem. We can do the calculations starting from point A and work slowly up to point B. But every time we run into something unknown it's like we have to make a big detour. Well, I'm not explaining it to you very well. Listen, Beffort, I have a theory too. But I don't even want to tell you because I'm afraid of being taken for a lunatic."

"I don't think anything could surprise me now, especially concerning Madame Atomos."

"Okay. During the research in Area 51, I started looking more closely at certain other parts of the flying saucer like the steering control, for example. My attention was drawn to a number of anomalies, things that didn't make sense. At first I couldn't figure out what was wrong but then it became clear to me. The flying saucer was meant to be miniaturized."

Smith Beffort's face showed no particular emotion.

The doctor continued, "It must be said that we haven't been able to bring up the main parts of the machine, which crashed into a difficult area to reach. Some of the debris literally evaporated on impact. Not to mention that the saucer is spread over several miles on the bottom of the sea. But I still think, and we should be pursuing this, that the main function of this machine was to be miniaturized."

"So, Madame Atomos managed to do it! It's incredible."

"I'm not sure the saucer was fully operational when it crashed. Maybe the diabolical woman needed more time to finish the work. But one thing I can tell you, Beffort, is that we must have seriously thwarted her plans. The fact that this flying saucer fell into the hands of the army is one more reason for Madame Atomos to want to disappear. Sooner or later we'll end up discovering everything. It's too bad the crash caused so much damage. It reduces our chances. But Madame Atomos doesn't know how far we've gotten. Maybe she thinks we've already found everything out."

"And your colleagues? What do they think about your theory?"

"Their opinions are split. I just thought of this recently, so it'll take some time before everyone can accept it. That's why I haven't told the military about it yet."

"You'll have to prove it too."

"Just like your theory about the bomb, Beffort, just like you…"

It was almost midnight when Ralph Bender finally decided to take off his Stetson. He put it on the only chair in his room and slowly started to undress. Like the rest of the house, the temperature in the room was cool. An oasis in the desert. The sheriff loved this house. It was his. It was his wife's. It was where they came to settle after the accident. Yomi was very weak now but she still managed to get around. From their first meeting Ralph Bender never stopped loving her and he sometimes wondered if it was mutual.

We've lived through too much together, he thought. *We've been through too many trials. But in spite of everything we're still here. I don't see what can destroy us now.*

Sitting on the big, impeccably neat bed he stared at the wall in front of him, his mind lost in a fog. His lips parted and he started to mumble slowly. "Kanoto Yoshimuta. She is Kanoto Yoshimuta. The spirits sent her. I can't imagine that she is here by chance. I believe in God. I believe in our gods."

While the house itself seemed to be dozing and Madame Atomos had fallen into a strangely calm and peaceful sleep, noises could be heard on the other side of the bedroom wall. Bender got up, went to the door and opened it slowly for his wife who stood there, like a shadow, in front of him.

"Come in, Yomi. We can sleep together tonight. Nothing would bring me more pleasure, you know that."

The giant delicately took the hand of his wife, the tiny, frail creature, and helped her lay down on the bed.

"I know you're anxious to see her, Yomi. But you have to be patient. I'll introduce you to her tomorrow night. I need to take a few precautions. I don't know how she'll react. We can't forget that she's a dangerous woman."

While speaking he rubbed her shoulders and then lay down beside her.

"Now I'm going to turn off the lights, Yomi and we'll sleep together like we did so often and like we'll do again many times. But before that I'm going to talk to you for a little while. I'm going to tell you about some of our time together because I know you love when I talk about that. Do you want to talk about your country? Or when we got to Long Island?"

Ralph Bender felt his wife's hand squeeze his arm. What might have been an innocent gesture of affection was really a clumsy attempt at a sensual caress. The sheriff tensed up. It was harder and harder to get used to these awkward signs of desire; they were making him more and more uncomfortable.

"I'll tell you about Long Island, Yomi. The day we moved, you remember?"

The small Japanese hand slid down Bender's body and stopped abruptly between his legs. This time Bender felt all the muscles become taut. In every part of his brain and soul panic set in.

"No, Yomi, not tonight," he stammered, ready to start screaming.

Yomi loosened his grip and Bender curled up into a fetal position. The air in the room had become almost unbreathable. As his eyes tried to pierce the darkness, he felt every pore of his body sweating.

He tried to focus his thoughts on Long Island but the images would not settled down in his mind. The happy days, the strolls, the weekends hand in hand… and then the accident, the attack, all the bodies destroyed, mutilated. The dreadful Madame Atomos!

But both of them got out of it. They escaped death and Yomi was still with him. Her body ruined, of course, but she was still there, alive, and that was all that mattered. At least, he tried to convince himself of that.

But he did not want to touch her or her to ask him to. His love for her was much more mental than physical now. Of course he accepted her presence and of course he still loved her, but it was more and more difficult for him to bear her gaze.

His wife's body moved beside him. Yomi still wanted to fondle. Yomi still wanted to make love.

The sheriff reached over and grabbed his belt. He put it between his teeth and bit down as hard as possible. Whatever he did, he could not scream.

Since his arrival in Las Vegas Hunter Robinson had started binging on all kinds of illegal substances. Not enough to crash out, however. No, the man could hold his stuff. But it was enough for him to spend a night in hell in Las Vegas. He was still lucid and when he hailed a cab he almost looked normal. He got inside without stumbling and he managed to give the cabbie the address of the finest casino without stuttering even once.

The taxi driver gave him a long speech about the hip casinos in Las Vegas that he knew like the back of his hand and that it was better to avoid if he did not want to be ripped off like a sucker of a tourist. Robinson agreed to be taken to a place less popular with the jet set but where he would have a better chance of hitting his bets. He had even agreed enthusiastically and for the rest of the trip they talked about the space race and the invasion of Martians among the communists.

The journalist had been in the place for 15 minutes leaning on the bar and had no run-ins with anyone. He congratulated himself. At the hotel he had done two big lines of coke and swallowed a handful of amphetamines like they were M&Ms, so now he could use a little booze to calm down. As an experienced practitioner he knew that this kind of mix was no good. The important thing was "to keep the mind clear during all the psychedelic experiences." The phrase was not his but he like to repeat it: it went well with the new journalism that he wanted to espouse.

He was relieved that the bats that had followed him in the taxi had not entered this establishment. He sauntered over to one of the clinking machines that blinked with a thousand colors. Tonight luck was with him, he was sure. He rummaged through his pockets in search of a token that would inevitably make him rich.

An hour later he had tried at least 50 of the One-Armed Bandits but they had not fed him much. The people kept flowing in and room was starting to get scarce in this casino that was turning out to be a pretty dreary place. Hunter Robinson was starting to get seriously bored and was thinking of going back to the hotel.

He slipped his last tokens into a machine that he must have already played before. The goal was to line up four fruits or whatever symbols in order to pay out. But to the great surprise of the journalist a crudely drawn human head now replaced the banana and the melon. It was the face of woman, recognizable, unmistakable: it was the face of Madame Atomos with two crossed bones, like a bow tie, at her neck, which highlighted, as if there were need, the skull-like apparition. It was still necessary to line up four of them to hit the jackpot. In spite of his somewhat radical leanings, Hunter Robinson found the joke in bad taste. What kind of company made this kind of slot machine? He would have a quick word about it with the bartender before he left.

The heads were spinning and blurring with the other symbols. When they stopped Robinson saw that he had only lined up two and he had no more money. He headed for the bar to ask them to call him a taxi.

Smith Beffort had spent the evening with Dr. Creighton but their discussion had not produced any satisfactory answers to their questions. It was relatively late when they finally called it a night.

If Las Vegas blows up, no one will have time to suspect a thing. Well, that's not the kind of statement that's going to get us very far! The agent thought before drifting off into a dreamless sleep.

225

He was still sleeping when someone knocked on the door. It took Beffort a few seconds to understand what it was. The knocking got louder and faster. There was obviously an emergency. Smith jumped out of bed and opened the door to see a man from the Green Dragon Force.

"Sorry for the early morning intrusion," the man said, "but we got a call from the Atomos Organization at the LVMPD Headquarters. If the source of the call is confirmed, it'll be some pretty surprising news. They're calling back in less than an hour and they want to talk to you, Mr. Beffort. They know you're in Las Vegas and we didn't deny it."

"You did fine," he said as he got dressed. "What do they want?"

"That's pretty surprising too. Madame Atomos has disappeared!"

"What? What kind of joke is this?"

In spite of the early hour, the police stations were already buzzing with excitement. Sergeant Wood and Smith Beffort rushed into an office to wait for the call from the Organization. The technical services were there to try to locate the origin of the phone call. At the appointed time the phone rang. Beffort picked up on the first ring.

"Is this Smith Beffort?" a male voice asked.

"It is," the agent answered. "I just found out about your first call."

"Are you holding Madame Atomos?"

"Not that I know of, at least for the moment," Beffort replied. "Listen, I've just been pulled out of bed and things might have happened that I don't know about, but if Madame Atomos is in the hands of the police right now, I can only congratulate them."

"Don't be so sure, Mr. Beffort. We have strict orders in such a case."

"If your boss is out of commission, the Atomos Organization has no more mastermind and I wouldn't bet on its survival."

"It'd be better for you if that wasn't the case. We have the means to reduce the United States to ashes."

"By placing bombs in strategic cities, for example?"

There was a pause before the voice answered.

"We have even more destructive means, Mr. Beffort. But let's not get off track. Once again my question is simple. Are you holding Madame Atomos?"

"It's still too early to say one way or another," the agent repeated. "Is your Organization in possession of the bomb that was stolen from the army eight years ago?"

"I'm going to hang up. I don't think I want to keep playing 20 questions. Maybe I'll call back. But if Madame Atomos is your prisoner, I advise you to release her as soon as possible."

The line went dead before Beffort could reply. A member of the technical team shook his head. The call was not traced.

"We'll have to wait," Beffort sighed. "But it looks like no one on either side knows what's going on."

"You think it's a bluff?" Sergeant Wood asked.

"First thing I need is coffee because my mind's a little fuzzy. If Madame Atomos was arrested by a local sheriff, for example, how long would it take us to get the information?"

"I can't say exactly. Assuming that Madame Atomos really has disappeared, we don't even know where in the states she might have been nabbed. It might have even happened in Mexico or in South America.

"That's possible. In any case the phone call came to me and the Organization knows that I'm in Las Vegas. I think there's been enough commotion around here lately for us to limit our search to Nevada, at least for the moment."

"What kind of commotion?" Wood asked, holding out a cup of coffee for Beffort.

"I know that this won't seem very important to anyone, but there was a certain car accident involving a young driver and a Nazi scientist who were both working for the Atomos Organization. A bunch of other things as well. A lot of indications really. Madame Atomos might have disappeared right around here. I'm going out to the site of the accident to get a better look. Maybe I'll find something interesting."

Chapter VIII

Dr. Creighton was glad to be accompanying Smith Beffort. The two men got on the road early to find the site of the accident. Beffort had insisted that Dr. Creighton bring a Geiger counter to spot the slightest traces of radioactivity. The scientist did so, but against his will. Sitting in the passenger seat he kept complaining about it.

"They've already inspected the car. There was absolutely no trace of radioactivity. Besides, we wouldn't find any even if it had a detonator. You know perfectly well, Smith, that something like that isn't radioactive. You're making me lug around completely useless equipment."

"Listen, it's just a favor I asked of you as a friend. I know you're cranky in the morning and we left in a hurry. I very well could be wrong. The Geiger counter might be unnecessary but it's not that heavy. Anyway, I'll be carrying it, so now you can stop complaining for the rest of the day."

Dr. Creighton did not respond right away. He got a cigarette out of the glove compartment. "You're right, Smith. The thing might come in handy trying to find Madame Atomos."

"Come again?"

"Since she's tried to drop a couple of nuclear bombs on our beautiful country for so long, she herself must be a little radioactive by now. I think she might even glow in the dark! No, really, Beffort, you were right to insist. Thanks to this device it won't take us long to find her."

The agent cracked a smile. Creighton, who rarely saw this expression on Beffort's face, was delighted.

The Ford, an unmarked police car, drove west for 20 miles or so down Highway 93, then at Boulder City it veered off to the left to reach the scene of the accident. The two men took no more than 15 minutes to inspect the site that had already been examined several times, first by the police and the FBI, then by the Green Dragon Force.

As the doctor had predicted, the Geiger counter found absolutely no trace of radioactivity. Beffort was thankful that Creighton was sensitive enough not to say anything like "I told you so."

Smith Beffort scrutinized the horizon pensively. The dry and rocky landscape stretched out around them. The sun was barely up over the desert surrounding the two men. Beffort's gaze stopped on an unpaved road that led into the mountains.

"According to our maps there's a town out there, right? A deserted town guarded by a sheriff by the name of Ralph Bender... maybe it'd be interesting to pay him a visit."

"Didn't your men already see him?"

"No. It was some employees of a motel that called for help. They were the closest ones around, so the Green Dragon questioned them, but without any fruitful results. The sheriff lives farther back behind that mountain. The sergeant told me about him. According to our information he's an old cop with a reputation of being very competent and very athletic. He was working in New York when his path crossed Madame Atomos. His wife was banged up badly in one of her attacks. Straightaway he transferred out here thanks to his past service. Anyway, it's a cushy set-up. Ralph Bender became sheriff of a ghost town that requires a minimum of upkeep, so he has all the time in the world to take care of his wife."

"What's wrong with his wife?"

"She's an invalid. Her husband gets her up and around sometimes. That's what the motel employees said. Because this Bender practically never leaves. He just goes to the motel for supplies once a week. Sometimes a guy goes to see him to bring the mail or whatever… but the sheriff has a reputation of being pretty reserved. He doesn't let many people get close to him."

"Well, you seem pretty well informed about the whole subject."

"Yes, I even got the impression that the sergeant was making sure I knew everything there was to know. He really wanted me to be interested in him. I guess we're all a little curious to know what our colleagues do with themselves in a situation like that. But I have to admit that it's a lead that might turn something up. Maybe Ralph Bender can tell us something about the accident."

"A sheriff with a screw loose and a physically handicapped sidekick… that could be pretty exciting," Creighton remarked as he got back in the car.

"I sense some sarcasm. But you'll be pleasantly surprised when I tell you that his wife is Japanese."

Smith Beffort started the car and headed down the path that became more and more windy the farther they went.

"I don't have the same personality as you do," Beffort said. "I can't laugh at everything to do with Madame Atomos. Whatever it is, the sheriff's life must be a living hell. They know him pretty well at the motel and they say that sometimes Bender comes down drunk as a skunk and one the employees has to take him back home, late at night, in a very bad state. I wouldn't want to be in his shoes."

"I'm sorry if I sounded sarcastic, Smith. We've all known tragedy since that dreadful Japanese woman declared war on the United States and it seems to me that there's no limit to her will to destroy. A little humor and levity can't hurt."

"You're probably right. I don't always think like you, but you're probably right," Beffort admitted, trying his best to avoid the potholes.

"This road, or rather this path is a real pain!" the doctor complained. "I wonder how the guys at the motel do it to get the drunken sheriff back home at 3 am. Is this town of yours far from here?"

"This town has a name: Salvation. And even driving slow like this we should see it very soon."

Ralph Bender touched the mask with his huge hands. It was a mask from Japanese theater. There were several of them in the room. He was alone now. Yomi had slipped away at dawn. Through the open door Bender saw the first rays of sunlight shine in the hallway at the end of which was the kitchen and behind the kitchen the cell. All the open doors made Bender feel better. Like this he could always keep an eye on his prisoner. He kept fingering the mask as if he were in a store full of Japanese theater articles and he was trying to chose the best one.

I'll need the kabuki mask, he told himself. *The kabuki is better suited for dinner. What would Yomi think? No, I won't ask her. She'll be wearing it but I won't ask which one she prefers. I'll choose for her. She won't refuse. She always agrees with my choice.*

He contemplated the masks one by one before he stopped at Yasha. It was a feminine deity with a ferocious smile.

"That's the one! That's the one Yomi will wear tonight!"

Ralph Bender was talking to himself out loud. He grabbed the mask and unhooked it from the wall.

"Tonight Yomi will wear the kabuki mask, the mask of epic drama!"

Then he left the room and went to the cell where Madame Atomos was finishing her breakfast of green tea and rye bread with honey. Bender took the plate and left the cell calmly, without a sound, like he had come.

Madame Atomos had not once tried to flee since her arrival. At no time, especially when the sheriff entered her prison cell, did she think it was possible or the opportune moment. Ralph Bender was very quick. His way of moving, almost supernatural, removed her desire to try anything at all.

For a full day she had closed herself up in almost total silence, which let her rest her mind and reflect. She had slept well and enjoyed her small breakfast. Moreover the smell of that revolting perfume was slowly dissipating, which made the start of this day a little more bearable.

Madame Atomos knew that the operation in Las Vegas was set in motion the night before. She knew that at any moment she might disappear from the face of the earth. The bomb was operational now and it could explode any time between this exact moment in the cell finishing her breakfast and the next four days according to her calculations of probability. In Las Vegas, the gambling capital of the USA, the probabilities were almost infinite. The system that she masterminded and that the Organization was responsible for implementing had put the moment of explosion between now and the next four days. Nobody could do anything to stop it.

The fact of being imprisoned by this psycho sheriff had certainly not been foreseen in Madame Atomos' plan but she accepted it. Japan might have surrendered but her world was still at war.

Ralph Bender had put the plate on the table and was turning over and over an object in his big hands that seemed to fascinate him. Kanoto Yoshimuta was astonished to see a kabuki mask. She wondered what this theater prop was doing here and what farce this hick sheriff was planning with a traditional mask meant for epic drama.

Bender approached the cell, still holding the mask. "I'm not going to insult you by explaining the traditions of your country. You certainly know what this mask represents."

The sheriff waited for an answer that did not come. He continued. "As I told you yesterday, I'm going to introduce you to wife and we'll have dinner together. My wife will be hidden behind this kabuki mask but I'm afraid you'll have the wrong idea, Madame Atomos. You're bound to think—see, you aren't the first one in this situation—you'll think, *This bastard sheriff doesn't want me to see his wife's ugly mug because she's really hideous!*"

Ralph Bender's voice had gradually become louder. His face had sudden turned red with anger. He was so close to the cell that his body was pressing through the bars.

Surprised by the change in attitude and expecting a sudden outburst of violence, she was slightly trembling but she still had enough self-control not to let it show.

Bender went on bawling. "Everybody thinks my wife is hideously ugly. The whole county! This whole goddamn town of hillbilly ghosts! But I'll tell you something: Everybody's wrong!"

The sheriff calmed down a little. He was almost laughing but his face had lost none of its crimson hue. He dried his wet eyes with a big, checkered handkerchief.

"Everybody's wrong," he said with a kind of hiccup due to his euphoria. "Everybody's wrong." His voice faded out and he was almost back to normal.

Kanoto Yoshimuta remained unfazed. Her wary eyes studied the face of this strange man, of this impressive human mass who was panting slowly in front of her. She waited for the peace and quiet to come back.

All of a sudden Ralph Bender tilted his head and his expression changed as if his mind had jumped back into his body.

"Someone's coming," he told the Japanese woman in a conspiratorial whisper. "A car just pulled up."

The Ford was parked a few feet from Ralph Bender's house. What was surprising about this ghost town was that it looked like no other. There was the one, main street like in the times of the Wild West along with the narrow, dark and gloomy alleys that ran off the square with the church. But what was most striking was how clean it all was, as if the town had never stopped living. As if the faces of the inhabitants might pop out from behind the curtains at any moment. There was not a shred of paper on the ground; not even a fallen stone at the foot of a ruined wall.

The sheriff must have been working hard to keep his deserted town in good condition.

When the bell rang and he went to open the door for the two visitors, the sheriff noticed that he had not had the presence of mind to check his clothes. He was usually very careful about his appearance: a neat brush cut, always freshly shaved and impeccably dressed, a spotless Stetson and a tailored uniform from Stalten Brothers. Moreover, his pants and shirt were custom-made for his impressive build. However, at the moment he had not thought that his appearance might need a little sprucing up.

Beffort and Creighton stood face to face with a guy whose face was flushed and sweating like he had just run a marathon. But the face was frozen in a weird way, like a wax mask. All together the sheriff gave off the impression of stillness and stiffness, an almost exaggerated stiffness that bordered on the comic.

Smith Beffort told him briefly the reason for their visit. Bender did not invite them in. Always courteous and professional he answered their questions with remarkable calm and good faith. Only a lie detector would have reacted when he answered the question, "Have you seen anything unusual around here in the last 24 hours?" Bender stood still and said that he had seen nothing, nothing out of the ordinary and he was very sorry.

After that the conversation drifted into the usual small talk: that it was getting really hot for this early hour and this altitude and of course the fact that he could not have been the sheriff of a ghost town without a living soul.

Bender suddenly felt that he had control of the situation and that he could invite the two visitors in for coffee or a beer. But just as he suspected, they declined his offer. At the end of their conversation Beffort and

Creighton firmly shook hands with Bender and went back to their car.

"What'd you think of the guy, doctor?" Beffort asked when he was seated behind the wheel. "Did you think there was anything fishy about him?"

"I don't know. You can't forget that we obviously interrupted something he was doing. It looked like he'd just run up the 375 stairs of the Empire State Building before opening the door."

"He can do whatever he wants. Besides, the guy's a sheriff and above all suspicion. We have nothing to go after him for. In fact, we have nothing to go after anyone for right now."

Nevertheless, Beffort looked pensive when he continued. "His face was pretty weird. And there was that smell, that perfume coming from the house. Did you smell it when he opened the door? Didn't you think it was strange?"

"It's the place that does it," the doctor replied. "It's the whole town that makes me feel uncomfortable. Everything's weird here. Bender's just like everything else."

Beffort started the car. "We don't have much time to figure this out."

"But we haven't received an ultimatum! There's nothing to prove that there's a link with the stolen bomb."

The FBI agent turned the Ford slowly onto the bumpy road.

"You know," Creighton continued, "I know what bothers me about this place. I've seen deserted towns before but none like this one. Salvation isn't like any other ghost town. In fact, Salvation isn't like any other place at all and that's disturbing to me."

"I like your thinking," Beffort joked. "You must not get bored with your learned colleagues in Area 51."

"I'm serious! Didn't you feel on edge in the town?"

"I didn't have time to feel anything at all, doc. I have too many things to do. But I'm still going to stop at the motel and talk with the employees there. They know Ralph Bender as well as anyone like that can be known. It won't bother you if we make a little detour, will it?"

"Not at all. I'll go with you, Smith. It's a nice change from the base and the flying saucer. Anyway, I guess I don't have much choice."

The sheriff closed the front door quietly. He knew that the cops would come pay him a visit sooner or later but he did not figure that it would be so soon. Anyway, they will have a hard time finding the Japanese woman's car.

There were exactly 132 houses in Salvation, the same number of garages and a bunch of sheds. Well, the sheds were not all in good shape but the garages still had locks and Bender had the keys.

Madame Atomos' car had no chance of being found in the Mosley's garage because no one would go looking for it there and even if they did... Making a car disappear for good was no easy task and might attract unwanted attention to him. In the present case Ralph Bender knew that his greatest advantage was knowing the lay of the land.

When he had arrived here with Yomi five years ago Salvation was already a ghost town but it was also his hometown and that of his ancestors. His father, grandfather and other Benders before them had lived here. No name on the gravestones in the old cemetery was unfamiliar to him. The sheriff was home. He and Yomi were home.

He had taken possession of his family home. The Bender house was the biggest house in Salvation second only to the old Bowley family. But the Bowleys had been dead for years.

Bender, therefore, had arranged the ancestral home of his family into two parts separated by a long hallway. He could very well have let the policemen in and led them to the left, even if he was sure that they would not accept his invitation. The part on the right had all the rooms he lived in now except the cell. He was the one who built it by adapting his office. He had welded the bars and installed an electronic door because a police-man worthy of his name needed a jail cell. He was espe-cially happy about it now because for one whole day it has held a distinguished guest.

Ralph Bender went into the kitchen and even though it was early he popped opened a can of beer. When the refreshing liquid ran down his throat he started thinking about all this again. He was sure that, although he was only conscious of it today, the cell had always been destined for Madame Atomos. Everything was written at the start.

He and Yomi had lived through many things. They had come too close to the sinister woman's path. Yes, everything was written at the start.

The sheriff put down the empty can and opened the office door. She was at the back of the cell with her eyes wide open and she was looking at him. Despite the bars separating them, Bender was impressed. This woman really looked like an evil statue. Perfect immobility. But Bender was not afraid of her any more than he was afraid of the policemen. Because everything was already written and it would happen as foretold. He felt a little like a puppet whose strings were being pulled by forces beyond him that were going to control all his movements from now on.

Yomi, Madame Atomos and him. They were finally reunited. Their destiny was about to be sealed.

The sheriff was already smiling with satisfaction when all of a sudden he saw the kabuki mask. In his hurry to answer the door for his visitors he had accidentally dropped it on the floor and it was lying on the wooden planks broken in pieces.

Ralph Bender could not hold back a shiver on seeing the shattered object. Madame Atomos stood still and expressionless staring at him like a researcher watching a lab rat.

Just as the Ford was picking up speed Smith Beffort slammed on the brakes. "Do you hear anything, doc?"

At his passenger's look of surprise Beffort turned off the engine and this time Creighton shuddered, turned around and shouted, "The Geiger counter. It's picked something up!"

Beffort looked at the meter. "Damn, it's showing more than 60 rem."

"That's a lot higher than normal," Creighton stated.

The scientist got out of the car and grabbed the device. He walked straight ahead for ten paces or so and slowly started walking in circles.

"It's absolutely incredible," he said. "The counter isn't indicating a particular spot. The reading is the same wherever I go. No, the whole ground around here is radioactive."

He continued moving forward.

"Come on," Beffort said. "There's no need to attract attention. We're not far from the Bender house and I don't trust that guy. Get back in. We'll go back to Las Vegas and tell my men what we've found. Then we'll come back and inspect the land no matter what the Sheriff of Salvation thinks."

Chapter IX

The two men stopped at the motel where they did not learn much. Bender sometimes went there to get a drink. He was not talkative and the only one with whom he conversed was Yahto, the Indian cook who was, unfortunately, not there at the moment because it was his day off.

The bartender babbled on forever about nothing and with the same energy as the waitress put in laughing at the truck drivers' jokes. The conversation was going nowhere fast but Beffort had to ask about the sheriff's wife.

"Only Yahto's seen her," the bartender replied, "because Yahto's the only one who goes up to Salvation. He goes to deliver stuff to Bender, like the mail. He even goes up to play cards with him, so he's seen the wife."

"Did he ever tell you about her?"

"Yeah. Since we don't have a hell of a lot to do here. She had an accident a long time ago apparently. Since then she's been handicapped or something like that. Well, it's real sad but it's none of our business."

"And... did she ever come down here with her husband?"

"No, I don't think so. But come back tomorrow and you can see Yahto. He'll tell you whatever you need to know better than me."

"One last thing, please. Since the accident the other day, the one nearby with the Mercury, have you seen anyone or anything unusual?"

"Nothing at all. The days here are no different than before the dude screwed himself with his car."

Beffort and Dr. Creighton thanked him and finished their coffee without saying a word. Maybe it would be wise to come back and question Yahto the cook. There were so many things to do that they did not know where to begin. Consequently, Beffort got back on the road to Las Vegas.

When the FBI agent and Dr. Creighton got to the police headquarters in Las Vegas the sergeant told them that they had received another call from the Organization. The message was the same: Madame Atomos' men are convinced that their boss is being held by the police. This time, however, they made explicit threats saying that they were ready to blow up Las Vegas.

The good news was that the evacuation of the city was going to start sooner than expected. The various municipal departments all agreed on the pressing issues.

"I'll explain everything in detail, Mr. Beffort," the sergeant said, "but first you two should listen to the tape of the conversation. Then I'll fill you in on the decisions we made."

Smith Beffort recognized the voice of the man he had spoken with before. The only difference was that this time he was more straightforward, as if he were reading from a text. The message contained, first of all, a warning. It was obvious that Madame Atomos was in the hands of the FBI. An ultimatum was laid down: Free her unconditionally or else watch Las Vegas and the rest of Nevada be blown to bits.

They're starting to reveal their project, Beffort thought. *I was right.*

Nevertheless, one phrase intrigued him. The man clearly said that the city would be destroyed within four days. "That's the probability established by Madame

Atomos because we are in Las Vegas, the city of gambling," the monotone voice announced. "And Madame Atomos is betting on death."

The sergeant stopped the tape. "Given what happened recently in Los Angeles, we figured that if there's a bomb Madame Atomos would make it so that the Americans pressed the detonator themselves."

"That's not a bad idea," Beffort remarked. "What do you have in mind?"

"There's more than 15,000 gaming machines in this city. If one of them were connected to a bomb as its detonator, it's the jackpot! And everything goes Boom! That's the possibility we have to keep in mind."

"In that case, why would they be so reckless as to warn us?"

"Because there's not much we can do. The guy said four days maximum, which isn't enough to evacuate everyone."

"Let's cut the electricity to the casinos and close all gaming rooms. That might be doable."

"Doable, yes, but not easy to implement because there's too much money in gambling and the Organization knows it as well as we do. Madame Atomos figured on it and she wasn't entirely wrong in the fact that the army, police, Mr. White the mayor, and especially the casino owners are unable to reach an agreement on whether to start evacuating immediately or purely and simply to stop all activity."

The sergeant paused and smiled. "Well, Madame Atomos made a mistake! See, Mr. Beffort, I succeeded in the impossible. For once the army and the police, I mean all the competent authorities, as well as the mayor, might be, what am I saying, they *are* in agreement. The evacuation started while you were gone. Some casinos have even closed their doors already and the others are on the way. I believe the Atomos Organization didn't count on the total and effective cooperation of all our forces."

"What happened in Los Angeles is obviously well known here."

"Without a doubt. And this time the Organization showed its hand too soon."

"In any case, I tip my hat to such fast action," Beffort said.

The federal agent told the police sergeant about the visit to the sheriff of Salvation as well as the high level of radioactivity near the town.

"I have to go back to Salvation. We're sure that Madame Atomos disappeared around there. She might even have been in the Mercury when it crashed. That's why the members of the Organization are on red alert. They were caught off guard. Between the crash of the flying saucer and its recovery by the army and now their boss has disappeared without leaving a trace…"

"No, something's not right," Dr. Creighton interrupted. "You say the operation's been planned for a long time but then you say the Organization was caught in the middle of something…"

"Yes, the bomb's been in their hands for many years. They they've had all the time in the world to hide it somewhere inaccessible. Under any building or casino in Las Vegas… there are 15,000! The Organization has had more than eight years to prepare its attack. They just had to bide their time…"

"Or hire a specialist to make the detonator. Like Professor Ernst Hartmann, for example."

"Exactly, doctor. Of course the operation's been planned for a long time, so freeing Madame Atomos, if we had her, wouldn't change a thing. But that doesn't take away the fact that her disappearance caught them off guard. It doesn't matter. With a little luck we'll succeed in frustrating the monster's plans."

Smith Beffort glanced out the window. The streets were busy, more crowded than usual. A traffic jam was already forming at the intersection. The evacuation of the city had started and was running pretty smoothly, which reassured him. It looked like orders were being followed. If things continued like this until the end, many lives would be saved.

However, if Beffort guessed right, the evacuation should not be limited to Las Vegas but concerned the whole State of Nevada, surely an impossible feat. Beffort immediately thought that he might still be mistaken.

Though Kanoto Yoshimuta had given up trying to escape, she was now trying to find a way to put a quick end to her life if circumstances demanded. The attitude of her jailor left no room for doubt: she was not faced with a normal individual but rather a seriously disturbed man and obviously gravely ill.

Her expert eye had scrutinized the sheriff's face. Even when he was angry, like she had just witnessed, his features remained frozen. On the upper right side of his face there was a spot of skin, an unsightly spot that looked dead compared to the rest of his face. Nothing to do with plastic surgery like she had first thought. Nor with an ugly scar. She knew about this kind of degeneration, which is what it was. She had seen it affect the survivors of the nuclear bomb. Radiation that continually ate away at human flesh, year after year, and made the victims wish they had died on the spot.

But he was not in Hiroshima or Nagasaki and no H-bomb had ever exploded in the United States. She knew that the breakdown of the skin had probably affected other parts of the body. Maybe the top of his head, which explained why Ralph Bender always kept his hat on.

She, too, had domesticated atomic energy. She had sent hordes of atomized zombies into different parts of the United States. Could there be a connection between her and this couple? Could they have been her victims?

Madame Atomos also knew that radioactivity influenced the nerve cells and certain parts of the brain. She had to face reality: she was here with two lunatics who knew her identity and might have reasons to hold grudge against her.

The Japanese woman was still watching Bender who was picking up the kabuki mask like a clumsy child and who looked particularly unhappy.

"I'm going to have to find another mask for Yomi," he said. "I hope it won't affect our dinner tonight..." He put the remains gently on a table and turned to his prisoner. "I'll make you some tea and then I'll tell you our story. You don't want to talk to me but I'm sure you'll be a good listener. You have to know what happened to us before you meet my wife."

The giant left and came back a few minutes later carrying a tray. With his exaggerated manners he served two cups of tea, holding one out for Madame Atomos. It was a positively revolting brew.

Then he sat on the ground. "When I met Yomi in Japan she was a stripper in a cheap club." He laughed. "She was young and beautiful. We were both young. And that's when my life really began, when really important things happened to me..." And the sheriff told in colorful detail how Yomi left Japan and arrived in America.

Kanoto Yoshimuta listened, almost sure of the outcome of the story. She still refused to say a single word. She was alive and her men were certainly looking for her. When Bender had to answer the door this morning she was hoping that it was them coming to free her, but according to the sheriff it was just two policemen, two colleagues from work. Did his colleagues know how crazy Bender was? Didn't it alarm them that a guy like him could live in a remote place like this with no neighbors. Was he really even a sheriff? The two policemen's visit seemed to indicate that he was but she could not be sure that Bender was telling the truth. In fact, Madame Atomos was not sure of many things at all. The United States could still surprise her.

"We went to New York in the beginning of the 60s," the sheriff continued. "We lived near Central Park but it was not very practical because I was assigned to the Long Island station. I asked for housing closer to my work but there was nothing available. I commuted for three years and Yomi felt more and more alone in the house. I advised her to get more involved in the New York life but she never went out. You know, in those days we lived in a dive. My father had been sheriff of Salvation; it's my hometown. That's where Yomi went when she came here from Japan. But in New York everything was different."

Bender stared at his empty cup.

"I think that Yomi started sinking into depression. And I had my job. I got a promotion. I was transferred to the 52nd precinct in the Bronx. You really screwed things up there, Madame!"

Here it comes, the Japanese thought. *Finally. A little trip down memory lane.*

"But all in good time," Bender continued. "I'll tell you about Yomi and the difficulty she had adjusting to life in the city. When I can, I'll bring her out, believe me. I think she had everything she wants materially but she suffered when I was away. I didn't see it coming. When I think back on it, I believe there's nothing I could have done anyway. Until tragedy struck, Madame Atomos, until tragedy struck…

Everything seemed to be happening inside the LVMPD headquarters. The local police, the FBI and now the men from the Green Dragon Force were milling around the crowded rooms. It was a beehive of activity.

Swamped by phone calls Smith Beffort did not even have time to go back to his hotel and change clothes.

"In less than an hour Las Vegas will become a ghost town," the sergeant said. "Our priority is to cut the electricity by sectors." He pointed at the map of the city on the big table in the center of the room. "The northeast quarter is already blacked out. Las Vegas is fed by different plants so we can't cut all electricity at once. The hospitals and other emergency services will continue to have juice but the casinos and gaming rooms will be cut off within 24 hours. I think we should be proud, Beffort, that the authorities have granted us so much authority because our conclusion could have seemed unreasonable. You think a bomb under a casino hooked up to a slot machine…"

"I'm not the one who thought it up," Beffort cut in. "Even though it seems totally reasonable… In any case the Organization's threats are being taken seriously."

"Yes. The army sent 2,000 men to search the basements of the city with a fine-toothed comb over the next 24 hours. That might seem too short a time but it's all I got. Okay, the evacuation of Las Vegas is put on the back burner because to evacuate everyone in less than 24 hours is totally unfeasible."

"I think you're managing just fine. I'm going back to take a look at Salvation. I'm sure there's something to find around there."

The sergeant agreed and took the phone that a policeman held out to him. He listened and spoke and Beffort could tell by his answers that it was the mayor. Out of discretion he moved away. He saw the sergeant's face change color but could not understand what he was saying as he was talking faster and faster, waving his left arm, then suddenly stopped, listened again for a long time before raising his voice. There was obviously a problem. The conversation lasted 20 minutes.

After hanging up the phone the sergeant threw up his hands. "Something's come up. Some bastard is screwing us up."

"What's wrong?"

"A big shot is refusing to close some casinos. His influence reached all the way to our dear President who call the mayor in person to make sure his demands are met."

"What does that mean?"

"As far as I understand, more than a third of Las Vegas will keep their electricity so that a few casinos can stay in business. Of course, this considerably reduces our chances of avoiding an explosion."

"And the President is okay with that?"

"It won't be the first stupid thing he's done during his term. And he seems to be doing more and more of them…"

"I'm going to have a talk with this influential gentleman. It's awful and irresponsible. In fact, it's criminal to demand such a thing. What's the name of his casino?"

"He's not a casino owner. He's a show biz manager. His headliner is singing in Las Vegas right now at the International Hotel and the guy wants that whole part of the city to continue functioning during his singer's tour of Las Vegas."

"And this guy convinced the President for the sake of his little crooner. I can't believe it! What kind of world are we living in?"

"Well, the crooner's a close friend of Nixon and been decorated a few times. I really think he's untouchable, Beffort."

"Madame Atomos is lucky to be attacking a world of madmen. So, what's this impresario's name?"

"Parker. Colonel Tom Parker."

Chapter X

Ralph Bender stopped talking. All of a sudden he jumped up and headed for the door.

"We'll continue this conversation later. It was a real pleasure talking to you about Yomi but my household chores await. Besides, I have to make sure that nobody will disturb us. The three of us are at a crossroads in our lives, a time when important things can happen, and I'm leery about what might come from the outside. There were already policemen here this morning and others might follow. I also have to prepare something to eat. I guess you're hungry."

As usual Madame Atomos just stared without answering. The sheriff disappeared behind the door but came back a few minutes later. To her great disappointment he was not carrying a plate of food. Except for breakfast Madame Atomos had eaten nothing since the day before but she knew how to live on little when need be. She did some calisthenics to loosen up and scowled when she saw how dirty her clothes were. Luckily there were basic toiletries in the corner and a sink with cold water so she could clean up a little.

In any case, the situation would not last forever. The sheriff had interrupted his story just before the attacks on Long Island and the Bronx. Now he would get to his wife's actual accident. Madame Atomos had no soft spot. If this girl had become American she betrayed her country and paid for it.

But Ralph Bender had left the room without finishing his story.

An hour later Madame Atomos heard faint footsteps behind the door. With her keen sense of hearing she thought that the person walking was in the hallway just outside the kitchen. She recognized Yomi's walk as she entered the room. Her footsteps sounded weird. They were not really those of an invalid. Madame Atomos had heard this kind of jerky walk before but she could not remember where.

Daylight flooded the room and Kanoto Yoshimuta finally saw Yomi when she entered the room. She stood there motionless in front of the door. She was wearing a mask, one of the theater masks like Bender had broken accidentally. She thought that the woman must be disfigured.

Out of the mask came long, jet black hair past her narrow shoulders. She wore a dark sweat suit that was too big for her and completely hid her puny body. The effect was striking.

Evidently she needed no help to stand up, so Madame Atomos figured that her sickness must be internal. And then, all of a sudden Yomi started moving. The prisoner in her cell felt all the horror one could feel faced with something truly inhuman. All her movements were jerky.

She stopped just a couple of feet in front of the bars and Madame Atomos hoped that she would not move again. Instinctively she had backed away to the far wall. It was the first time in her life she had ever backed away.

How could this sickly little creature with her ratty old sweat suit and ridiculous mask terrorize and disgust her so?

Bender had probably drugged her tea so that all her senses were peaked to fill her with fear. The sheriff's exit was, in fact, a ploy. He had planned it with his wife down to the last detail. It was all staged for her benefit. She was the prisoner of a couple of lunatics out for revenge.

Madame Atomos closed her eyes for a minute and when she opened them Yomi had disappeared. She had heard her leaving but did not want to see her monstrous movements again. She sighed in relief. After the creature had left, so too did her fear dissipate. All that was left was an uneasy feeling and bewilderment. What had really happened? Apparently she had not been drugged since she was back to her normal self...

She had to face facts: the mere presence of the sheriff's wife had scared her. But it was not really her presence but rather her way of moving and walking. This feeling, almost dread, that Kanoto Yoshimuta had never known before was growing and she hoped deep down inside that she would never see that creature again.

The car was parked in the motel lot. It was a black Chevrolet Monte Carlo with Mexican plates. Three men climbed out.

When Yahto saw them come into the bar he thought of the cops right away but he changed his mind when he got a closer look. Two of them were certainly Mexican and had to be younger than 30. The third man was older and stood stiffly. All three wore neatly ironed white shirts.

Yahto had heard that two FBI agents were looking for him and was glad that his colleagues were so discreet. He had spent some nights drinking heavily with Ralph Bender during which the usually quiet sheriff had revealed things that Yahto had no desire to repeat to the cops. But these men were obviously not cops.

They introduced themselves as relatives and friends of the victim of the car accident. It was the older man who spoke. The two Mexicans stood back. The discussion first revolved around the Mercury. The guy apparently wanted to know if Yahto had noticed anything special. The motel employee answered in the negative.

Then the man cleverly shifted the conversation to Salvation and what a sheriff was doing in a deserted town. Yahto was immediately suspicious and eluded the question. He could have said a lot about Bender but certainly not to these three characters. Besides, he did not want to be thought crazy.

The three men thanked him politely, finished their drinks and left. The Chevy headed into the mountains. Yahto watched them go and thought the time had come to call the cops. He could not keep it all bottled up inside. Especially when two FBI agents had already shown up and these three guys looked so shady. It was getting to be too much.

Yahto asked his colleague for the name of the cop who had come around in the morning.

"Beffort," the bartender replied. "Smith Beffort. He left his card in case you wanted to reach him."

The guy driving the Chevy did all he could to avoid the ruts but the narrow mountain road did not leave much room to maneuver. Sitting in the backseat Ernst Hartmann watched the desert landscape, remembering his nocturnal march after the accident. He was back in Salvation.

A lot of things had happened since the night he spent in the ghost town and especially since the disappearance of Madame Atomos. Given that he was one of the last people to see the Japanese woman, Ernst Hartmann had been questioned for a long time by members of the Organization. He had to repeat the tiniest details of that frightful night in Salvation. All the same it was Madame Atomos' agents who came to get him and bring him to Las Vegas, so they must have known that the old scientist had absolutely nothing to do with their boss' disappearance.

Moreover, he had completed his mission. He had primed the bomb and set up the detonator in a different way than the original prototype. In short, he had taken care of everything. Now, even though he knew it was not safe in Nevada, he had to stay here, a prisoner in this place where a bomb could explode at any minute whereas he should be long gone in a safe haven with enough money to last the rest of his life.

I'm always getting conned, he thought. *My entire life. Ever since I started selling myself.*

He preferred not to think that he might never be on the right side of the fence. His thoughts were interrupted by the Mexican sitting in the passenger seat.

"We're going to stop before the town, Mr. Hartmann. It's better to be careful and go on foot. It wouldn't be good for us to be spotted by the sheriff."

Hartmann nodded.

It was Lopez Castillo who had spoken. He was a pure blood Mexican. He had been part of the team that had picked up the scientist and the detonator and he had come with Madame Atomos to find Hartmann in Salvation. Lopez Castillo liked to act tough, being part of the Organization for many years. He could not help his condescending tone when speaking to Hartmann and the scientist hated him for it. Even if the thug called him Mister, he still thought he was the boss.

The other was not much better. A thug by the name of Alonzo Acosta, a driver when needed.

In fact, these two were killers and despite having brains the size of lizards their physical superiority over Hartmann was obvious. They were so stupid that he figured he could never manipulate them. He, the superior German, the scientist who was the authority in many domains of thermo-dynamics, was trapped by these two idiots and had to put up with their arrogance. Fortunately when they wanted to crack jokes the jerks spoke in Spanish.

Alonzo stopped the Chevy around 100 yards before the first houses appeared. "Show us where you spent the night, Mr. Hartmann. Maybe we'll find a clue."

The scientist nodded again and the three men got out of the car. In the sunlight the German found Salvation even weirder than the first time.

"To think there's a sheriff guarding this dump," Lopez muttered. "Everyone's gotta work, okay, but this is too much!"

"We gotta find out where he's holing up," his partner said. "Before he finds us…"

"Not to worry," Lopez responded. "We have every right to be walking around here. And our purpose isn't written all over our face, is it Mr. Hartmann?"

Ernst Hartmann just shrugged. The two Mexicans were walking two steps behind him, which made him feel like France during the Occupation, but this time he was not on the good side.

"Here it is," Hartmann pointed to a falling down chapel.

"You spent the night in there?" Alonzo was surprised. "It's one of the few buildings without a roof!"

"It was dark and I was injured and exhausted. I didn't go looking around," the German was getting angry.

The two Mexicans walked around in front of the chapel before going inside. Alonzo finally observed, "There's nothing here. But it's all cleaned up. Not a piece of trash."

"What exactly are you looking for?" Hartmann asked.

Neither of the Mexicans answered. They looked up to examine the top of the walls.

"We're going to inspect every damn inch of this town," Lopez said after a moment of silence. "One house at a time. Then we'll pay the sheriff a little visit."

"Unless he finds us first," Hartmann replied. "Maybe this place is going to be crawling with cops anytime. Stopping to ask for information at the motel was already a careless move. So, if I were you, I'd get a move on, make a quick inspection and not press my luck."

"I don't need luck," Lopez stepped up to Hartmann with a menacing look on his face. "We'll stay here as long as we need to. Alonzo will stash the wheels so we'll be able to take off fast if there's a problem."

Alonzo did as he was told.

"We'll split up and each explore a part of the town," Lopez said when his partner had returned. "Search the houses and check in every 15 minutes. This is no time to lose contact with each other. If you see a cop, get back to the car as soon as possible, unless, of course, it's the sheriff."

"That's a little flimsy as a backup plan," Hartmann commented, "but I guess we have no choice."

The farther into town they walked, the quieter it grew. The Mexicans were affected by the strangeness of the place and ended up not saying a word. Main Street was deserted and the alleyways narrow and empty. It was eerily like the ship *Mary Celeste* whose passengers disappeared without leaving a trace.

Hartmann and Lopez took the first alleys on the right side while Alonzo continued down Main Street. It did not take long to recognize the sheriff's house on the other end of town. His car was parked right out front and Bender himself was carrying packages that the Mexican, from his distance, could not identify. Anyway, the sheriff was there in town while they were inspecting the houses one by one.

Alonzo backtracked to tell the others and found Lopez crawling out of a window because the door was locked.

"If the sheriff is busy on the other side of town," Lopez decided, "then we have plenty of time to search over here. We'll go see him after."

"We might not have to," Alonzo said. "And we should keep it quiet."

Lopez did not respond as his partner headed down another alley. Ernst Hartmann was still searching without much confidence. At first because he did not really know what he was looking for and then because he did not like the place at all and could not concentrate on the task at hand.

The German could not hold back a shudder. The town was like a cemetery and the houses like well-kept tombs. Inside them was only a little furniture that looked very carefully arranged and all the rooms were neat and clean. Hartmann would often glance through a window because he did not want to lose sight of the other two, but the Mexican killers were never far away, which was starting to be a comforting thought.

Hunter Robinson was in a pretty bad mood. Nothing was going as he had planned. He had come to Las Vegas to be with Smith Beffort but he had not seen the FBI agent since they arrived. And now a guy at the hotel was knocking on the door telling him he had to evacuate the premises. Robinson had barely arrived and the authorities were evacuating Las Vegas! This would make one hell of a paper. A bang-up opening for his article.

From his window the journalist watched the commotion in the street that grew as the hours passed. He sat on his bed and opened his travel bag. It still contained a good number of illegal substances that Robinson needed in order to progress in the new journalism. For five minutes his eyes wandered back and forth from the suitcase to window. In the end, being thoroughly professional, he decided that it would be better in the first place, given this turn of events, to go down to the bar and get stinking drunk on tequila.

Dressed in red shorts and a neatly ironed beige sweatshirt he entered the bar and ordered a drink, all the while questioning the bartender about the reasons for all the fuss.

"At the start it was supposed to be a general evacuation," he explained from behind the bar," but then they decided to cut the electricity. From what I heard they're not going to cut off the whole city because there are certain people who don't want it done. So, obviously, it's kind of a mess."

Hunter Robinson stared hard at the bottom of his glass thinking that he was probably not the only one taking acid in this crazy world; there must have been a good batch circulating among the officials.

"Maybe because of Madame Atomos," the bartender proposed. "I heard about a bomb and a bunch of other things. To tell you the truth it's not really being taken seriously. But hey, since it was only an evacuation some people were just having fun with it. Now that they've cut the power in the casinos, they're not laughing anymore. You know, Las Vegas is only full of gamblers, alcoholics and big kids."

"And the people who work here," the journalist added, still too sober to feel in tune with the general atmosphere.

"Maybe it's better not to take this too lightly," the bartender continued. "I've already decided to leave. Tomorrow I'm going to my sister's house in Los Angeles. You can never be too careful."

Robinson looked up from his glass and eyed the man. "Before leaving, could you call the taxi who picked me up the other night? He brought me to a really nice place, a casino whose name I forget but with really funky slot machines. Little Chinese death's heads lining up and blinking. I'd love to break the bank just once in my life."

Chapter XI

It was the 7th or 8th house that Ernst Hartmann had been in. He was not really counting and they all looked exactly the same with the same number of rooms and the same layout designed, no doubt, by the same architect.

Where he was now, therefore, was the same as the others with its rooms cleaned as if waiting for some unlikely occupants to arrive. Exactly like the others except for one thing: a wooden door was in the middle of the living room wall. Hartmann had seen enough living rooms in this town to know that this was unusual.

To his great surprise the metal doorknob turned easily and the door opened onto a staircase leading down into darkness. The German felt for a light switch along the wall but found nothing. He stood still for a few seconds in front of the black hole that foretold nothing good. He waited for his eyes to adjust but the darkness remained impenetrable.

Hartmann decided to leave the house and call the two Mexicans. Lopez showed up first followed by Alonzo a few seconds later. They went together into the house and Hartmann led them to the staircase he had found.

"It probably just goes down into a basement," Alonzo said.

"It's too dark," Lopez observed. "Go back to the car and dig up a flashlight or something."

Lopez grabbed the handrail, ready to go down. "Like this if the steps are rotted I won't break my neck. The basement can't be too far down. I'll look for a switch down there."

Ernst Hartmann admired his courage. Nothing in the world could make him go down into that gloom.

The Mexican stepped carefully and Hartmann watched him slowly disappear into the dark. The wood creaked ominously under the young man's feet. After what seemed an eternity, while he was waiting for Lopez to say something, Hartmann suddenly saw a faint glow coming from the basement. The Mexican had found the light switch.

"You can come down now, Mr. Hartmann. My God, what is this thing?"

In spite of the light the stairs were steep and relatively dangerous because of their condition but Hartmann scurried down anyway. When he finally reached the basement, he saw a completely empty room. Lopez was kneeling in the middle of the floor examining a padlocked trapdoor.

"Look at this! A trapdoor in a basement! It must lead directly to hell!"

"Maybe it's a wine cellar."

"That's a European for you. Look at how they locked it up. With these thick chains and locks I'd be amazed if all we find are some bottles of wine."

"What then?"

"No idea. Stay here. I'm going up to get Alonzo. We need more than a flashlight now. Some bolt cutters and tools to open this thing. I hope we've got something in the car."

The idea of staying alone did not please the physicist but he had no choice. To pass the time waiting for the Mexicans Ernst Hartmann started examining the bare, white walls that crumbled at his touch, but he could not tell if it was only plaster. He would have to know the origin of the house to know what they used to cover the walls. Then Hartmann examined the trapdoor meticulously. It was a heavy steel plate that looked indestructible. It could just as easily be used to keep something from getting out. The chains were thick, too.

Once again the scientist thought of Germany at the start of the war and the weird turn events sometimes took. Events that could end up in places like this behind heavy doors, heavy trapdoors... Always the same systems to separate the healthy mind from the unspeakable.

Hartmann jumped when the toolbox landed at his feet making an infernal racket after which he heard, "Hey, Alonzo, don't throw stuff around like that!"

The two Mexicans were back and trying to figure out the best way to open the trapdoor. The huge steel chains looked unbreakable so they were left with the two padlocks that should be easier to open.

"It's our only chance," Lopez said. "You think you can do it?"

"Shouldn't be too tough," Alonzo replied. "They're new locks so I know their weak points. Give me 15 minutes."

The Mexican started working on the locks like a professional while Hartmann looked on. He asked them, "What's going to happen after it's open?"

Lopez did not bother to answer, as if the question was completely idiotic. He held the lock delicately while his partner picked at it with a sharp tool and a screwdriver.

"We'll need brighter lights to go down there," Lopez ended up saying. "I'll go back to the car."

"Hey, my car's not a mobile hardware store," Alonzo sneered. "I'm pretty well equipped but you can't expect miracles. If we're gonna explore this hole, we're gonna use the flashlights I brought."

Lopez was obviously annoyed and turned to Hartmann. "Can you go back to the car, Mr. Hartmann? See if there's something in trunk to improve our visibility."

Hartmann smiled at the deliberately pompous phrase. He suspected that the Mexican was making fun of him but he wanted to get some fresh air and smoke a cigarette, so he accepted.

"What should I be looking for exactly?"

"Some kind of bright light," Lopez sounded exasperated.

When he was out in the open Ernst Hartmann felt a little better. Alonzo had given precise directions to the Chevrolet, just outside the entrance to the town, ready to take them far away if anything unexpected arose. Hartmann searched the trunk without much enthusiasm. There were still some tools but nothing of any use. They would have to continue their search with the lights they had.

He was starting to hope that the Mexicans would not be able to open the trapdoor. He took a break to smoke another cigarette. In the distance, at least 300 yards away, stood the sheriff's house, which they would certainly visit soon. Maybe this Ralph Bender had already spotted them. For the moment, however, everything was calm in Salvation. The cops and FBI had not yet invaded the area. They had enough to do in Las Vegas.

Thinking of the bomb, Ernst Hartmann felt uneasy. A member of the Organization would have to defuse it until they were all safely out of range, but no one wanted to defy the orders of the dreadful Madame Atomos. Their lives were clearly not worth much in the eyes of this woman who had made no backup plan in case of a problem. The German was always aware of this. He crushed his cigarette with the heel of his shoe and headed back to the house, submissively.

The second padlock had popped open and the two Mexicans took the chains off. Now they had to open the steel trapdoor, which did not look like it would be easy. The only part they could grab it was a long groove on the right side.

"It looks more like a tombstone than a trapdoor," Alonzo said, straining his muscles and pulling with all his might next to his partner.

They lifted the steel plate a few inches.

"Don't drop it," Lopez shouted. "A little more and we can swing it over."

When it was vertical the heavy door stood on its own, suspended in the air. All of a sudden the huge weight crashed to the floor. Lopez barely had time to step away. Then the two of them leaned over the empty space. It was a shallow space opening onto a corridor or rather a tunnel. All they had to do was jump down and they would be in.

The Mexicans looked at each other in a daze. Because there was something weird: the corridor they saw was lit up. The light was dim but they could see clearly enough. The two men could imagine that the town had generators, but they were surprised to see the energy being used to light up underground tunnels. And then the heady odor of perfume rose out of the hole. A cheap, vanilla-scented perfume. The smell brought back some not very pleasant memories for Alonzo.

"The funeral home in Guanagatos," he said. "Where my father was laid out before they buried him. It's the same damn smell. It's not vanilla, it's a funeral home. The smell of death!"

Lopez' eyes were bulging. There was something not right. The German was taking his time coming back. "Hartman should be back by now. The old geezer must've got nabbed by the sheriff."

He had barely finished speaking when the German appeared on the stairs. When he joined the Mexican he looked haggard but they paid no attention to him in their excitement.

"Look, Mr. Hartmann," Lopez was almost friendly. "We got it. The trapdoor's open and I think this town still has a few surprises in store for us. Lean over and take a look down there. We just might have stumbled on Satan worshippers or some crap like that. And they use cheap perfume. Do you smell that, Mr. Hartmann?"

The German did not answer. He was turning pale.

"Don't be scared," the Mexican went on. "We've never been afraid of crazy people, isn't that right Alonzo? We'll go down to say hello and then go say hi to the sheriff."

"You seem to have forgotten the real purpose of our coming to Salvation," Hartmann's voice was shaky.

Lopez suddenly looked aggressive. "I didn't forget, Hartmann. We're here to look for Madame Atomos and that's what we're doing. Why do you have to say stupid things like that?"

Ernst Hartmann gulped. It was not easy for him to get the words out of his mouth. "Because I just found Madame Atomos' car. It's sitting almost right next to ours."

Smith Beffort ended up convincing Dr. Creighton to stay in Las Vegas with the other competent engineers in order to study the bomb built more than 30 years ago and whose design was partly unfinished, which did not make the specialists' work very easy.

In fact, the bomb, considered obsolete, had practically disappeared from the military archives and the army engineers had not rendered it harmless, although it was considered safe since it had no detonator. They were guilty of negligence and mistakes over the years and Madame Atomos had capitalized on it. But Smith Beffort was very confident that Dr. Creighton would figure out how the bomb worked and find a way to defuse it.

Now that the threat was overt thanks to the Atomos Organization's phone calls, which had confirmed the warnings that the federal agent had announced to his superiors, Smith Beffort had been able to assign Dr. Creighton as the specialist assigned to defuse the bomb when it was found. The scientist agreed to stay in Las Vegas, although he was aware of the enormous responsibility on his shoulders. They shook hands for a long time before Beffort left for Salvation.

On the way Smith Beffort decided to stop at the motel. One of the employees had left a message asking him to get in touch as soon as possible. Apparently he had some important information.

When he got there the bartender introduced him to Yahto who had been waiting for Beffort for two hours. The man seemed slightly drunk so the federal agent wondered if he should believe what he would say. The cook invited him up his room because the bar always had ears.

"I can't stay long," Beffort told the small, olive-skinned man. "I see you've been drinking, which is going to affect your speech and waste my time."

Yahto sat on his bed with an empty glass in his hand. "I have good reason to get drunk," he spoke seriously. "Alcohol is also Ralph Bender's friend. Without it his life would be unbearable."

The cook pulled up his knees. With his already tiny frame, it looked like he was trying to disappear. Smith Beffort waited for him to speak, not hiding his impatience.

"Well," Yahto broke his silence. "I'm an Indian, you probably guessed, just like Bender. So we've got a bond."

"Okay, you're an Indian like the sheriff, but that's no reason to get drunk every time you see each other. What's the story?"

"We both come from a tribe called that even the Shoshone don't want to talk about."

"And?"

"Very few people have heard of this tribe and those who have would rather forget it ever existed. Our tribe comes out of the Shoshone and it devoted itself to a kind of worship that others didn't out up with. Pagan worship come directly from Europe. That was the time of Cortez during the great invasions and massacres. A white man, a Portuguese priest, had taken control of some of our people. Most of the Shoshone didn't like seeing him force his doctrine on us. Only a few members of the tribe were lured in by the white man but some of them were killed by their blood brothers. The others were banished and built the town of Salvation to live in peace and keep their unholy worship. They were called the Cthugha."

"I've never heard this story," Beffort confessed.

"Of course not. Nowadays nobody cares and the descendants of this tribe don't really brag about it. So, Ralph Bender and I are both descendants of the Cthugha, which gives us good reason to get drunk together, Mr. Beffort."

"And what kind of worship did this tribe practice?" Beffort asked.

"It was a death cult, only a death cult."

"A death cult? You mean black masses and pacts with the devil?"

"Not at all. Only a death cult and the place is perfectly suited for it. It's still suited for it today, Mr. Beffort, which is why I wanted to see you, to advise you not to go to Salvation alone."

"So the town's dangerous? We already know that it's radioactive."

Yahto got up to get the bottle of Jack Daniels, then flopped back onto the bed. "The town is radioactive," the Indian sounded more sure of himself. "The town is everything you want it to be! You could even say that all the curses on earth are in Salvation. The place is a catalyst. That's why Bender went there with his wife after the accident. And that's why no stranger should go there alone. There's no way you'll stand up to it, Mr. FBI agent!"

"His wife? You mean the Japanese woman who survived one of Madame Atomos' attacks?"

"The very same, Mr. Beffort. Yomi Bender, Ralph's wife. No one more in love than those two! Might as well call them Romeo and Juliette. They're inseparable. Except you're wrong, Mr. Beffort, Yomi didn't survive the attack. Yomi died over ten years ago."

Chapter XII

Ralph Bender was more and more disagreeable. He had suspected that the capture of Madame Atomos would probably set things in motion, but he had not thought that Yomi's behavior would be affected.

"She came to see you, didn't she?" he asked his prisoner without really expecting an answer. "I can see in your terrified eyes that she came to see you. Because you're scared, Kanoto. It's all over your face. Have no fear, you didn't really see anything otherwise you wouldn't be here listening to me."

The sheriff leaned over to look out the window.

"There are two guys outside. Maybe they're your men out here looking for you. Anyway, they think they're very clever. They think I haven't seen them."

He started laughing.

"I'm not deluding myself. Soon there will be a lot of people here. The cops will be all over this place too. Maybe it'll be the apocalypse but I don't care because our destiny is sealed and the finishing touches will soon be applied. You will learn about this destiny now, Kanoto. I just need a little time to finish my story. It's not your men that worry me. They'll show up here before too long but I can give them a warm welcome. No, it's Yomi's attitude that bothers me. She's more agitated than usual. I thought she would take this all more calmly but your presence and these men outside... I'm not sure I'll get you two together tonight. I'm afraid I'll have to cancel dinner, which really irks me."

Ralph Bender came away from the window and sat cross-legged in front of the cell, just two feet away.

Madame Atomos was standing up, still silent, but her expression had changed.

"Well, I was in New York," the sheriff resumed. "As I told you, Yomi was alone most of the time and she didn't make any friends in the neighborhood. Time passed. The routine... but does it matter? I came home almost every night and we were always happy to see each other. And then one day in March 1963 a colleague and I were given an ordinary assignment but while I was getting changed my boss came to tell me that I should get home right away. Something had happened. In fact, Yomi had been hit by a taxi and was killed on the spot. She wasn't hit extremely hard but with her small body... She was still beautiful when I saw her in the morgue. I didn't bang my head against the wall because I hadn't really absorbed it. But of course I'd have to grieve and accept living without her, which even today I can't imagine."

He paused before continuing.

"Do you remember, Kanoto, the attacks in the Bronx, the living dead that you sent to blow up all of New York[4]? It was chaos that week, the start of hostilities. I still wonder how you managed to do such things, to raise the dead and use them as walking bombs. And radioactive to boot! It's certainly not a little sheriff from the desert who can understand your Japanese technology... Me, at the time, I just cleaned up. Helped the victims and counted the dead."

He cleared his throat and made sure that Madame Atomos was still listening.

"Plus, you obviously understand better than me what happened. Because your thing, your ray, I never

---

[4] See *The Terror of Madame Atomos.*

found out how it worked. In that month of March, while the roads were being cleared with a flame-thrower to get rid of the few corpses still left standing, I went back to the morgue to make sure Yomi was okay before she was buried. The morgue was total mess, Kanoto. It had suffered the effects of your damned ray. A bunch of corpses had come back to life and then disappeared. But Yomi was still there. When I opened the drawer where her body lay, she started moving. Since the drawer had been closed she couldn't get out to join the other corpses who had left, but she was... let's say 'animated'. I worked fast, without thinking. She didn't weigh a thing. I wrapped her in a sheet and carried her out of the building. There was panic everywhere. The people were too crazy to see anything. I brought Yomi home. We stayed there for a few days and when I went to work she stayed on the bed, just twitching a little. She didn't talk or eat, of course, because she was dead. But she watched me. The spark in her eye was still weak but she watched me and she recognized me. Every night I lay down next to her and we slept together. At least, the first few nights... because I quickly saw that she was slowly decomposing, that the smell was becoming unbearable and that the neighbors were going to start asking questions. I decided to ask for a transfer to Salvation. It had been expected for a while that I would go back there and what happened in New York sped things up. My father had been sheriff of Salvation and I was simply going back to take his place. But someone had to take care of Yomi for the few weeks I had to stay in the city. Someone to watch over her. I sent her in a coffin and an old, trusty friend received her and took care of her before I could get here."

Madame Atomos approached the bars and for the first time in days came out of her silence. "What you're telling me is utterly impossible. I know how the ray works since I invented it. The bodies I animated were just bomb-toting corpses. There's no way my invention could have brought your wife back to life or given her back her soul."

"You must have missed something, Madame Atomos. Whoever made such a weapon was obviously not aware of all its secrets."

"Your wife wasn't dead, sheriff. It's not too complicated. Either your wife is still living today or you're completely off your rocker. Let's say you could live the rest of your life with a corpse, a corpse rots. A corpse can't recognize you... Okay, let's change the subject. My men are outside. You'd be better off letting me go before you get hurt."

"I see you haven't understood," Bender sounded desolated. "But see, I won't hold it against you. Yomi and I owe you a lot and our story isn't over yet."

Smith Beffort was back on the road to Salvation. The motel cook was with him, sitting in the passenger seat. During the drive Yahto continued telling his incredible story.

"I helped Ralph because he's my friend and always will be. We're united by blood and nothing's stronger than blood. So, I picked up Yomi's coffin and brought it to Salvation. Ralph didn't officially declare her dead in New York and no one paid attention. After the tragic events caused by Madame Atomos New York State was completely disorganized and in the confusion Ralph managed to get the body transferred out of state without a problem."

"I still can't believe... The living dead sent off by Madame Atomos were autopsied at the time," Beffort said. "They were only bodies reanimated for a few hours... and when the effects of the ray wore off they went back to being just dead bodies."

"Yes, but there was a little difference with Yomi. She had already been exposed to atomic radiation in Hiroshima. She was even seriously irradiated, which is why she couldn't have children or at least that's what the doctors told Ralph and Yomi. That might explain her different reaction to Madame Atomos' ray, don't you think? Anyway, I can tell you that Yomi was definitely alive when she got to Salvation."

"Then Yomi's a living corpse?"

"When I took care of her she was more than a living corpse, Mr. Beffort. Yomi was Yomi again. I think something must have happened to her during her trip to limbo. Her soul had come back into her body."

"Did she recognize you? Maybe she was just in a coma or something like that?"

"No, there's something else. Ralph advised me not to look into her eyes. He even covered her face with a mask so I wouldn't see her when she got out of the coffin. He told me that she had brought something back from the Beyond, something too much for humans to look at without losing their mind."

"But he obviously looked at her?"

"Yes, certainly, but the two of them are inseparable. That's their history and it belongs to them."

"What happened next?"

"As I said, Salvation is a façade. Way back when, my ancestors practiced their worship in rooms built under the town. They dug miles of tunnels that became a real maze. But this underground network was abandoned a long time ago. Ralph got the idea to fix up part of it for Yomi. He thought the earth in the tunnels might slow down his wife's decomposition. Our tribe has always known that the ground in Salvation has magical qualities."

The FBI agent had to pay close attention to follow the Indian's story while avoiding the ruts and potholes in the road. "I really don't understand everything you're saying. What you're telling me is hard to believe."

And I haven't told you everything yet, Yahto thought. *I had to tone it down or you'd pull the car over immediately. But if you knew what I know, maybe you'd want to just drop a bomb on the cursed place.*

Lopez and Alonzo were stunned. Hartmann had found Madame Atomos' car! Therefore, she was being held prisoner by the sheriff.

"Why do look like that?" Lopez asked. "It's good news. Now we know she's here. We'll go have a word with the cop."

"Don't underestimate him," Alonzo jumped in. "The guy might be dangerous."

But Lopez was not listening to anybody but himself as he launched up the stairs. Hartmann and Alonzo followed. Rushing toward the sheriff's house he pulled out his gun but when he got within 50 feet he stopped short and examined the front of the house.

"Get back here," Hartmann said. "You're going to get yourself picked off."

Of course the Mexican paid no attention to the warning. He took careful aim at a window and pulled the trigger, shattering two panes of glass.

Madame Atomos stood up but her field of vision did not let her see anything at all. Nevertheless, she clearly heard Lopez' voice shouting. She knew then that she would not remain a prisoner for long.

All Ralph Bender did was check to make sure the doors were locked. Strangely calm he brought a cup of tea for his prisoner.

"They can't get in," he said. "The door is solid."

The Mexican standing in the middle of the road would have made a perfect target but the sheriff refused all acts of violence.

"It'll soon be over for you," Madame Atomos told him.

But Ralph Bender was not listening to her. He was worried about his wife's reaction to all the commotion. He checked the door again and went down the hallway.

"I'm in here," Madame Atomos yelled. "Inside the house!"

Lopez heard her voice but could not tell exactly where it was coming from. This time, however, there was no doubt about it. Madame Atomos was in the house. He lowered his weapon and joined the two others who were crouching behind a wall.

"Take me to Madame Atomos' car," he ordered the German. "There might be something inside that can help us get her out of there fast."

At the end of the hallway a door led down into the cellar where a trapdoor gave access to a tunnel on the west side of the underground town. The trapdoor was always open so that Yomi could come and go as she pleased between the two worlds. Ralph Bender had added a second generator for all the lights to let his wife travel easily through the tunnels.

The sheriff hurried. He shouted Yomi's name a few times but she did not show up. He was a little disturbed by the turn of events. He was ready to face any situation as long as it did not get between him and his wife. Yomi demanded very particular care and right now, in no time at all, everything was getting out of control.

His shouting was in vain. Yomi did not answer. She must be hiding in some secret corner. Bender finally decided to stop searching. Yomi knew the underground world much better than the surface so there was no need for him to worry. The important thing for the moment was to deal with the problems at hand. And the priority was the men raiding his town.

Madame Atomos' car was unlocked. The men searched it but found nothing of use. Lopez, who knew the Japanese woman rarely traveled without her disintegrator pistol, was discouraged.

"Okay, too bad. We'll go back there and kick down the door. The sheriff obviously doesn't want to come out and it can't be too hard to get inside there so we can blow his brains out."

Lopez rushed down main street again, the two others trailing behind him. He was walking fast, almost running, eager to get it over with. Again he stopped in front of the house and called out Madame Atomos' name.

When the door opened he did not even think of pulling out his gun. First because he was not expecting it and then because the sheriff looked totally normal, like a guy just coming out of his house to get the mail.

In a natural, fearless motion Ralph Bender raised the sawed-off rifle from his hip and put two bullets into Lopez, one in the stomach and the other in the head. It was the second bullet that killed the Mexican on the spot. He dropped onto the pavement as his two partners looked on in shock.

Smith Beffort stopped the car at the entrance to the town and with the cook headed to the sheriff's house on foot. The federal agent banged on the door but nobody answered.

"What do you think, Yahto? Is Bender really gone or does he just not want to open up?"

"He's probably fixing something around town. It's a lot of work keeping up Salvation and he's the only one here to do it."

"Don't take me for an idiot! You told me the underground goes directly to his house but there's got to be other entrances."

"There's three of them. One at Ralph's, a second one to the north and the other's in the east. I can show them to you."

"Please do, if it's not too much trouble."

Yahto looked nervous. He hesitated a moment before heading back to the Ford. "We'll need some tools. Some pliers and a little screwdriver or something like that. We've got to open a padlock. Do you have any tools in your car?"

After getting the necessary material, the two men went north into a part of town where all the houses were identical. The farther they went the tenser Yahto became. He stopped abruptly and turned to Beffort.

"It's not the best decision," he said.

"You scared? Listen, you insisted on coming with me. You said you'd be my guide, so now I'm following you. Taking you on your word…"

Yahto started walking again. "You're right. Besides, we're almost there and this has got to end someday."

Yahto pointed out a house like all the others. The door was cracked open when they entered. Instinctively Beffort waved to Yahto to stay back. The Indian also knew that something was awry. They were not the first ones here: an opening, probably leading to the basement, let a little light into room and proof that other people were in the place. The federal agent snuck up to the basement door and saw some wooden stairs. A bullet whizzed by and he jumped back.

"FBI," Beffort yelled. "Come out of there or you'll be forced out at your own risk."

"Come and get me, you rotten pig," a man's voice responded.

"You said there was another entrance?" Beffort whispered to the Indian.

"Yes. Those guys are stuck down there but we can get in through the east entrance."

"First I'd like to know who I'm dealing with. It's probably men from the Atomos Organization. For a ghost town there sure are a lot of people milling around." Then the federal agent shouted another ultimatum. "We have all night! You might as well just come out now."

This time there was no answer.

"It won't be easy getting them out of there," Beffort whispered. "I'm going to have to call for backup."

"By the time they get here... Besides, these guys certainly found the entrance to the tunnels and maybe already opened the trapdoor," the Indian said as an icy shiver ran down his spine.

Chapter XIII

Stobbart was in permanent contact with all the Las Vegas police stations. Over the past few years there had been a clearly dysfunctional relationship between the police and the army. After finally getting things cleared up, today it was all up in the air again because of an entertainer. The situation was surreal.

The evacuation of Las Vegas was taking its time, but they could not do otherwise without creating a panic. A circus, a joke, that was what the authorities were calling it when they blamed each other's powerlessness... until they all agreed on who was really responsible for the mess: an FBI agent by the name of Smith Beffort.

As for cutting the electricity, there too they proved to be ineffective in that a civilian had got the right to limit it, leaving a third of the city exposed to a possible threat.

That was what the chief of police was trying to explain to the FBI chief who was trying to explain it to the Secretary of Defense so he could convince the President.

In high places, however, they thought the telephone calls from the Organization seemed to indicate that the bomb was hooked up to a slot machine and the possibility could not be neglected. Very quickly most of the casinos looked like disaster zones where technicians and engineers were running all over the place, checking every machine, one by one, and inspecting the basements.

With the casinos closed, the city lost a lot more money in one hour than the manager of a factory in Boston would earn in his lifetime. Las Vegas watched huge amounts of profit slipping away, as the Mayor did not stop reminding them.

But Las Vegas also risked being wiped off the face of the earth.

Hunter Robinson had become a little more serious. He did not really think that being serious was necessarily a respectable form of behavior but present events had changed his view of things and encouraged a certain journalistic gravity. There was enough going on to furnish a smashing article. Several titles were already popping into his head: 'Las Vegas Losing Its Marbles' or 'Batty In The Desert'.

They kept coming to advise him to leave the city but he did not want to go before his assignment was finished. In truth it did not seem very urgent. The authorities looked pretty calm and aloof.

Hunter Robinson had stopped taking his usual drugs. He needed to take a break and keep his mind clear to start writing what would be the first page of this article. The night before he had decided not to sleep so he would not have to wake up at dawn. Therefore, he went to the police headquarters looking for Smith Beffort but the agent was nowhere to be found. Some policemen had told him that Beffort was on a hot lead and no one could get in touch with him. Besides, the police and the army were on red alert and had better things to do than answer a reporter's questions.

Robinson left the station empty-handed. He had trouble finding his bearings in the immense city, so he just started wandering down the wide sidewalk on Fremont Street. The army was at the ready. The game rooms were mostly closed and the hotels looked empty.

Some restaurants were open but it was impossible to get served.

Robinson, therefore, thought that Madame Atomos must have considerable power for a city to shut down at the mere mention of her name. Thinking of her brought him back to the place where he had gambled the night he arrived and that would be absolutely impossible for him to find again. The small gaming room with its multicolored neon lights and flashing machines could be anywhere in this huge, unknown city.

Likewise he thought about the machine with the diabolical Japanese woman's head he had to line up to hit the jackpot. What bad taste! How offensive! Even he would never imagine such a machine and he was no stranger to offending people...

Robinson started thinking. In spite of his more or less alcoholic states and his trips to an artificial paradise, he was not completely devoid of common sense when he came back down to earth. A swift connection was made in his mind and a bunch of little lights flashed red in his brain. The journalist did not even stop to hail a cab. He ran as fast as he could to the nearest police station.

Smith Beffort and Yahto had gone to the back of the room to stay out of range of the shooter but the agent grabbed the Indian by the arm and dragged him outside.

"Take me to the other entrance!"

"Hold on, I have a better idea. It'd be just as easy to go back to Ralph's. I know a way to get in. I know it's not polite but we have no choice. I didn't expect there to be so many people here."

Walking around the sheriff's house the Indian noticed the broken window.

"I haven't seen that before," he was surprised. "It must be recent. It's not like Ralph to neglect urgent repairs. Especially in his own house. Come on, we'll go through the garage."

Behind the house Yahto squeezed between the wall of the garage and the sheriff's car that was parked next to it. He felt along the top of the sliding door and found a small, silver key.

"It's the emergency key," he declared. "It opens the garage. I'm the only one knows about it. Besides Ralph and Yomi of course. You can't imagine how close we are."

The Indian forced a smile but Beffort could see how tense he was. His hand was trembling so much that it took several tries for him to get the key into the lock. The two of them slid the corrugated sheet metal door which opened with a loud, unpleasant grating sound. Yahto entered the dark room first and immediately switched on the lights. It was a big garage built to hold the sheriff's big pick-up truck. At the moment it was completely empty except for some shelves in the corner with a toolbox and gas cans neatly lined up. Yahto pointed to a door in the back of the garage reached by three small, stone stairs.

"That goes directly into his house. I don't like to enter people's houses like this. Ralph always trusted me so the best case scenario is he's waiting for us in there with a beer. The worst case scenario…"

Beffort followed the Indian with all his senses on alert. By reflex he put his hand on the gun in his shoulder holster. When he realized how nervous he was he tried to relax by taking a deep breathe.

They walked into the kitchen where everything was calm. Yahto called out for Bender but got no reply. They went through all the rooms in the house including the one with the cell. Everything was hopelessly empty. But everything was neat and clean also, except for the cell where a dinner plate with some food was sitting on the table. The front door was locked from the inside. Beffort examined the broken window then returned to the prison room.

"Something happened here very recently. Under this awful perfume that's stinking the place up I smell the faint odor of gunpowder."

Yahto agreed but he had nothing to add. The FBI agent was ignorant of too many things. They were not on equal footing, so the Indian just looked around without saying a word.

"You know the house," Beffort said. "You can lead the way to the underground."

"If you're looking for Ralph we can wait here. I'm sure he just went out to make his rounds in town."

"Stop deluding yourself, Yahto. You don't believe a word you're saying. I saw your hands trembling and I saw your face. You weren't showing much peace of mind. Why not take a look at the underground entrance?"

This time the Indian's face broke down so drastically that Beffort was stunned.

"Hold on. You told me about the living dead. You said you took care of her, which is not, I'm sorry, a normal routine. You also said you get along with this slightly deranged couple and there are underground tunnels that you know like the back of your hand. So I ask you: what are you afraid of? What else is there?"

"There are powers that it'd be better…"

"Yes, yes, I know the story," Beffort cut him off, becoming annoyed. "I, too, read *Weird Tales* when I was a kid. That was long before Madame Atomos entered my life and I can guarantee you that the shades crawling around here are cartoons compared to that terrible Japanese woman!

Ernst Hartmann and Alonzo stared down the tunnel, the only exit open to them. Now that the cops had arrived in Salvation it was more and more urgent that they find Madame Atomos and get her out safe and sound.

"We have no choice," Alonzo said. "We have to take this tunnel or else we'll be surrounded by the cops."

"I will remind you again that we don't hear anything from the surface. There doesn't seem to be too many of them and you obviously scared them away."

"Yeah but by the time they return with backup we'll be long gone. After you, Mr. German!"

Hartmann stepped cautiously into the dimly lit passage that was just big enough for a medium-sized adult.

"I'd like to know where this light's coming from," Hartmann said.

"We'll soon find out. Right now I'm happy we can both stand up, which'll make it easy going for us. Where do you think we are exactly, doctor?"

"I have absolutely no idea. With this heavy smell of vanilla there might be an underground candy factory or something like that."

They progressed slowly down the tunnel. Hartmann quickly realized that the light was coming from a row of bulbs set into the wall.

"So why so much electricity in an underground tunnel of a deserted town?" the German wondered aloud.

The tunnel sloped downhill until it suddenly leveled off. The height, luckily, did not change (about six and a half feet high) so they could still stand up. A few minutes later the scientist saw a second tunnel veer off to the left, then another one farther along.

"It's a maze down here," he remarked. "We're going to get lost. If we're not already."

"What should we do?" the Mexican asked. "Keep going?"

"I don't see what else we can do. I think the best solution is to continue straight ahead. We have to end up somewhere."

While walking the German sought a natural source of light or a draft of fresh air but he had to face the facts: they were surrounded by nothing but damp, compact earth.

After what seemed like ages they came into a small room with new tunnels.

"This is getting ridiculous!" Alonzo said. "We don't know where we are and we don't even know what we're doing here."

"We're looking for Madame Atomos and a way out. You said so yourself. But I agree that this place is too weird for us to find her down here."

"You think I can yell out?"

"My God... I don't see why not. The earth seems pretty solid. I don't think we have to worry about a cave-in."

Alonzo cupped his hands around his mouth and started yelling, "Madame Atomos! Madame Atomos!"

"This whole thing's kind of funny," Hartmann said. "Here we are lost in a maze under a ghost town and hollering 'Madame Atomos'. Never in my wildest dreams could I have imagined this."

"That's normal because you're smarter than everyone else, Hartmann. You studied a long time and so you think you can make fun of everyone. But me, I don't like you. In fact, nobody likes you in the Organization."

"The Organization, as far as I know, is not there to like people," Hartmann replied while kicking dirt off his shoes.

The Mexican did the same and took out his cigarettes. "It's not that I'm tired, but I'm going to do like you, Hartmann, and take a break while I smoke. You think it's okay to smoke down here?"

"You can do whatever you want down here, pal. You can smoke, scream, even just sit and wait. Anyway, we can listen to the silence. Maybe someone's trying to answer you."

Alonzo took a drag off his smoke and listened. He was going to talk, to ask a question of the German scientist, but he stopped himself—he had just heard something. At first he was the only one to react. The German's hearing was not as good so it took him longer but the sound was audible to both men soon enough. It was footsteps. Someone not very heavy who walked with a limp.

A woman, Hartmann thought. *She's coming from the left. The footsteps are coming from the left.*

The Mexican also thought it was a woman. It had to be a woman.

Frail, small, limping were the first adjectives that came to mind. And yet an uncomfortable feeling, a terror, which *a priori* was completely illogical, suddenly took hold of them. There was something bizarre in her walk.

Alonzo grabbed his gun and was surprised to see his hand trembling, which had never in his life happened.

The thing is coming here, Hartmann thought. *It'll be here any second at the entrance to the tunnel.*

Instinctively the two men stood up together, totally confused by the sudden panic they felt.

The footsteps were louder now, seeming to echo in their ears, maybe because of the peculiar underground acoustics. Alonzo kept his eyes glued to the tunnel. He could not keep his shaking arm aimed at the entrance.

When the woman appeared the young Mexican understood why her walk sounded so strange.

Ernst Hartmann saw nothing but the doorway on the opposite side of the room, the only exit whereby they could escape. He walked away from where the thing was coming. He wanted to speed up, to run as fast as he could but he felt like he was living in a nightmare, a nightmare in which his legs were weighed down so they could not run normally. Like being held back by some invisible force, the German was fleeing in slow motion.

However, even though he did not realize it, he had a huge advantage over Alonzo: he did not look back. He managed to look away before the creature appeared. Now his eyes were riveted on the entrance where they came in. When he got into the tunnel he heard Alonzo scream. A hellish, inhuman howl that literally froze his blood.

Something clicked in him and his legs were freed from the invisible shackles. Ernst Hartmann started running, running like he had never run in his life.

Chapter XIV

When Madame Atomos' men entered Salvation the sheriff had to make all his decisions in a hurry. First he stuck the Mexican's body in the house across the street, then he took care of Madame Atomos: he burst into her cell like a robber and fired a right hook whose speed and power surprised even himself. Then he threw her limp body over his shoulders, carried her to the trapdoor and went down into the first tunnel to the east, the best maintained part of the underground maze. That was where Bender had once built a room for Yomi which became a complete apartment, though quite Spartan, that his wife could enjoy in peace and quiet.

Laying Madame Atomos on Yomi's bed Bender waited for her to wake up. Yomi had not appreciated the intrusion into her apartment, so she fled into the tunnels. This was not the first time she had done so. Every time she became upset at something she disappeared.

The dinner for three was in jeopardy but at least Yomi had the chance to meet Madame Atomos.

Ralph Bender suddenly felt something warm leaking out of his mouth. Damn, another tooth falling out! He had lost two already this month alone. Luckily this one was a molar and would not show, but if he kept losing his front teeth he would have to go see Rafelson, which was not a pleasant thought. Especially since he was not feeling well. And when you do not feel well all the little crap comes raining down at the same time. Teeth, fever, headaches... Bender was not getting any younger and he knew it.

Kanoto Yoshimuta breathed heavily and fidgeted beneath the blanket. She was slowly but painfully coming to and she was no longer behind bars. The sheriff was going to be alone, face to face with his prisoner. Unless the situation were reversed...

Kanoto opened one eye. Then the other. Two magnificent, deep brown eyes in a face that immediately woke up to become as inexpressive as possible. Ralph Bender was stunned by the woman's beauty. It was as if the bars of her cell had also locked away her aura, an aura that was free now and that hit him full in the face. The scene was like a husband tending his wife on her sick bed.

A second later Madame Atomos was on her feet and gently rubbing her bruised chin. "I could kill you with my bare hands," she said looking around the room.

Ralph Bender did not deny it. He knew that it was not an empty threat. He never thought he could hit this woman and right now he could not doubt the truth of what she had just said. But he knew that besides his exceptional physical strength he had other advantages over her. First the terrible Japanese woman was in a strange and unknown place. Bender also knew that he could count on his ancestors' powers that could be felt in every inch of the underground town. Last but not least he held his precious 44 Magnum, a gun that did not come from the police but that he kept with him at all times and that could make a hole bigger than any service revolver.

Smith Beffort's throat was dry and he gladly accepted the beer offered by the Indian. The listened patiently to Yahto recount in detail certain legends of his tribe but it did not really interest him. None of it could explain the terror the Indian felt at going down into the tunnels. And none of it could put Beffort on Madame Atomos' trail. If it really was her in the cell, she was gone now and he had to idea where to start looking.

"We'll check out the tunnels," he decided. "After that I'll take off. I still have a lot to do in Las Vegas."

"Doesn't the radioactivity in Salvation interest you?"

"Of course, and there's obviously a logical explanation for it but right now my priority is to get my hands on that murderous Japanese woman and keep Las Vegas and the region from being destroyed. I don't want to waste any more time."

"I'm sure that if you pointed that machine of yours at the house it would beep like crazy," Yahto suggested.

"You're probably right and it's worth trying. I'll go get the Geiger counter and we'll see."

The federal agent put down his beer and left. The sun outside was so bright that Beffort was briefly blinded. Squinting through the glare he caught sight of a moving shadow. A shadow that must have been no more than 30 feet away. Instinctively he pulled out his gun while stepping back.

"Stop!" he shouted. "FBI! Hands in the air!"

He used his left hand to shield his eyes from the sunlight and saw a small man, well dressed, waving his arms in the air. The stranger was rather old and his face was twisted with fear. He stood still, trembling nervously waiting for a signal to scurry away.

Beffort recognized him. He had seen so many faces over his career that it was hard for him to put a name to all the crooks known to the United States, but this was a particular face and his name jumped out immediately.

"Ernst Hartmann!" he shouted, moving closer. "Ernst Hartmann!"

The man nodded anxiously.

"I've heard a lot about you lately," the FBI agent continued. "I see I've hit the jackpot. You're going to tell me about your boss, Madame Atomos, and about the bomb."

Beffort waited for an answer as Yahto came up behind him.

"What's wrong with you?" the G-man asked Hartmann. "You look like you've seen a ghost."

"Madame Atomos is here," the German stammered. "We found her car and we also found the tunnels."

"You went underground?" Yahto asked.

Hartmann nodded but uttered no sound.

Beffort thought the German might break down in tears any second. "Where's Madame Atomos?" he demanded. "Have you seen her?"

"It's that damned sheriff. He's holding her prisoner. I was with Alonzo. We started looking for her…"

As if relieved to be able to talk about it Hartmann started telling in detail about his wandering through the tunnels and meeting with a creature whom he could not describe without breaking into a cold sweat.

"He's more and more incoherent," Beffort turned to the Indian. "What do you think? What did he see? Could it have been the sheriff's wife?"

"It's a miracle that this man got back to the surface," Yahto answered. "As for his partner, if he's stuck down there, we'll never find him. I wouldn't bet two cents on the Mexican's survival."

"And if we went to see what it's all about?" Beffort suggested. "You got out through the north entrance, right, Hartmann? Where I almost got shot?"

The German nodded as Beffort frisked him summarily.

"I'll go with you," Yahto said. "But I won't go down into the tunnels."

"We're all going!" Beffort announced, watching Hartmann's face turn white.

The three men headed north. The federal agent was the first in the house, his gun at the ready, and he carefully opened the door leading to the basement. He went down. The small room was still lit up. At the bottom of the wooden stairs that creaked under his weight, Beffort found the trapdoor open. Through the opening, at the bottom of the shallow well, he could see the entrance to the tunnel.

"We can't go any farther," the Indian shouted. "The guy's scared stiff and refusing to go down the stairs."

"Okay, let him stay there. But keep an eye on him, please. I don't want him to escape."

"And you? What are you going to do?"

"I don't know," Beffort replied after a second's hesitation. "I think I'll try to go down there."

His brain was working overtime thinking about the best decision to make under these circumstances. If Madame Atomos' car was really in town, then was the Japanese herself still here? He also had to ask Hartmann about the bomb in Las Vegas. The German's presence in Salvation was proof positive that Beffort had been right all along.

All of a sudden he heard noises coming from the underground. At first he thought he heard men talking. Someone was walking through the tunnel and coming closer. In fact, it was not someone talking but someone laughing. And then the shadow appeared right under the trapdoor. The laugh was loud and raucous. A man looked up at him, laughing like a lunatic. Enough to send shivers down your spine. It was the Mexican whose face was frozen and whose eyes were lifeless. He was trying to climb up but his hands kept slipping on the walls that were too smooth for him to get a grip. But he kept laughing nonetheless, his frightening morbid laugh. He had obviously lost his mind.

"Close the trapdoor," Yahto yelled. "Leave him down there. That man is no longer in the land of the living. Listen, Beffort, do what I tell you, close the trapdoor! You can't do anything for him now. Madame Atomos is probably down there too. Oh well, so much the better. Everything that's Evil on earth is now trapped under Salvation. We just have to shut the doors and toss down a bomb to destroy them all. Let's be done with it!"

Beffort was taken aback at this outburst of violence. Between Yahto screaming his head off and the Mexican whose laugh was turning into an ominous howl, the place was suddenly shaking with sick vibrations.

He used all his strength to drag the trapdoor over the opening. Then he scrambled up the stairs and found Ernst Hartmann sitting on the ground, completely dazed, next to Yahto, who had calmed down. In any case, the two of them looked relieved that the trapdoor was closed and the tunnels shut off.

"He's right," the German finally snapped out of his silence. "Madame Atomos is down there. If you want to get rid of her, now's the moment."

"How can you be so sure? No one here has even seen her. Including you, I believe."

"I'll explain," the Indian said. "It's obvious she's down there because the forces of Evil had an appointment in Salvation. It's time to finish it. And Ralph would agree with me. Yomi too. They've lived through enough and want nothing but peace. Please, Mr. Beffort, listen to me. I've already told you how I feel about Ralph. He thinks Yomi brought something back from Beyond that human beings can't bear the sight of... It's true, I assure you."

"Yes, yes," Beffort said with a hint of impatience in his voice. "You already told me about Yomi's gaze, that she has to wear a mask..."

"Please," Yahto cut him off, "don't take me for a stupid, superstitious Indian. I was here when Yomi came back from Salvation after being reanimated by the Atomos ray. What she brought back with her from her voyage Beyond was never meant to come into the land of the living. No one should play around with such things, even if your name is Madame Atomos and you're a genius. It's like the sorcerer's apprentice. That's why we have to destroy this thing that is not from our world, that the dreadful Japanese woman woke up with her cursed experiments. You see, Yomi is nothing but a vehicle for Evil. I mean this thing that she's got inside her and that she hides behind a mask. It's a run of bad luck. Yomi ran into Madame Atomos after being irradiated in Hiroshima and Ralph brought her to Salvation where she could stay alive because Salvation wanted her to. Or the spirits of our ancestors in Salvation. Poor Ralph might have flooded his house and all the tunnels with that nasty stink of the mortuary but he couldn't stop smelling the slow, very slow, relentless decomposition of his beloved wife. And even though Yomi's body is falling apart, little by little every day, she's still alive because the thing is living inside her. That's the price Ralph paid to stay with his one and only love."

"Yes, it's very sad, but..."

"That's what the Mexican saw today. And you, Beffort, didn't have to be asked twice to close the trapdoor on the cursed thing because you couldn't stand it either. Am I right?"

Beffort felt a shiver run down his spine but he did not answer.

"Am I right, Beffort?" the Indian pressed. "You think you can open the trapdoor and help our Mexican friend climb out?"

"Well, hell," the agent confessed, "I'm afraid not."

"So you agree with me when I tell you that the underground evil has to be destroyed. One way or another."

Smith Beffort stared pensively at the stairs and the trapdoor sealing shut Salvation's tunnels. Then he asked Ernst Hartmann to take him to Madame Atomos' car. When he got there he gave it a quick search and found a few papers that had been left on the passenger seat.

"One never knows," he mumbled. He turned to the German and said, "My dear Dr. Hartmann, now you're going to tell me a little more about this bomb."

Sergeant Wallis had relayed to his superiors the information given to him by the journalist and everything speeded up. If Robinson could not remember the name of the casino in question, the bartender at the hotel could easily find the name of the taxi driver who took him there.

The gaming room located downtown around Fremont Street was, for Las Vegas, of modest size. As if by chance it was in one of the zones still with electricity thanks to Colonel Parker. Two members of the Green Dragon Force got there first and quickly spotted the machine described by Robinson. It was the only one of its kind inside the bar. Except for the woman's face in the small, square windows, it was no different from any other one-armed bandit.

The Green Dragon men thought of unplugging the machine but they changed their mind and decided to wait for the emergency team to arrive. Meanwhile they went to see the managers to close the bar since the owners were away for an indefinite period of time.

Dr. Creighton was informed immediately and when the first team arrived they found a secondary electrical apparatus inside the machine. The device had three copper wires wrapped in a blue plastic sheathing that ran down into the floor. In less than 30 minutes, long before Creighton got there, a crowd of policemen, firemen and soldiers took control of the building as the two managers looked on in amazement.

One of the men from the Green Dragon Force grabbed a telephone. "You have to inform Smith Beffort," he told headquarters. "We've got this whacked out machine and we hope it's the only one. Some guys are downstairs right now checking out what's under this place."

He barely finished speaking when a shout came from the basement. Then a fireman came running through the kitchen door.

"The bomb's down there! That's it, we've found it! And I've never seen such a weird thing that size."

After relating the news over the phone, the Green Dragon agent hung up. At first there was a lot of noise in the bar. Shouts of joy and congratulations. Then everyone realized that the game was just beginning and silence fell over them just when Creighton finally arrived. Now he had to defuse the bomb.

"This is your job," a lieutenant told the scientist. "I'll show you where it is. This way, please."

Creighton followed him down the service stairs, one flight after another, endlessly. The bomb was in the third-level basement, which looked like it had been built to house the huge device.

It was the size and shape of a small submarine. A model built during the troubled, post-war period, an antique! Dr. Creighton could not get over it. This thing was so huge that he could not even imagine that it could explode. Truthfully, he could not imagine that such a monstrous thing could exist.

The army had succeeded in letting it get stolen and in judging it inoffensive had given the Atomos Organization all the time in the world to build a working detonator...

Creighton looked at the detonator in the front of the bomb and thought about Ernst Hartmann, the only man in the world who could manage such a feat. He wondered where the German was right now. Then he thought he ought to get to work since he was the one who had to fuse it.

Creighton quickly felt more confident. Truck drivers will tell you, "The bigger it is, the easier it is!" He examined the detonator which was the size of a pressure cooker. He could do it. He knew that at least if he made a mistake it would happen in a flash and he would feel nothing.

When he put his sweating hands on the device he wondered if Elvis had started singing for all the old hags in Las Vegas and it was an extremely unpleasant thought.

Unfazed, Hartmann looked at Beffort. "The bomb does exist and I think the Atomos Organization wouldn't want me to tell you too much about it."

"Is it really the bomb stolen from the army eight years ago?"

"That's right, Mr. Beffort. I was recruited to build the detonator and as I'm speaking, if we're still alive it's because it hasn't been found yet."

"Are you ready to help me, Hartmann, to tell me where it is? We have some clues that make us think it was planted somewhere do with gambling."

"You're talking about the calls from the Organization? What was it... 'Madame Atomos is betting on death', is that right?"

"That's right. The Las Vegas police figured that the bomb is hooked up to a slot machine and when a particular combination hits it'll explode within four days."

"You see there, you're very smart in the police to figure things out so quickly."

The German started laughing. Beffort stared at him, then suddenly he understood and his blood froze.

"Good God! The probabilities of one to four days!"

"Oh yes. 'Madame Atomos is betting on death'. That's exactly right. Except that you didn't interpret the phrase correctly. We're not talking about the same probabilities."

The FBI agent ran to the Ford. "Quick!" he shouted to no one in particular. "The radio! We have to warn Las Vegas. They've been playing with us from the start!"

"Hurry up," Ernst Hartmann said as Beffort jumped into his car. "Better hope that your friends haven't found the superbomb yet."

Chapter XV

Ralph Bender passed his hand gently over his face to feel how deep the wound was. He was relieved that, in spite of the blood spreading over his fingers, it was only superficial. He did not really understand what had happened.

Just a minute ago he had the upper hand because he was holding the Magnum. Then Madame Atomos suddenly pounced like a tigress. Her fingernails dug into his face, gashing his irradiated skin and blinding him when they reached his eyes. A few seconds of dizziness and blur. The sheriff could not even use his weapon because he was too busy trying to protect his face. Then the Japanese woman vanished, leaving him alone with the pain glutting his cheeks.

"It's nothing," he told himself while dabbing his bloody face with a handkerchief.

Bender still had the gun in his hand but he did not see what good it would do now. Madame Atomos had escaped and taken the right way, seeing that there was no other. Somewhere in the tunnels she would inevitably meet Yomi. It had to be.

He had not imagined that things would end up like this. He had simply wanted to organize a dinner, a rendezvous… something almost intimate. And now the two women were going to run into each other unexpectedly…

The sheriff looked at the handkerchief. His cheek was still bleeding but it did not sting as much.

Dr. Creighton knew this model of detonator. The one before him, although made by hand, was exactly identical to another model made by the army a few years earlier. The difference was that a mitigator had been added here, but the basic structure was the same.

He heard a click while starting to separate it from the bomb. The detonator slid half an inch revealing a smooth, golden, metallic groove. Now he just had to rotate it 180 degrees clockwise so he could disconnect part of the device. The hardest thing would come after and Creighton estimated it would take an hour of work, certainly the longest hour in his life.

But the detonator was hard to move. There was resistance. Dr. Creighton could not get it to rotate correctly.

"I'll need a hand," he told the Marine standing behind him. "You have to help me turn this piece to the right. I think the two of us can do it."

The man nodded and stepped forward but a voice from the floor above cried out, "Don't touch anything! The detonator is booby-trapped! It's mounted backwards. It'll blow the bomb if you try to take it off."

For a long while Ernst Hartmann anxiously watched Beffort. They were waiting for an answer from Las Vegas. After five minutes the FBI agent's face finally lit up.

"That's it! The message got through! The bomb won't go off."

"And it'll stay like that as long as no one tries to defuse it," Hartmann added.

"I'll put you in contact with Dr. Creighton. He'll follow your instructions to shut it down completely. If you cooperate, the courts will go easy on you."

"More than the Atomos Organization anyway," the German said coldly. "I have a few years yet to live and I'd like to do it honorably. Besides, the United States might need my services."

Beffort saw the Indian suddenly pop into sight. He had a strange look on his face that might have been him smiling.

"It's finished," Yahto declared. "That's it, I did what I had to do. For Madame Atomos, Ralph and Yomi, I have sealed their fate for good."

"What have you done?" Beffort blurted out.

"I cut off the generators. Like that there's no more light in the tunnels and the fans will stop blowing that sweet smell of vanilla. It'll all rot. And if I were you, I'd bomb this town to smithereens to get rid of Madame Atomos for good."

"But there's the sheriff and Yomi! That's murder!"

"Ralph is contaminated too, Mr. Beffort. Unfortunately he was contaminated by Yomi a long time ago. They don't belong to the land of the living anymore. I think that after coming here to Salvation you've had more than enough proof."

When the lights went out Madame Atomos tried to feel her way along like a blind person by following the moist tunnel walls. Then she stopped and concentrated on listening for something that might help her to analyze her position and prove that the sheriff was not on her trail. There was obviously a way to get out of the tunnels, so her prodigious brain started working at full speed.

Beffort must be outside. There might even be a swarm of cops. They must have cut the electricity. Now, little by little, the stench of rot was replacing the usual perfume.

That's not so bad, she thought. *At least I can know the truth. The real America is showing its true face, and it's rotten to the core.*

She had to find a way to get out but it was not necessarily by going up that she would do it. After a little while she heard footsteps but not those of the sheriff. Yomi was walking slowly in her direction. Yomi who had terrified her! It was a trap! She was going to have to face this creature, but strange as it might seem Kanoto Yoshimuta was not scared. She felt ready for it and even ready to go and meet her compatriot.

The rotting stench was spreading fast and furious.

Madame Atomos, whose eyes were getting used to the dark, could see the end of the tunnel where the little footsteps were coming from. Yomi appeared with a bluish light that glowed faintly off the rocky walls.

She had taken off her sweat suit and put on a long, white robe that covered all her body. Her face was also covered by the Japanese mask that she apparently never took off. Madame Atomos approached her, confident and self-assured in spite of the smell of dead flesh flooding the place. She wanted to know. She had to take that mask off. The answer was behind it and Kanoto Yoshimuta was more and more convinced that she had not come here by accident.

Now she was right in front of Yomi. Her fingers grasped the mask, which represented "Kashiki", the starving woman, and she slowly pulled it off without the slightest shudder running through her body. Yomi stood still before her like a submissive woman letting herself be stripped naked.

When the mask fell to the ground Madame Atomos finally saw that face. A radiant face lit up by a big smile. The face of an extremely beautiful woman for whom time had stood still. The face of woman very alive as well.

"You're Kanoto Yoshimuta," the sheriff's wife said. "You were born in Nagasaki. You were a student at the university in that city."

Madame Atomos was dazed and amazed. This woman was calling up very strong memories in her. She remembered her university days like they were yesterday and yet it had been many long years since the last time she remembered any of it.

"I, too, was at the university," Yomi continued. "But I didn't know you. I wasn't a student. I worked in the kitchen sometimes. But in a little way I was part of your life. You remember the place where the students went to talk, down by the river on the Bunkyo campus?"

"The river, the Bunkyo campus..." Madame Atomos pronounced the words slowly, totally stunned. "That place has been wiped out of my memory for so long! It's absolutely incredible, Yomi. You're a part of my youth!"

"It's not so incredible. We're not here by accident. You know that, Kanoto."

"Your husband, Ralph Bender, told me everything. You died and came back to life and you're here."

"Yes, I came back to life, thanks to you, and Salvation has reunited us. You will get a lot here, Kanoto, because you're going to gain new strength to continue your fight. We have something in common, you and I. We both suffered the terrible effects of American imperialism. The people who used to live in Salvation many years ago also want revenge. Believe me, it is not by chance that we are meeting together here and now."

Madame Atomos looked up at the ceiling of the tunnel.

"They're coming, Kanoto. They'll bomb the town and to make sure they'll destroy everything around Salvation. But they'll have no idea that it will just make you stronger."

Madame Atomos realized that Yomi, while speaking, had taken her hand. The two women started laughing. Madame Atomos understood everything that this town had to offer her. The possibility of continuing her battle in a new way, in spheres unknown to the living but much more frightening!

The wound on his face had finally stopped bleeding as the sheriff stumbled through the underground maze of Salvation. The sudden darkness did not make it easy for him. When the air had been cut a dreadful odor of putrefaction rushed up his nostrils while infesting all the tunnels with the smell of death.

At length Bender saw a halo of light and heard voices. He knew that the two women had finally met and they were together now. Coming up to them he was surprised to see that Yomi had taken off her mask. It was harder and harder for him to tolerate the presence and smell of his wife. All the things that they had lived through together he could no longer endure and he was happy that it was finally over.

"Here's your husband," Madame Atomos said.

"Ralph and I were very much in love with each other for a long time," Yomi whispered to her. "He helped me enormously. He brought me to Salvation. I owe him a lot. This town has helped me too. And you, Kanoto, have also helped me. Without your ray I wouldn't be here today. We're two links in the chain and Ralph was just a middleman. I acknowledge everything this man has done for me and I have no regrets about being his wife. But now I don't love him anymore."

Ralph Bender was amazed to see his wife's face unmasked. It radiated such a force, such intensity that he was mortified when she turned to him. They were less than 15 feet from each other when Yomi took a few steps in his direction. The sheriff felt the shudder of fear run through his body.

All of a sudden she resumed her inhuman stride and Bender, who was seeing the true face of his wife for the first time in years, recognized nothing in her features like he had known and loved before and like he had seen a few moments earlier in front of Kanoto Yoshimuta. It was as if the years of living together were wiped out in one fell swoop. As if there was nothing left of his wife but the reflection of Death. And this, it must be said, had been the case for a long time. Since the accident that Yomi had suffered in New York.

The sheriff started backpedalling but Yomi's scrawny arms were hugging him and her legs were wrapped around his waist. Her greedy mouth was all over his face trying to sink her tiny sharp teeth into it.

Images flickered in his mind. Don't they say that your life flashes before your eyes right before you die?

Bender saw the Japanese countryside where Yomi and he used to walk years ago. But clouds quickly covered it over. Bender did not remember clouds during their walks together. Nor did he remember the sudden darkness.

Yomi snapped her jaws shut. There was a crack, like the sound of a chicken bone breaking, and she tore off a piece of skin.

The two of them were looking for shelter from the storm now but the trees were bare and Bender realized with horror that Yomi had let go of his hand.

The sheriff felt like he was losing an eye and his panic was as strong as the pain.

It was raining harder and harder and his mind kept falling apart. In any case, she had let him go and seemed not to want to follow him.

It didn't happen like this, he told himself. *Or I don't remember. Or I don't want to remember.*

Bender fell on his knees and put his hands over his gouged out face. He felt the muscles and bones from the flesh she had bitten off and he trembled in fear. The pain was unbearable and Bender screamed. His sight was blurred by blood that was spurting out of the top of his skull now but before dying he had time to see Kanoto Yoshimuta through the reddening veil.

Yomi was eating him and the sinister Madame Atomos looked on, smiling, enjoying the spectacle, thoroughly satisfied.

Weary but happy, Mie was lying on her bed in the maternity ward of Washington Adventist Hospital. She had just given birth to a baby girl whom the couple decided to name Dawn. Smith Beffort was telling her about the latest developments in the Atomos affair.

"I think we're done with this now. The bomb was neutralized and things are pretty much back to normal in Las Vegas."

"Did you destroy that weird town?"

"Truthfully, the official order came from Stobben. He made the decision to demolish a 30-mile radius around Salvation. To a certain extent I agreed with him but I regret not being able to get everyone out of there."

"Yomi Bender? You're thinking about her? Is she included in the 'people' you're talking about?"

"We ended up finding her death certificate in New York from a few years ago. After that was total chaos. All I know is that the town is gone. It was bombed out of existence by the US Air Force. As for Madame Atomos..."

The federal agent looked at all the flower bouquets around Mie's room. There were so many that some had to be put on the floor.

"We'll soon have plenty of space for these flowers. All of Washington seems to know about our daughter," Beffort tried to avoid a subject that never completely left his mind, even at a time as intimate and happy as this.

Mie watched her husband joke and smile but she knew perfectly well that Smith Beffort's mind would never be at peace until the corpse of that dreadful Japanese woman was lying at his feet.

He made a great effort to appear relaxed. The time he had just lived through had been grueling and he could not forget the Indian's words about Salvation's curse. He was, however, too logical and far too busy with work to go off studying old Indian legends.

In one of the bouquets was a card that Mie had not yet had the time to read. He grabbed it and said to his wife, "It's from the Joyces. With their sincere congratulations."

"The Joyces are still in Washington? I thought they moved..."

"I'm working too hard and you're too busy. We're neglecting our friends. You should call them and invite them over one of these days."

"That's true, we have a lot of invitations to catch up on," Mie responded. "But I'm going to straighten everything out. Look at all these cards. You see they haven't forgotten us."

Like a child looking for Easter eggs Beffort started rummaging around in the flowers in search of cards.

"The Larsons from Washington, the O'Neals, the Browns and... well, I'll be..."

"Who is it?"

"We have the compliments of Colonel Parker, the guy who threw a monkey wrench in the works in Las Vegas. I'll have to tell you about that crazy story."

Mie was glad to see him smiling. This time he seemed to have momentarily left his usual obsession behind him. It was time that he started thinking about the future. Mie watched their daughter sleeping in the crib.

"There's more. The Thompsons, the Millers... Hold on, I don't know any Miller." He picked out the card and began reading, "With compliments of..." But the words got stuck in his throat.

Mie saw Smith's face turn pale as he read the little white card that looked like all the others. For a few seconds he stood as still as a statue. Someone else would probably have already broken down in despair but Mie knew that her husband could control himself.

I really was lucky to have married such a man, she mused. *The journey is not over, my dear, and I'm proud to be travelling it with you.*

#2

#3

#4

313

#5

#6

315

#7

316

#9

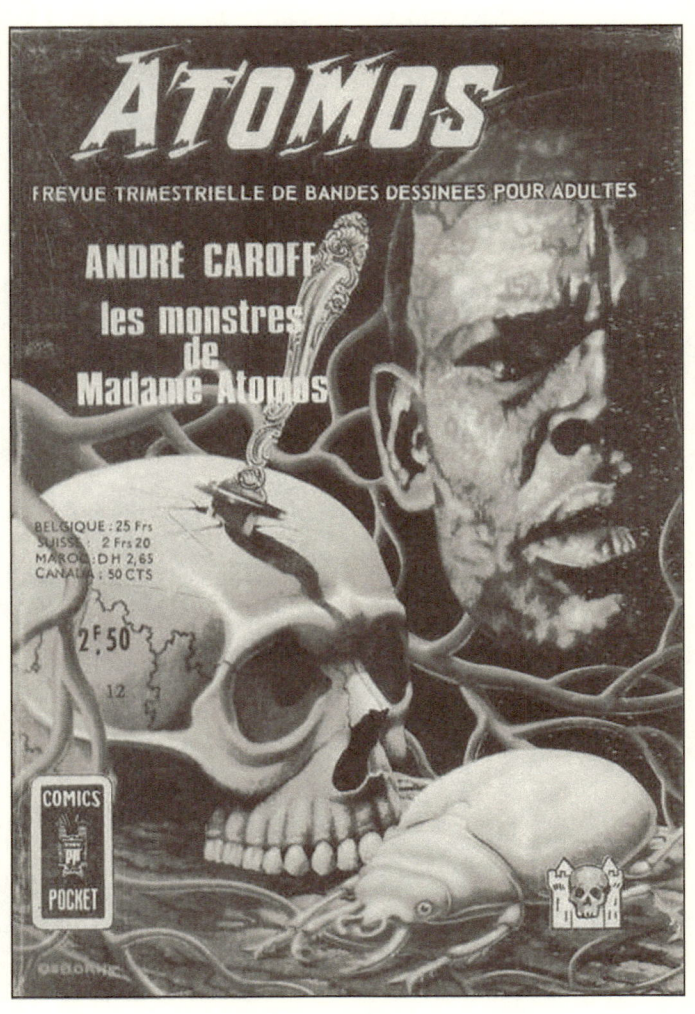

#12